Promises, Promises

D1557385

Sandy Loyd

Published by Sandy Loyd
Copyright 2012 Sandy Loyd
Cover design by Kelli Ann Morgan
Interior layout: www.formatting4U.com

For more information on the author and her works, please see www.SandyLoyd.com

This book is also available in electronic form from some online retailers.

Dedication

As with all my stories, <u>Promises, Promises</u> is dedicated to my husband. Without him behind me I wouldn't have written so much.

I also want to dedicate this story to my first editing partner, Lori Larson. We don't work as closely on manuscripts any longer, but she and I reworked Promises, Promises together. Her support and encouragement as a peer were paramount. Without both, I may not have come so far.

Chapter 1

Judith Reid lifted her face to the sun's warm rays, enjoying a light breeze. It was one of those glorious, sun-soaked days rarely experienced in San Francisco, especially during this time of the year. Late June was usually socked in with fog, but today the sun shone high in the sky and no clouds marred the horizon. That had to be a good omen.

She slowed her pace when she caught her reflection in the storefront window. A confident woman dressed for success stared back. Her posture straightened an inch. The navy suit offered the perfect professional touch.

Her cell phone beeped. She weaved in and out of a few tourists before answering the text from her best friend, Kate, wishing her good luck. She stuck the phone back in her bag and continued past the bakery. The scent of freshly baked bread floated out the door and added to her sense of well-being.

Yes! She was totally prepared to tackle the challenge of redesigning a building, not just any old building, but *her* building. Besides a personal connection with the four-story structure, this project had the potential to catapult her career to the next level. She'd trained and worked for years for an opportunity like this to showcase her talent as a commercial interior designer in the Bay Area.

Outside her destination, she paused to take a deep breath. She gave herself a mental pat on the back and headed through the heavy glass door, not stopping until the elevator doors closed and reopened to a huge, airy reception area on the fourth floor.

"I'm Judith Reid and I have an appointment to see a Mr. D.A. McAllister," she said calmly to the receptionist.

"Please be seated." She nodded. "I'll let Mr. McAllister's assistant know you're here."

Judith slid into a plush, comfy chair and took a moment to observe her surroundings. She'd tried to learn as much as she could about the reclusive CEO, but googling had provided only a

1

sketchy idea of a man who kept to himself and shied away from the limelight. Still, he had a reputation for being a mover and shaker in Northern California.

Whoever he was, he knew how to create a statement. Details such as spacing, lighting, and building materials were subtle tricks designers used to work their magic. The granite, glass, and dark wood had the look of success and polish. The owner of this company had extravagant taste, but it wasn't overdone. From the big windows overlooking the bay to the Chagall and Monet prints gracing the walls, this entire operation shouted class, something she understood.

"Ms. Reid?"

Judith glanced up. A petite auburn-haired woman wearing a no-nonsense smile approached. Dressed in a dark tailored dress, she appeared sixtyish, given the telltale lines around her eyes and mouth. Clearly a dynamic woman who doesn't miss much, Judith thought, also noting those shrewd brown eyes.

"I'm Ms. Abrams." She extended her hand. "Mr. McAllister's assistant."

Judith stood. "It's nice to meet you." The woman's handshake was firm.

"Mr. McAllister is ready to see you now." She turned and led her through a hallway.

Ms. Abrams saw her inside a spacious office, then efficiently closed the door behind her.

Judith's gaze made a quick sweep of a room that was even more impressive than the reception area. She took two more steps, then stopped. Her smile froze in place. The instant she focused on the man seated behind the huge walnut desk, her beautiful day and optimistic mood ended.

Mac...

"Hello, Judith." The familiar deep voice wrapped around her ears and tossed her senses into chaos. "It's good to see you again. You're looking better than at our last meeting."

This had to be a mistake. Tongue-tied, she eyed the imposing man and prodded her brain to work. How could the same Mac from her worst college nightmare be sitting in front of her, impersonating Devon A. McAllister, the CEO and majority owner of McAllister, Inc., a business now trading on the

NASDAQ?

The strong features of his face would never be considered pretty, but together with his wavy black hair and alert blue eyes, they only added to his appeal.

She tamped down the urge to run when he stood and offered a polite hand. All six feet two inches of this solidly built male presented an image of power. His firm grip confirmed the idea. A slight tingle shot up her arm as her hand was engulfed in his bigger one. The feeling alarmed her. The calculated look in his eyes troubled her more, especially when she noticed him scanning the length of her body. He quickly extinguished the look and suddenly was all business.

"Have a seat." He let go of her hand and pointed to a chair. "I was pleased to learn you've decided to join in the bidding fray and submit plans. I've heard good things about your work from Smith and Kline."

Having spent most of her youth hiding her feelings behind a mask of calm reserve, Judith quickly recovered from the shock of seeing Mac after all these years. Thankful for the ability to hold others at a distance with a cool stare, another self-protective skill learned early on, she adopted that detached expression now. That didn't stop her thoughts from racing. Or her insides from twisting.

Relax! Stay cool and play out this chance meeting. Get through the interview.

If she could, everything would be fine. Except that things weren't fine, her mind screamed. They were, in fact, just the opposite. Her galloping heartbeat wouldn't let her relax and the energy humming through her veins hindered her efforts to remain in control. She'd forgotten how much he affected her. Thirty seconds in his company and every sensation she'd felt that long-ago night returned with tornado-like speed. How would she ever survive the next half hour?

Buck up! Remember, this is an opportunity of a lifetime. A chance to bring my building, something I love, back to its natural beauty and glory. That's worth more than the heartache of seeing Mac again.

"I'm honored to learn my work's been noticed, *Mr. McAllister.*" She pasted on her most serene smile, the same one she'd perfected in high school to survive the taunts from cruel kids. She had to keep everything in the past where it belonged, just as he seemed to be doing. It was a matter of pride. He'd never know how much this meeting bothered her. Her smile grew an inch. "I've been on my own for a little over a year now, since I left Smith and Kline."

"Please, call me Dev. After all, it seems silly not to, considering our past." His devilish grin told her he hadn't forgotten either, even though the past they shared consisted of a few scant hours spent together ten years ago.

He cleared his throat and his business mien was in place once again. "Several design firms have offered bids. The building's a real mess and needs almost everything from the inside out. Innovative and fresh...isn't that what they say about your work?" When she nodded, he added, "So I couldn't leave your plans out of the process."

The project in question was a renovation, an especially attractive prospect because the office building itself was on the historic preservation list, creating an even heftier challenge for anyone daring to undertake something of this magnitude. Old buildings all over San Francisco needed twenty-first century updates. But this was *her building.*

Well, not hers, exactly, since McAllister, Inc. owned it.

She clenched a fist. Ownership didn't matter. She just had to make sure she got the job. Her plans were solid. Nothing would stop her from seeing them through to completion. Not even the inconvenience and pain of dealing with the sexy hunk in front of her, one whose grin had suddenly become smug. Her spine stiffened. She could do this. She refused to let him affect her any more than he already had.

As Judith reached into her bag, her confidence returned. "I have my plans right here." She handed him her proposal. "They meet all of your specifications."

McAllister, Inc. wanted all of the frills, including heating and air conditioning, updated electrical, lighting, and security systems, the best technology offered, as well as making the building resistant to earthquakes and fire. Being historic meant all of these improvements had to be made without taking away the integrity of its age and beauty.

Dev placed the folder on the desk in front of him.

She bit her lip and watched him thumb through it. Second by second, her delicate thread of self-assurance slipped. She tucked a lock of hair behind her ear and resisted the urge to fidget. Judith cleared her throat and said with much more certainty than she felt, "Once you've had a chance to review it, we can meet to go over specifics. I can answer any of your questions at the same time. Or if you'd rather, we can do it right now, step by step. It shouldn't take too long."

"I'd like nothing better than to go over this right now, but there's a slight problem." He glanced at his watch. "Something unexpected's come up and I need to be somewhere in fifteen minutes. How about meeting later tonight for dinner? My treat."

Dinner? He was asking her to dinner? Crossing her fingers to negate the small lie, she replied, striving for casual, "I can't this evening. I have plans. How about lunch tomorrow?" Lunch was doable, but dinner was another matter entirely.

"I know it's short notice and I apologize." Though he spoke with a twinge of regret, the amusement dancing in his shrewd gaze belied his sincerity. So did the half grin he still sported. He straightened and added in a more businesslike tone, "I'll review your proposal during my spare time this afternoon. However, I want to discuss it with you, along with any questions. I'm presenting my decision at a board meeting tomorrow morning."

He sat back with fingers together, tips touching his chin, and scrutinized her.

Finally, he sighed. "I'll be honest. I'm leaning toward a solid plan from another firm. But, before I finalize anything and because you were highly recommended, I felt you deserved a shot. So it comes down to timing and availability. I have no preference, but I thought a busy restaurant would be a more comfortable environment than an empty office after hours."

His lopsided grin was back as well as that amused gleam in his eyes. "It's up to you as to where, but if you want a shot at the job, we'll be meeting tonight. It's the only time I'm free."

Judith groaned inwardly. The last thing she wanted to do was have dinner with *him*. It wasn't in her best interest to be anywhere near the man in such a setting, considering their last meeting. But the building was hers. She couldn't back down now.

She flashed a Gucci knockoff smile. "I guess my plans can

change." She'd deal with any client, even if it meant tangling with Satan, or one Devon A. McAllister in this instance. She could resist his charm. After all, she'd already had practice. Back then she'd been so green, a naïve girl who'd never met anyone like him. "When and where shall I meet you?"

"I'll make reservations for seven and pick you up a little before."

"I don't think so," she said with finality, noticing that smug gleam in his eyes. "I'll meet you. You'll be pleased with what I've done, so tell me where and I'll leave you to your next appointment."

A determined gaze met hers. She held her breath… waiting… praying. His confident expression told her that even though round one wasn't ending in a complete knockout, he felt secure in the outcome of their skirmish. The game had begun and he was definitely playing.

"Vincente's, and don't be late." He released her stare and stood, then picked up his briefcase and stuffed the proposal inside, along with a laptop. "Now, I should get going."

He was beside her in seconds.

"Allow me," he said, as she straightened after retrieving her bag. "I'll walk you out." When his hand touched her elbow, the connection sent a small burst of energy straight through her.

Judith glanced at him, noting his startled reaction, and at that precise moment realization set in. How would she ever survive dinner when a decade had done nothing to alleviate the strong current of attraction that had sprung up between them?

Remember my building.

She sighed and preceded him out, hoping she could stay focused on her objective.

Dev stopped by his assistant's office. "If you need me, call my cell," he said, before accompanying Judith to the elevator.

Neither spoke during the short ride.

He walked her out to the street. When he neared the door of a white limo, he turned. "Can I drop you anywhere?"

"No, thanks. I'll see you at seven." She smiled to cover a sudden rush of panic and strode away briskly without caring that her destination was in the opposite direction.

~

Dev stood watching her retreat as his driver jogged around to open his door. He stepped inside the limo, relaxed into the seat cushions, and stretched.

"Let's go home, Mike."

"You're supposed to call me Jeeves, boss," Mike Andrews said, as a wide grin split his face.

Dev chuckled.

"I'm serious. You have to act the part."

"I'd sooner die than have a stuffy chauffeur named Jeeves. Having one named Mike is bad enough."

Mike's exhale came out in an audible, exaggerated huff. "Yeah, but how are people going to know how rich you are if you don't have servants with stuffy names?"

"Just drive." Dev grinned, shaking his head. "I'm not worried about people knowing about my money." Now that he'd achieved success on his own terms, he didn't give a damn what others thought of him, especially those with deep pockets. He'd grown up in a working-class neighborhood with only his single mom for support. Maggie had given him her best, something that money couldn't buy. Basic values.

Like anyone, he'd rather have money than not, but that had never been one of his motivators. The trappings of wealth certainly didn't impress him. He glanced out the window, suddenly happy to have a hefty bank account. Money gave him the means. Finally, his plans were jelling. Thoughts of Judith Reid and the building he'd bought years ago to lure her into his path filled his brain. Despite one or two glitches, things were panning out exactly as he had hoped.

As the car sped on, his mind drifted back ten years to his last year of grad school at Stanford, where he'd earned his MBA. Immersed in several start-up projects by then, he'd needed the letters after his name, since they gave a person of his background more credibility.

His humble upbringing was something others, namely a few wealthier classmates with family connections, deemed a social disadvantage. Those who thought the world owed them for no other reason than they had the good luck to be born with not only the silver spoon, but also the whole meal.

He'd kept his opinion to himself of these spoiled rich kids

he'd met through James Morrison, his college roommate and frat brother. Secretly, he'd pitied them. After all, they hadn't had his edge. His drive to succeed came from a hunger his peers could never experience because they had never gone without, had never wanted for anything. Dev had. He knew what it was like to be considered inferior simply because of status, and he hungered for what some called unattainable. Dev's hunger to be the best…to have the best…led him to take risks no one but the most brazen could stomach.

His thoughts shifted to a graduation party James had hosted right after final exams. Most in his friend's wealthy crowd remembered the wild night as a rite of passage before moving on to adulthood. He had another reason for remembering.

That was the night he met and was completely taken in by Judith Reid. His mind cleared of everything but the memory of the time he still went by his old nickname, Mac.

~

"Thanks," Mac said, grabbing the beer someone had just untapped from the keg. While the foam subsided, his gaze swept the room. In the middle of taking a sip, he blinked and swallowed hard. He knew he gawked like a star-struck fan, but he couldn't look away from a blonde not twenty feet in front of him. She was a woman worth noting, a goddess holding court with mere mortals.

Once he could breathe again, his scan appraised without hiding male appreciation. He'd already made a fool of himself with staring, so why stop now?

Her tall, slender frame wasn't Barbie-doll perfect, but he never liked that kind of perfection anyway. He much preferred hers. Small but rounded breasts, a slim waist, and she had just enough curves on her hips to attract him. And being a leg man, he couldn't ignore hers. Long, never ending, and sexy—legs that even Barbie would envy.

His gaze moved higher. Natural highlights streaked through hair the color of wheat before harvest, catching and reflecting the light whenever her head moved.

She laughed at something one of her friends said and he felt a strong jolt, as expressive jade green eyes lit with intelligent humor met his for the briefest moment.

He finally found his common sense and quit gaping outright. Yet, he couldn't contain his interest, hiding it behind sipping at his beer.

Her regal bearing and expensive clothes reeked of money, so he prayed she wasn't one of those spoiled sorority partiers he had no use for. She only seemed interested in her group of girlfriends, and she nursed one drink the entire time he watched her, another good sign.

His number one rule of dating was never get involved with someone who drank too much. Mac rarely drank more than two drinks at any event, party or not. He'd made it through grad school on his own merits, not on Mommy and Daddy's money, so he had little time for hangovers. Nor did he waste time on someone who did. He wasn't one to spend time with someone too wasted to know who she was with. If he chose to acknowledge someone by putting out the effort of getting to know her at a party like this one, he was arrogant enough to want her to make the same effort. Call it a quirk, but that's how he felt.

He finally excused himself from a partier hanging on his every word and started toward the angel he'd been observing. She looked up and noticed his advance. His gaze caught hers and held the contact, electrifying him with a sensation of connection.

Her only reaction, once he stopped at a point where he could fully appreciate the way her eyes assessed him, was a cool smile. There was a bit of a dare thrown out in that smile. And Mac never backed away from a challenge, especially one promising to be as entertaining as this beautiful creature presented.

"Dance with me," he commanded in the firm tone of a man used to getting what he wanted. He reached for her hand, linked fingers, and propelled her with him to the middle of the crowded room.

Mac only had eyes for *her*. With an enormous amount of willpower, he resisted the zing of attraction surging through his veins and gently placed her arms on his shoulders. Sensing wariness, he worked to soothe, keeping a bit of distance for the simple reason he didn't want her to bolt.

"Now that we're so close, I guess I should introduce myself. My friends call me Mac." When she didn't respond right away, he prodded, "How about you? What do your friends call you?"

"Jude." She offered another cool smile that was beginning to drive him nuts. "You can call me Judith."

Undaunted, he laughed. *Definitely a challenge.* But he decided he preferred one when the women he usually met seemed too available, until they discovered his lowly status.

He sensed Judith was different. Or maybe he just wanted her to be different from all those social-climbing parasites who thought him the perfect man to have a good time with, but not good enough for happily-ever-after.

He pushed the disturbing thoughts aside. It didn't matter. He wasn't looking for long term. Not anymore. Right now, getting to know her was his main priority.

"I'm surprised we haven't met before," Mac said. "I thought I knew all of James' friends." Slowly they danced, moving in the direction of an open door leading to a huge deck.

"Let's find someplace we can talk, okay?" Mac's hold tightened when he felt her stepping away.

"I think you have the wrong idea about me," she said, drawing his gaze.

Her cool smile had taken on a touch of haughtiness that now mocked as she held his attention without flinching. His blonde goddess had spunk.

"What idea?"

"I'm not into going to bed with anyone, especially you."

Mac stared at her, totally taken aback. Maybe he had come on a little strong, but usually he was the one who slowed things down. It was bad enough that she thought so little of him, but that she could dismiss him so readily, really stung.

"I'm crushed that you'd think such a thing about me." Her haughty brow rose an inch. "Am I wrong?" "Um…um…"

Shit, he was too stunned to answer her. "Thought so," she said in a clipped, annoyed tone, pulling abruptly out of his grasp. With a straight spine, she turned to leave.

His jaw dropped lower and he gaped. She was actually walking away. "Wait. Don't go." He grabbed for her hand, but caught air instead.

Instantly, Mac knew he had made a tactical error and had to figure out what to say to keep her from fleeing. Now, more than ever, he knew she was someone worth pursuing. And more than anything, he wanted to break through her calm, aloof barrier.

"I didn't mean to come on so strong. I'm sorry if I offended you. Please stay." Once the apology was out, he couldn't help but notice the sincerity in his voice. He meant every word.

She stopped and turned around. She did a good job of hiding her emotions, but for an instant he spied indecision in those bright green eyes before the calm, cool smile returned.

"Okay. But don't disappoint me."

Relief swept through him as he reached for her hand, this time connecting and bringing it to his lips in a silent thank-you.

They headed outside and sat on the steps of the crowded deck. Mac had to shout to be heard over the noise despite her sitting only inches away. The two yelled back and forth for several minutes.

Finally, Mac stood and held out his hand. "Come on. It's too noisy here. I know a place we can go where it's quiet and we can talk. That's all, I promise."

She nodded and locked fingers with his. He guided her through a maze of trees and bushes.

Green space, and lots of it, surrounded the house tucked away in the hills of Woodside, California. Having been a frequent visitor over the last five years, Mac headed through the familiar terrain for one of his favorite spots, knowing it would be secluded and quiet.

No one from the party knew about the spot but him…and James, of course.

When they reached the gazebo, faint strains of distant music drifted from the house creating a romantic setting complete with bushes blocking the structure from view.

Mac led her to the one of the outdoor sofas. She sat and looked at him expectantly, waiting.

"Now that we can hear each other, let's start over." He put on an innocent grin in an effort to charm. "Pretend you just met me and have no preconceived notions about my personality. I'm Mac. I live in Palo Alto, and I'm about to graduate from Stanford with an MBA. And yes, I'm trying like hell to impress you by telling you that." He paused. His grin stretched. "Now it's your turn."

His introduction earned a slight smile and the knot in his stomach eased a bit.

"I'm Judith. I'm majoring in interior design at San Jose State."

"Really? What year?" Good. She was talking.

"I'll be a junior next year." Judith's breath came out in a small sigh while the firm line of her shoulders softened into a curve.

"So, you're a decorator?"

"That's one facet." She shook her head and laughed softly. "But I'm more interested in designing commercial buildings, from the outside in." Judith gave him a brief description of the planning involved, ending with, "Once the walls are in place, I'll be the one adding lighting and flooring and everything in between. Business interiors are difficult to design because of the expense involved and amount of wear and tear commercial buildings endure."

She stopped to take a breath.

Mac smiled. Her feminine voice rose and fell in a pleasing cadence as she continued explaining a subject she obviously loved. He couldn't take his gaze off her face.

"I'm really interested in refurbishing old buildings, especially from the early nineteen hundreds or earlier. Sometimes they're easier to tear down, but if that happens, we lose a part of history. And many of those buildings are so well built, it's better to update them. San Francisco has hundreds of them, one I especially love."

"That's awesome." He asked question after question, unable to hide his interest. She was fascinating to listen to. He could do it all night.

"Have you ever felt you were destined to do something?" she asked earnestly, once the conversation died down.

"I don't know," he answered honestly. He shrugged. "I've never thought about it before. I'm driven, but I'm not sure if it's destiny or, as my mother says, plain obstinacy."

"Well, I believe in destiny now." When he allowed the question to form in his eyes, she grinned. "I used to feel as if I never fit in anywhere. When I was younger, I was kind of a shy loner and hated school."

He chuckled and shook his head. "I can't imagine you being shy."

"I was. I daydreamed a lot, especially on the way to school. There's this run-down building. On Hyde Street, close to Geary. I passed by it every day."

She stopped talking as if lost in thought. Mac watched her. Before his eyes, Judith's expression turned diffident, giving him a glimpse of the girl she used to be.

"I'm being silly." She glanced at her hands, twisting them as his stare remained fastened on her lips. She cleared her throat and offered another shy smile. "You're probably laughing at this."

"No. Tell me. I'm dying to know," he shot back, realizing he was dead serious. He wanted to learn everything about her.

"Okay," she said, laughing. "But you asked for it."

Damn, if she didn't have the sweetest laugh.

"It was a lonely building, as if it didn't belong or fit in either. I don't know why, but whenever I'd walk past it, I'd feel something. Though old and worn-out, sitting out of place among the newer buildings on the street, I noticed so much beauty. I forgot about it once I went to high school. In college I discovered commercial designing, and the memory came back." She shrugged. "I remembered how my building used to make me feel. Special. Like we shared something in common. I found out why I exist. To bring buildings like that one back to life."

"I'll never look at an old building again in the same way." His answer produced another one of her heart-stopping smiles, and instantly his empty notions of long term and love vanished.

"I know you're teasing, but I don't care. Someday I'll have my own business specializing in refurbishing because there's so much hidden beauty in those old buildings."

"I take it you'll be doing this in San Francisco, not San Jose?"

"I hope to. I'm from the city," Judith said, nodding. "My family's been there for generations. They're very old-fashioned and a little overprotective." She sighed. "I'm sure they think I was dropped on their doorstep because I'm so different."

Mac's eyebrows shot up. "How so?"

"My mom's the typical wife of her generation, a whiz at

organizing parties, and she's always involved with several committees. She's never held a job and doesn't understand my need to work when I don't have to. Chairing a committee is about as far away as you can get from what I want for my life." She tugged at the hem of her shorts. "I don't mean to disappoint either of them, but they just don't get me."

"You're lucky to have two caring parents," he said softly a moment later. This time Judith's eyebrows rose in question.

He laughed. "I have my mom, but my dad's a loser who never paid child support. I haven't seen him since I was little. So it was just the two of us."

Her eyes reflected compassion.

"Oh, don't get me wrong," he quickly added. "My mom's the best. She's my biggest supporter, but I know it was hard for her, being a single parent and all."

He told Judith all about his unprivileged childhood in San Leandro, California.

Usually, he never talked freely to the wealthy women he met in his best friend's crowd, having become cynical regarding them for good reason.

Judith definitely came from money, but she was nothing like those social-climbing vultures. Mac found himself opening up. Like a faucet going full blast, the story of his life poured forth.

"In high school, computers fascinated me," he said. Wanting to impress her, he detailed his successes. "I had a great teacher in my freshman year, Mr. Dobson. I used to help him after school. He taught me how business works, and showed me how to use my brain to earn money. My first company was so successful, I created a couple more."

"So you just started companies? In high school? How exciting."

"It was nothing, especially since there was a big demand for what I knew." He couldn't keep the pride out of his voice after glimpsing admiration in her animated expression. "My small companies are centered on computers and are very profitable. I create websites and design systems most people have no clue about. But it's only the beginning. I made it through Stanford on full scholarship. I'm going to the top and I won't stop till I have my own major company. My plans are already in the works."

They sat talking in the gazebo for hours, but to Mac it seemed like minutes. He'd never felt so alive. He felt a true connection with her. Only James and his mother knew more about him after the time spent alone with her. He'd certainly never shared such a big part of himself with any other woman.

When their conversation ebbed, a quiet peacefulness surrounded them. He was very comfortable with the silence and considering her relaxed pose, she was too.

Finally, Mac glanced at Judith. Their gazes locked. He saw a soul mate in those liquid jade eyes. Her cool expression was gone. In its place was a warm, inviting smile, drawing him in deeper with the force of a riptide.

He had to kiss that mouth. He angled his head. Slowly, his lips met hers. The moment they did, he knew he'd found paradise.

When her mouth opened on a small sigh, giving him all the invitation he needed, he deepened the kiss. His tongue invaded, eliciting her response. She wrapped her arms around him, pulling him closer as sensation after sensation rolled over him. Like waves hitting the beach, his blood pounded, filling him with need.

He couldn't get enough. He couldn't stop. She was as intoxicating as the most potent drug.

Her soft moans set him on fire. He burned for her. Too swept away with the pleasure her lips gave, he positioned her pliant body underneath his on the sofa, still kissing.

She was perfection. So soft. So warm. So yielding.

His hands moved of their own volition. Roaming, straying, feeling, and touching. After unsnapping her bra, one hand found exactly what it had been searching for, heaven in his palm, as he kneaded and squeezed the perfect breast.

His movements intensified as his hunger and want grew. She was made for him. No one had ever held him this close to the edge of losing sanity before. And that's right where he was. The edge of sanity.

She seemed as caught up in the moment as he and this urged him forward. He unzipped her shorts.

He was hard with a driving need to be inside of her, to get as close to her as possible.

Someone called her name from a distance. She stiffened. His brain registered the fact, but they were secluded. No one knew where they were. Now, more than ever, Mac needed to be inside her.

He broke contact with her lips. "It's okay," he soothed, as someone called her name again. Only this time, the sound was louder and much closer.

His hands left her body and he caught Judith's look of horror. She redid the clasp on her bra with shaking hands, zipped up her shorts, then jumped up and ran from the gazebo.

When the full magnitude of her actions hit Mac, he sat back in stunned silence and stared at the empty space. What the hell?

Did she have a boyfriend and not tell him?

He slammed a fist into a post. It took minutes for his breathing and other body parts to return to normal. Then he started after her.

Mac entered the house from the deck, hurried to the foyer, and strode briskly toward James Morrison, who was at the front door waving good-bye to someone.

James closed the door, spun around, then noticed him and smiled broadly. "Hey, Mac, where've you been hiding?"

"Did you see Judith?" he asked.

"Yeah, she just left in a hurry. Why?"

Mac ran to the door and jerked it open as a sporty car shot down the street.

"Damn!" he said under his breath and turned back to see James following with a puzzled expression.

"Hey, you're not interested in her, are you? If so, you should rethink. I call her the Ice Queen. Even your charm and good looks can't break through all her cold."

"You know her?" Mac asked, glancing at James.

"Paul's interested in her. He's known her for years. I've always thought her a little aloof, above us underlings." He offered a careless shrug. "She's a lot younger than our crowd, so I was surprised to see her here tonight. I assumed she came with Paul."

"I don't even know her last name," Mac whispered, looking down the road the car had taken.

"It's Reid...Judith Reid. She may be gorgeous to look at, but no's her favorite word. Paul's been trying for the last year to get a date with her and she shoots him down every time he asks. I don't know why he still tries."

Mac remembered James' younger brother; they'd met a time or two before. Paul was younger than them, about three years or so. He looked a lot like his older brother, but was a little taller and leaner.

James focused on Mac's face. His grin spread. Then he broke into a full-blown laugh. "You struck out with her, didn't you?" he taunted.

"No," Mac snorted. "But I think I might like to try," he added, before heading back inside.

Chapter 2

Judith couldn't keep her hands steady while sticking the gold post into her ear. She took a deep breath and tried again.

All afternoon, she'd obsessed over tonight.

The idea of going out with Mac…no, not Mac, *Dev*…was terrifying, but deep down, if she was honest with herself, it also thrilled her. There was something above and beyond Dev's good looks that grabbed her and made her take notice, exactly as it had that night so long ago.

Etched into her memory, those few hours had made her even more wary of men. If only she hadn't accompanied her best friend, Kate Winters, now Kate Morrison, to James Morrison's graduation party and tried to pretend to be something she wasn't. She'd never fit in with cool, popular guys like Dev or James, and after that night, she realized why.

"Yeah!" she muttered, as she padded to her closet. "I was too inexperienced for that coeds-gone-wild crowd." A gazelle in the midst of cheetahs came to mind. She definitely should have paid more attention to the signs.

She reached for the new sea-blue dress that enhanced the color of her eyes, then stepped into it and pulled up the zipper.

Thank God for Paul Morrison's intervention. If he hadn't come looking for her… A flush of embarrassment crept up her face and she closed her eyes, unwilling to think about the alternative.

Her only defense? She hadn't wanted to believe Mac could be like the guys in high school, those conniving little weasels who'd placed bets on 'nailing her' as their leader, Tommy Ridgeway, had so aptly phrased it. He'd had a hard time accepting the word no, but he certainly didn't have any power over her now. He was just a bad memory of an ill-mannered jerk.

Unfortunately, Dev was another unforgettable matter entirely.

She gave a disgusted snort and pulled a brush through her

hair, chiding herself for being such an easy target. An idiot. She should have known better than to trust his promise. And to think he'd gotten so close to her, so quickly.

That he'd considered her a conquest back then had pierced deeply into her soul. In order to avoid similar pain, she'd made a conscious choice to avoid involvement. She'd already proven she wasn't the best judge of character, leaving her with only one conclusion. Men, and the quest for happily-ever-after, simply weren't worth the price.

How upsetting to realize that after one brief meeting with Dev, the door she'd barred years ago had reopened an inch. She'd forgotten how thrilling just talking to him had been, before things had gotten out of hand.

She checked herself out in the mirror, indulged in a satisfied smile, and determined then and there her past would not intrude on tonight. In fact, now, after thinking on it, she rather liked the idea of a dinner meeting.

Remember, this is work. Nothing else.

Despite the reminder, she couldn't quite quell the excitement sizzling inside of her at the thought of spending time with *him* again, even if it was work.

He was so gorgeous and she still found him attractive. Just like the first time she saw him strutting in her direction. He was such a hunk, Dr. McSteamy and Dr. McDreamy rolled into one, so how could she not be attracted when he took her hand? She was just an inexperienced seventeen-year-old trying to act cool, whose only wish was to fit in. It was scary, yet exhilarating at the same time.

Judith headed out her front door, refusing to dwell on her stupidity. Why berate herself over one mistake in judgment? After all, she'd been a child on the verge of adulthood, so it was pointless.

She crossed the road and walked toward Union Street with resolve. This dinner was long overdue. It was time to quit running. She needed to put that night in the past where it belonged and quit being a scared, naïve girl.

It was time to meet the man as a mature woman.

She neared Vincente's and glanced at her watch, pushing the memories aside.

Six fifty-seven. Perfect timing.

"Has Mr. McAllister arrived?" she asked the maître d' after entering.

"Yes, right this way." He led her through a maze of tables to a dark corner in the back.

Mac stood at their approach. *Good grief, I really need to think of him as Dev now.* He pulled out a chair and had her seated in a smooth, sleek move, reminding her of the same sexy hunk she first met ten years ago.

Whoa! Don't even go there. She had to focus on the building, not on him.

"I've ordered a bottle of cabernet. What will you have?" he asked, while catching the waiter's attention.

"Cabernet's fine. I love red wine."

She surreptitiously watched Dev tell the waiter to hold their dinner orders so they could discuss business. The man was simply too attractive for his own good. Though he'd dressed casually, in Dockers and a maroon sports shirt that complemented his blue eyes and black hair, power emanated from him. He was a hard man to ignore, even for someone who'd spent her life ignoring men.

She made eye contact with him once the waiter sped away and quickly wished she hadn't.

More memories of their heated encounter all those years ago rushed back. Instantly, she realized the girl of her youth had never stood a chance against his dynamic charm and killer looks. She wasn't entirely sure of his motives, but one thing she did know. If she was his intended target, she couldn't delude herself into thinking he wouldn't hit a bull's-eye. Heck, just look at him. Who wouldn't want to be his target? The idea of a relationship with him held a certain appeal, but such chumminess and business seldom mixed well.

She had no intention of allowing anything to muck up this project.

"I've gone over your proposal and I'm very impressed." Dev's rich voice broke into her thoughts and she gave him her full attention, as he added, "I'm not well-schooled in design, but I can see why you're considered fresh, creative, and innovative. I suspected your plans would be good, but they're the best I've seen. They show the building the way it should be." The edges of his lips curled into a warm smile. "I don't give praise lightly, Judith, but I do give it where it's due."

His praise shocked her. She glanced down at her hands as a hint of heat slid up her face. She certainly hadn't expected to see such approval shining from his eyes. No matter how good their work is, every artist is vulnerable to how other people see it. She took a deep breath and met his gaze without letting him perceive how much his opinion meant.

"Okay, so you like my plans. Now what? Where do we go from here?"

He proceeded to tell her, and they spent the next hour engrossed in business.

One thing Judith learned about Dev during that time, he was thorough where his business was concerned. She let him know early on she was a savvy negotiator with a quick mind who didn't miss any details.

They drank their first glass of wine. He promptly poured a second and they ordered in between the negotiations. Just as dinner was served, they came to an agreement.

"So, now that we've got that out of the way, how about telling me more about yourself?"

She threw him a wary look and he shrugged. "I like to get to know the people I work closely with, and this project qualifies since we are going to be spending a considerable amount of time together."

Judith took a long sip of wine and set the glass back on the table, keeping her hand on the stem. She cleared her throat. "What would you like to know?"

"Personal stuff. I already know you relocated from San Jose to San Francisco a little over a year ago to start your own business. I also know that you've struggled more than your fair share because a lot of fools in the building industry are chauvinists who don't like working for a company run by a woman."

"Good grief. I didn't realize you were that interested."

"I do background checks on all of my prospective business associates. What's lacking is the personal."

"I see." His answer made sense. Hadn't she done her own

investigating? The only difference was that her life was pretty much an open book, while his was hidden from the public eye. Dev had offered a ton of information that night, though. She probably knew more about him after their time in that gazebo than most people who'd known him for years, considering what little was available about his past. *Yeah, but don't forget, he had ulterior motives for opening up.*

She hadn't wanted to believe his interest in her hadn't been real, but what other explanation was there when Paul told her Mac was a love 'em and leave 'em kind of guy. In a pained instant, their kiss and how quickly it spun out of control came hurling back. What hurt her pride, more than being thought of as a notch on his bedpost, was that she'd totally misread him. She thought she'd found a soul mate. Someone like her who understood her loneliness.

Looking at him now, she wondered how she'd ever come to that conclusion. "Before I answer, I have one question." She hesitated, then added, "Since we're getting so personal."

He smiled and nodded. "Okay."

"So tell me, Dev. How did you happen to pick that building?"

His forehead furrowed. "That building?"

"Yes. I want to know why you bought it."

~

"Why?" Dev struggled to sound nonchalant, but it was damned hard considering the question. He certainly hadn't expected her to ask about anything that alluded to their shared past. He glanced at her, noting how much she appeared like the woman he originally perceived her to be. But he knew better. She was a viper of the most vicious kind, dangerous because she came across as all innocent and sweet. "Funny you should ask that."

He expected attraction, especially since his first glimpse of her was one of those unforgettable moments. Physically, she hadn't changed one bit, except maybe to grow more beautiful.

"Well?" she asked, her voice pulling him back to her question. "I'm waiting for an answer."

He shrugged and went for honesty, or as much as he could allow considering his plans. "Let's just say those few hours swayed me enough to check it out. Once I did, I took a closer look at what appeared to be a pile of rubble and was able to see what you'd described." He picked up his wineglass. Before taking a drink, he added, "It was a good investment. Nothing more. And who better to refurbish it than the person who brought it to my attention in the first place?"

She didn't have to know the whole truth. The memory of her story had touched him, so much so that he'd wanted to please her and had leased the building she'd told him about with an option to buy. Imagine him thinking they could join forces and take on the world together. He'd buy run-down properties and she could help renovate them. What a wasted effort, when she wouldn't even take his phone calls. Yet, when it came time to give up the lease, he couldn't. Instead, he bought the building and bided his time.

He'd kept up with Judith over the years through his best friend James, hoping for an opportunity to make his move. Many times he'd stayed away from events to avoid a chance meeting. His connection to James and his family had created several close calls.

He'd almost given up his quest since she and Paul Morrison had remained an item. Rumors even floated about that they were close to being engaged. Then one day James came by his office and told him everything was off. Even more surprising, James and Kate had broken up too, and within months, Paul married Kate Winters.

The news of the breakup had been a stroke of luck for Dev. Judith Reid and that night were still etched in his brain and he had to find a way to erase them from his mind forever.

Nothing would stop him now.

Nothing but the cool smile she offered him, the same one he remembered. Damn if he didn't feel as if she were issuing a challenge all over again.

He needed to do something to knock her off balance. Otherwise, she could throw him off course. "So, back to the personal. What happened between you and Paul? Why didn't you marry him?"

She opened her mouth as if shocked. "That's personal."

"Which is exactly why I want to know. We have mutual friends. I'm just curious, especially since Paul was one of those

23

who recommended you highly."

Judith focused on her plate. "We came to a mutual understanding." She stirred the food around, hesitating. "We weren't meant to be together."

It took her long enough to realize the fact. Too bad she never gave him a chance. They would have been good together. For a few hours there, he'd believed in love at first sight.

The thought stopped him. Is that why he'd never forgotten her? He shook it off. No way. He was simply collecting on a long-standing debt.

Dev no longer believed in love. Judith was the woman who completely obliterated his faith in the stupid emotion. He'd foolishly let his guard down by thinking she was something special.

He'd just have to be careful. Wouldn't do to slip up now.

They ate their meal in silence, then ordered dessert.

"Would you like another glass of wine?" Dev asked, once the waiter was out of earshot.

She nodded and he finished off the bottle.

He knew damned well he shouldn't prolong this meeting, but he found himself lingering.

~

Judith dug into her tiramisu, developing an unforeseen respect for D.A. McAllister. Glimpses of the Dev she remembered emerged during their meal. She couldn't help liking him all over again, or noting the same sincerity she'd sensed that night so long ago when he'd told her of his plans to make it big someday with his own company.

It was probably an act, she thought, remembering Paul's warning. Just like back then, when she'd prayed he was different from those jerks from high school. Men like him didn't change their stripes. Thank God hindsight was twenty-twenty.

She took another bite of the custard and savored the flavor. She willed herself to not be taken in again, but the task was nearly impossible. She swallowed hard, wishing her experience tonight hadn't opened her memory's floodgates. His absorbed interest throughout their meal reminded her too much of those few hours when he'd flattered her....had made her feel beautiful, special even...like what she said mattered, which was something

Judith had never forgotten. Especially for someone who'd spent her early teen years as a gangly adolescent whose facial features were in place long before her growth spurts had a chance to catch up. Though her looks had improved with age, she still felt like an awkward, funny-looking kid at times. But not then. Not while talking to Mac. And not tonight. Not while talking to Dev.

Judith set her spoon down and pushed the bowl aside. Needing to place distance between them, she said, "It's getting late."

Dev nodded. "This has been a productive dinner. I'm pleased with the results." He pushed away from the table and stood. "I'll get in touch with you about the contract as soon as my board convenes tomorrow."

He was beside her quickly and offered a hand.

Dev's charming business persona was back as he held her elbow and led her out of the now empty restaurant.

"Can I walk you to your car?"

"I walked." Now that their time together was actually coming to an end, she suddenly wanted more time with him. "My house isn't far."

"Then I'll walk you home."

"Okay." Judith offered him a warm smile. She shouldn't encourage him, but what harm could there be in walking? "That would be nice."

Traffic noise died as they headed away from Union Street, ambling up the hill to quieter blocks where storefronts gave way to residential houses. Both were lost in their thoughts. The mood was mellow, aided by the good food and wine they'd imbibed.

"This is it," she said, when they neared her house. "Thanks for a nice evening."

She had her keys in her hand. He took them from her, and continued up the walkway. After unlocking and opening her door, he bent to drop a quick kiss on her cheek before handing back her keys.

Dev turned and bounded down the porch steps, saying over his shoulder, "You'll hear from me, Judith. Good night."

Judith stood inside, slightly dazed by the speed at which he'd put her completely at ease. She hadn't expected it, but should have. At this point, she'd totally revised her opinion of Dev 'Mac'

25

McAllister. Oh, he was charming, all right, and she loved his quick, challenging mind. And she had to admit, he was damned sexy. Yet, despite his easygoing manner, at dinner she'd detected an underlying tension behind his smile and conversation. Suddenly, she felt much like a mouse caught under a cat's paw, while the cat waits motionless for the mouse to respond so it can move in for the kill.

Was Dev a cat on the prowl?

She snorted. Who knew? She only knew that she enjoyed dinner and she was going to enjoy refurbishing his building.

Shaking her head, she started for her bedroom. She could handle her attraction. Right now, sleep beckoned. Things always looked better by daylight. She was a pro at figuring ways to put up her guard to keep guys at bay. She would merely stay ten steps ahead of Dev. If she could manage that, she might survive this project intact.

Chapter 3

Dev took the steps two at a time before ringing Judith's doorbell. He glanced around, taking a closer look at her house by daylight. He'd always known Judith had money, but this two-story, well-maintained Victorian shouted megabucks, the kind that came from earned interest, not earned income.

He waited. When nothing happened after a full minute, he pressed again, this time keeping his finger on the buzzer.

He caught movement through the bay window, open at the top, and the sound of Judith's annoyed voice floated down.

"Stupid neighborhood kids."

The door jerked open and he took his finger off the button.

The warnings she was about to yell died a quick death when she saw him leaning against the jamb. She swallowed hard and threw him a suspicious glance.

"What are you doing here at..." Judith turned back to glance at a clock on the hall table, "...7:30 a.m. and why are you laying on my doorbell?"

"Sheath your claws, woman, I'm here on a mission of mercy," he said, stepping over the threshold when she moved aside to let him in.

"Nice place. I take it you decorated it yourself?" He turned a full three-sixty while he absorbed her taste.

"Yes, but that still doesn't answer my question. Why are you here?"

The foyer split a formal dining area on one side of the hall and the formal living room on the other. Both rooms were decorated with flair, could make the cover of one of those home magazines his mother was always reading. Cream and a cranberry-red color were juxtaposed throughout to create an inviting atmosphere despite the formality of expensive and traditional furniture. He liked the rooms because they told him that while Judith followed convention, she couldn't hide her creative streak.

"Well?" The one word drew his attention. She stood and stared at him with hands on her hips.

Grinning, he gave her body a slow perusal, starting at the top of her head and ending at her elegantly shaped bare feet, made sexier with red toenails. He'd obviously gotten her out of bed. Her shoulder-length blonde hair was a mess and she had no makeup on this morning. She wore a knee-length sleeveless t-shirt with a scalloped edge and no collar. The shirt fell over an elegant shoulder, exposing it, while also outlining a perfect pair of breasts.

An instant shot of lust hit him. Thoughts of bending over to kiss one of those breasts bounced around his brain before he could catch and subdue them. Her allure was tempting. Almost too tempting, but he quickly willed his libido to shut down. Lust would have to wait.

"Get dressed." Since grabbing her and heading for the nearest bed were out of the question, he added, "I came to take you to the building for an early inspection before they start gutting the inside this afternoon. I want to snap a few 'before' shots."

"Really?" Judith appeared torn. Dev could plainly read the mental debate on her face; her longing to tell him he was nuts warring with her desire to be at the site.

He relaxed when he saw her smile. He'd won this round.

"I'm usually an early riser, but not this morning. It's going to take me a few minutes and I need coffee. So, while I'm showering make yourself useful. You can make coffee, can't you?" she said in a voice full of laughter. "It's easy, you just grind and pour."

Fascinated, Dev watched her turn and sashay toward her bedroom. Such a contradiction. An enticing, arousing goddess one minute and a laughing, innocent kid the next.

Before she could take another step, he grabbed her hand, twirled her around, and hauled her up to him. Her surprised expression had his grin widening. He rather liked surprising her.

"Such a smart mouth and so demanding this early in the morning. Punishment for a comment like that is a kiss." His mouth then descended over hers.

At first, the kiss was playful, meant only to be a flirtation and she responded in kind. Yet, it deepened and changed to something more serious.

Judith's lips were soft and yielding and, as he remembered, the contact electric. From the moment he'd spotted her walking into his office the day before, he'd been dying to see if she tasted as good as he remembered. Reality was better. The woman was made for him. She twisted his stomach inside out now as easily as she had all those years ago.

When her hand slid tentatively around his neck, he didn't hesitate to take advantage, maneuvering them both against the wall. Fully aroused and under her spell, he stepped closer to her warmth so she could feel his need.

A powerful, primal urge to lift her shirt and seduce her with sensation was all encompassing and too much like their last encounter.

Somehow through the erotic haze he sensed her withdrawal. Immediately, he stopped. She managed to turn her head and break the connnection with his lips. When she tried to pull away, his arms tightened. He rested his chin on her head, closed his eyes to gain control of his senses, and didn't allow her to move.

"I'm sorry," he whispered a moment later. "I never meant for that to happen. Why don't you go in and shower and I'll get coffee?"

He then let her go and turned toward what he thought was her kitchen.

~

Judith scampered into her room and stood with her back against the closed door for support, taking countless deep breaths. She was in big trouble. No, she was in humongous trouble.

How could she not be, after awakening to *him* standing in her living room all sexy and tempting? She'd have to be dead not to appreciate Dev's blatant masculine appeal. How could she deny an attraction to him, especially after that kiss? Who wouldn't be unsettled after that? Paul's kisses had never curled her toes. If they had, she might have married him.

She tried to block the mental image of Dev dressed casually in a navy polo that brought out the blue of his eyes. His worn jeans were old, faded, and had shrunk a bit, fitting him like a second skin, hugging his butt and showing off muscular, well-developed thighs. Her insides quivered from the memory.

Oh, good grief! Why was she having such thoughts? It was so unlike her. She closed her eyes and continued breathing slowly, trying to forget—everything.

By choice, she still rarely dated, and she was used to keeping guys at a distance. She certainly didn't kiss many. What was it about him? None of the men she currently knew made her want to have hot, uninhibited sex after only one dinner and a kiss.

Sighing, she headed for the bathroom.

She needed to keep her equilibrium and not let sex get in the way. If she succumbed to lust, it could screw things up, making it difficult to work together. She turned on the shower and stepped into it. While soaping up, she thought about how she could slow things.

Judith resolved right then to talk to Dev and get his agreement to keep his hands to himself if he wanted her to work on his project. It was an empty threat because nothing would keep her off the project at this point, but the decision made her feel better.

~

In the kitchen, Dev found the coffeepot, beans, and grinder. Thankfully, she liked fresh-ground coffee. He needed a jolt of caffeine to settle his nerves and get his mind off sex.

He wasn't a teenage boy who couldn't keep it in his pants, for God's sake. He was thirty-three years old and proud of the fact that his control made women moan with pleasure. The one person who had ever made him lose his control was taking a shower at that very moment.

It took supreme effort not to run in and take her there, wet and slippery. He seriously considered it, knowing he could achieve his objective considering her response.

Hell, what was wrong with him? Where was his control? His resolve?

If he acted on his urges, the game would be over and he'd be the loser. *Again.* The thought kept him in the kitchen.

He was truly in deep shit. Judith affected him too much. Much more than he'd anticipated, so he had to rethink his strategy.

Dev's original plan hadn't taken into account this strong

sexual pull between them. Eventually he'd get what he wanted out of her, but he wanted it to be on his terms, with her out of control, not him. Besides, he enjoyed her company...didn't want the game to be over so quickly. Once he walked away, their ties would be severed forever. That thought unsettled him.

He heard the bedroom door open. Seconds later Judith rounded the doorway and walked toward him wearing an expression etched in determination.

She'd applied her makeup sparingly. Now fully dressed in jeans and a casual shirt, she had a fresh, youthful look about her, seeming so calm and reserved, not at all like the siren in his arms moments ago. Dev grinned. He doubted many knew about those hidden passions lurking just below the surface of her cool detachment.

Steeling himself for the verbal battle obviously about to begin, he watched her walk up to the coffeepot and pour the fragrant, steaming liquid into a cup he'd set out.

She took a drink and inhaled.

When she looked over at him, all he could see was her soft, kissable mouth, slightly swollen from their antics not fifteen minutes earlier.

With effort, he moved his focus higher and met her defiant gaze. Damn, if she only knew how provocative she was when she stared at him with those icy, calm eyes.

"Look, Mac—I mean, Dev. I've been thinking."

Oh boy, here it comes.

"I've always tried to be honest in my dealings with people. Because I'm not about to stop the habit now, I won't sugarcoat this, so here goes." Judith inhaled deeply, as if extra air gave her added courage, and continued. "I find you extremely attractive. I'd love nothing better than to jump into the nearest bed and have what I think would be a mind-blowing experience. However, I'm going to refrain because I want to work with you on this job. We can't let sex and feelings get involved, so we need to come to an understanding."

"I'm listening," he said, her honesty drawing his admiration. He certainly hadn't expected this tack.

"The way I see it, we need to set a couple of ground rules. We're both adults who should be able to work together without falling all over each other."

He nodded in agreement. "Tell me your rules and I'll see if I can live with them."

"Okay, first…no kissing. Kissing only gets us into trouble."

"No!" Dev stated firmly. He could never agree to anything so ludicrous. Whenever he got within a foot of her, all he could think about was kissing her; when he was kissing her, all he could think of was getting her flat on her back. So the rule was definitely out of the question.

"What do you mean, no?" she asked, straightening her shoulders and eyeing him cautiously.

"I mean no, I won't agree. I'll never agree to something when I know I can't follow through. However, I'll promise to try not to kiss you." He offered his most charming smile and said, "How's that?"

"You're something else," Judith said, grinning back and shaking her head. Then sobering, she added, "I don't know. We need to keep our distance. We're embarking on a professional endeavor, so let's keep everything on a business level. Surely you can agree to that?"

"I always keep business and pleasure separated. I promise you when we're working together, it'll be about business and only business. However, I reserve the right to pursue you when the whistle blows at the end of the day."

"But I don't want you to. Haven't you been listening?"

Dev's smile grew when he caught her frustration. Frustration was good. Kept her off balance. "That's not what your lips told me a few minutes ago."

~

Judith gaped at him. Was he serious? This wasn't going as planned. She had to make him understand.

"Dev, I'm not going to sleep with you." At least not until after the building was done.

"Oh?" His eyebrows shot up. Then his manner turned smug. "Honesty begets honesty, Judith. I want you and your reaction tells me you want me. I'll never force myself on you, but I'm giving you fair warning. A sexual relationship is my main goal, and exactly where my efforts will be directed. All you have to do is say no and I will stop. But…make no mistake, we will make love…eventually. When it happens, you'll definitely be saying yes."

His arrogant confidence irritated her. Still, she wasn't naïve enough to ignore his warning. Not when he spoke the truth. Unsure how she got herself into this position, she could only sigh. At least she understood his intentions. Hopefully, her stay of execution would allow her to hold him off until she could come up with another plan.

"Can we get croissants on the way?" she asked. "I'm starving."

Dev chuckled at her obvious diversion and didn't answer.

She walked to the cupboard over the sink, reached in to take out two travel mugs, and proceeded to fill one up. "I have an extra travel cup if you want more coffee. We can drink it on the way. I'm anxious to get to the building, so let's go."

"Yeah, I'd like more." His eyes bore into hers, the implication clear.

Judith averted her gaze, feeling heat seep into her face. She bit her lower lip to avoid answering, and held out the extra cup.

His self-satisfied expression told her he hadn't missed her uneasiness as he took the pot and filled the cup she handed him. He snapped on the lid and started toward the door.

"I'll drive. No sense taking two cars when parking's such a pain."

Judith wasn't exactly thrilled with his suggestion, but she kept it to herself and followed him out. "I'll agree to anything as long as I get my croissants."

Dev hit the keyless entry and the locks clicked on a sporty black Lexus parked in front of her house. He opened the passenger door and waited. Once she was seated, he raced around and slid behind the wheel in a fluid motion.

"Do you have a favorite bakery in mind?" He spared her a brief nod after driving a block. "If not, there's one on the way."

"No, I'm not fussy about my indulgences." She bit her tongue, wishing she'd chosen her words more carefully. She chanced a glance at him.

Judging by his smirk, he definitely caught the double meaning.

"Well, I can certainly try to satisfy one of your cravings."

"Will you stop?" She tried not to smile.

"What? I'm stopping for croissants."

Dev's expression turned so innocent she couldn't stop the laugh that burst free. "Behave," she warned. "You promised to be professional."

"You started it. Remember, Judith. Don't start something if you're not willing to finish it. I only have so much patience."

Though spoken in jest, what she glimpsed in his intense gaze told her he wasn't joking. She swallowed hard and looked away.

Neither spoke until he stopped in front of a bakery and glanced at her with eyebrows raised.

"I'll buy, if you'll run in." He reached into his wallet and pulled out a ten. "Get me a couple of cheese croissants."

"Sure. I'll be right back."

She was in and out in no time.

Minutes later he parked the Lexus in front of the building because it was still early and no other cars lined the street. At the entrance, Dev was about to hand his coffee over to her when Judith shrugged, holding up coffee in one hand and the croissants in the other.

He nodded. One-handed, he finagled the key into the lock and turned it, then used his shoulder to push open the big heavy door. He held the door open with his body, waiting for her to go in ahead of him. As soon as he stepped inside, it slammed shut.

"Let's eat first. I left the camera in the car. I'll go back and get it when we're ready to take pictures."

Dev headed toward a window ledge about thigh high. He shoved clutter to the floor and sat. "Come on, Judith, you can sit here." He patted the spot next to him. "I won't bite. It's not a four-star restaurant, but it'll do."

Judith walked over and sat down, setting down the bag between them.

They ate for a moment in silence that was easy rather than awkward.

When he finished with his first croissant, Dev started talking, telling her about the building. He knew most of its eighty-year history. After they finished their quick meal, he took her on a tour.

He led her up the first floor stairwell to the second floor.

34

"Watch your step."

She avoided piles of debris and glanced around. The ravages of time and use had taken their toll. Rotten wood was noticeable everywhere. So was rust.

"You can tell this building hasn't been remodeled since the fifties." Wherever she turned, she saw faded wallpaper or paint that begged to be redone, or outdated fixtures that needed replacing.

"It's pretty ugly," he replied, brushing a smudge of dust off his pants. Looking at the mess, he added, "I'm sure we'll see big differences in before and after."

Judith walked over to a corner and pulled at a piece of curling linoleum. "Look at this." She knocked on what lie underneath. "Thick. Hard. Wood. What I call hidden treasure. Most old buildings were built using wood and stone meant to last centuries. After this old junk is removed and it's refinished, this floor will shine like new." When he merely nodded, she said, unable to keep the excitement out of her voice, "They don't make solid wood plank floors like this anymore."

She made a sweeping motion with her hand. "In a couple of months, once the place is gutted, new walls put in, moldings repaired and new fixtures installed, it'll look like new."

"Hidden treasures. Hmmm." Dev smiled. "I trust your talent." He started for the stairwell door. "I want to get my camera. I'll be right back."

Judith nodded. As promised, his business demeanor hadn't slipped once. While he was gone, she began to relax and inspected further. Before long, she lowered her guard even more; she was enjoying herself too much to continue worrying when worrying took some of the fun out of the experience.

Dev eventually returned with his camera in hand and began snapping pictures as they finished the tour.

It wasn't until they headed in the direction of his car when Judith remembered his board meeting. She waited until he pulled away from the curb, before asking, "I thought you had to get approval from your board today. Wasn't the meeting supposed to be at eleven? If so, you're late."

Startled by the question, Dev's eyes narrowed in confusion. Then he smiled and replied smoothly, "Oh, I took care of it and had a subordinate submit your plans. With my stamp of approval, it was merely a formality anyway."

"I thought you were going to be busy this morning. How come you're free all of a sudden?" Judith asked, suddenly suspicious.

Dev shrugged. "Those plans included inspecting the building. I decided you might want to join me is all."

She accepted his reasonable answer and for the rest of the drive neither felt they had to entertain the other with inane chatter.

Soon he pulled up to her house and turned off the ignition, shrouding them in complete silence. Instantly, the space in the car shrank.

After long seconds he finally spoke. "My assistant's drawing up a contract with the stipulations we negotiated last night. I'd like to bring it by later this afternoon, if that's okay?"

"No," she said, wanting to keep contact with him at a minimum. "I have a few errands to run and don't want you to waste your time."

Dev nodded. "Okay. How about if my assistant gives you a call when it's ready to sign and she can drop it off. Then you can bring it by the office when it's convenient." He caught her gaze. "By avoiding me you're only prolonging the inevitable, you know."

"I'm only avoiding potential problems."

"Oh?" His eyebrows rose as he regarded her intently. "Admit it. You're afraid of me. Of what might happen when the whistle blows and I pursue you."

There was challenge in his tone.

She snorted. "I'm not afraid of you." She avoided his eyes, afraid he'd see how close to the mark his statement really was.

Dev reached over and took her chin with his fingers, turning her to face him. Their gazes locked. Finally, he smiled. "You're lying."

"No," she said on a breathless sigh, shaking her head.

"Then prove it."

The whispered dare swirled inside her brain as she watched him lower his head in slow motion. She should turn away. Kissing wasn't in her best interest, but she didn't move. Instead, she closed her eyes and felt his soft lips touch hers, wanting to savor something she'd never gotten to experience as a teen. It was only a kiss. What could it hurt?

He took his time, kissing her thoroughly and for an extended moment, Judith lost herself in his mouth and gave in to the need to respond. She let go of her reserve and melted against him. Let his lips and tongue work magic. And that's how it felt. Magical. He swept her away to never-never land, just like he had that first night, only this time she was fully aware of what his lips and mouth were doing to her senses.

A full minute passed before she realized he'd broken the connection. His breathing was labored. It took an enormous amount of effort for Judith to clear her mind and take in air, especially when her lungs seemed impaired.

She tried to turn away, but he gripped her chin again, forcing her to hold his gaze. The raw desire she saw in his eyes should have scared her off. It didn't. She felt drawn to him. If she were a rose, he'd be her sunshine. Without him, she wouldn't be able to fully bloom. Shaking the thought and coming to her senses, she pulled her chin free, reached for the handle, and opened the car door.

Once out, she leaned in. "I'm not afraid, merely cautious. I think we should keep to my plan and see each other only when necessary."

She turned and strode up the walk without looking back, feeling the heat of his gaze with every step. Safely inside her house, she lowered her forehead against the cool wood and exhaled a sigh of relief when she heard him drive away.

For a long while Judith stood with her head against the door, taking deep breaths and wondering about her sanity. She might as well face facts. She was no match for Dev or guys like him. Not that she was afraid of him, she wasn't. What bothered her more was making a fool of herself. She felt like an inexperienced kid again and she hated that feeling. It bothered her so much she briefly considered pulling out of the project. The paperwork wasn't signed yet. She still had an out, a small window of time to decide.

Her kitchen beckoned. Nothing could be decided until she ate.

While scouting out lunch in the refrigerator, she reviewed the last twenty-four hours.

She grinned. The guy was too much. When he wasn't terrifying her with his blatant sex appeal, his dynamic personality was tugging at her mental strings. There was nothing about him she didn't like. Dev "Mac' McAllister was too appealing, especially when he turned his attention to melting her resistance. His smile could melt an iceberg.

She carried a loaf of bread, sliced ham, lettuce, and cheese over to the cutting board.

Maybe if they'd just met, had no history, she might be tempted to ride Dev's sensual wave to see where it led. The time they spent together, last night and at the site, along with his kisses, made her realize she could really fall for him. She already liked him...liked being with him, and they were sexually attracted to each other. That hadn't changed in ten years.

Judith picked up the glass of milk she'd poured, along with her plate, and drifted to the table. She instinctively knew it would simply be a matter of time before he wore her down. Look at what had happened earlier. He had her up against the wall, literally. It took all of her willpower to walk away, just like in the car.

Self-preservation made her want to run as far away from Dev as possible.

Her biggest problem? Part of her wanted to stay and find out what would happen. It was this part she was so afraid of because she knew after today she had very little resistance against him.

As she ate, her mind spun. She *should* back out of the job. A pang of regret hit her.

She fell in love with the building all over again after spending the morning traipsing through it. Dev, shrewd as he was, had taken her there for that very reason. She had to give him credit. He'd found her Achilles' heel.

She finished lunch, then went into her home office and sat at her desk, which was really a drafting table spanning an entire wall. She didn't bother with turning on the lamp. Plenty of natural light poured in from wall-to-wall windows.

She focused on a tree in the yard, still debating.

While she wasn't dependent on her business for survival, for things like paying rent and eating, her business was every bit as important to her for a different reason. Her work gave her a sense of accomplishment, a sense of who she was. Having a job like the building remodel on her resume would increase her sense of satisfaction, and show those who said she couldn't do a man's job that they were wrong. She needed to explore all options before giving it up.

The buzzer interrupted Judith's thoughts.

She opened her front door and recognized the no-nonsense woman from Dev's office.

"Ms. Reid?" Her eyebrows quirked. "We met earlier, remember? I'm Maude Abrams, Mr. McAllister's assistant. I have a contract for you to sign." She handed Judith the contract.

"I guess I should read it and make sure there aren't any surprises," Judith said, glancing at the pages.

"It's a fair document, very up-front. You won't find anything in it not discussed earlier," Maude said, dismissing Judith's concerns with the wave of her hand.

"Oh?" Judith's eyes narrowed. "You sound so sure."

"I am. I read it as I typed. In fact, it seems to benefit you more than Dev." Then she smiled in such an engaging way that Judith had no doubt the grin could be used to win over board members and small children alike. "So, I'm curious. And because I'm nosy by nature and make it my job to stay on top of things, I couldn't let it pass without seeing for myself what's what. I'm supposed to drop this off and leave, but I'm hoping you'll invite me in to satisfy my curiosity."

Her honesty caught Judith off guard. *Definitely a shrewd lady.*

"Well then, come on in." Maude Abrams reminded Judith of her outspoken grandmother and she felt an instant rapport with the feisty woman. Before her death, Grandmother Reid had been Judith's confidante, someone who understood her perfectly and never made her feel like an outsider. "And since you're so candid, I'll return the favor. I'm just as interested in Dev as you are in me. Maybe we can swap information."

"I'm sure the next few minutes will be beneficial to both of us." The grin on Maude's face transformed into one that now could only be called mischievous.

"I have apple pie, if you'd like a piece," Judith offered. She

Sandy Loyd

just might learn something useful.

"Sounds wonderful. I like your place," Maude said, looking around. "Who's your decorator?"

"I did it myself." She couldn't contain her pleasure as her gaze followed Maude's. "You really like it?"

"I do. You have a flair for putting colors and textures together."

Maude trailed behind her to the kitchen, where the two chitchatted about her decorating while Judith poured coffee and cut two pieces of pie. She set two steaming cups, then filled plates, in front of them as they settled themselves at the table. "There you go."

Judith decided she more than liked Maude Abrams. Her nonstop compliments over her taste had Judith readily dropping her natural reserve. She was pragmatic and friendly with a great sense of humor. Soon both were joking around and talking about inconsequential things.

"You seem to know Dev pretty well, Ms. Abrams," Judith commented after Maude told her they'd been working together for almost ten years.

"I do. But what's this 'Ms. Abrams' stuff. Call me Maude. Everyone does. Since you're going to be working with the company, I'd say we'll be seeing a lot of each other."

Judith nodded. The two continued talking until, without thinking, she revealed information she'd never told anyone concerning her connection to Devon McAllister. Not even Kate knew about that night. She certainly never meant to unload so much, but the woman's sympathetic questioning had her revealing more than she'd intended.

"I know he's pursuing me again and I'm having second thoughts about the project." Her brow furrowed as she twisted her napkin.

"I see." Maude nodded. "I wondered about your history, given Dev's actions lately."

"I can't say I'm not flattered, but I don't see Dev as long term and I'm not into getting hurt again. What do you think?"

Maude shook her head and tutted, then remained silent for a few minutes. Finally, she said, "Since you were so honest with me, I'll be honest with you. I've known Dev a long time. I admire

40

him and would never do anything to destroy our working relationship, but I sensed there was more going on here than merely business, which is why I butted in. Now that I know of your past, I'd like to help if I can." She expelled a long sigh. "While I've never known Dev to be cruel, I do know he's not perfect. He has both a healthy ego and a strong drive, and can be an arrogant bastard at times."

"Tell me something I don't know," Judith said, meeting the older woman's compassionate gaze.

"Okay." Maude smiled. "He has such heart, but he also has wounds and they go deep. This sometimes affects his judgment." She chuckled softly at Judith's raised eyebrows. "Oh, he's a ladies' man all right, exacerbated by the fact that there're so many available women at his disposal. He's become cynical."

"Cynical? I've never been after him, so why's he pursuing me?"

"Good question."

Judith's gaze moved to her hands and she studied her fingernails for too long before she asked, "Do you think fate brought us back together? I mean, the attraction's always been there right from the start. Maybe I'm worrying for nothing."

"I'm not sure." Maude shook her head and tutted again. The sound sent the swelling hope inside of Judith plummeting. After a moment of apparent deep thought, Maude's revelation allowed hope to swell again. "I've watched his business strategies over the years and I know how his mind works. I could swear Dev's scheming and this bothers me because I somehow think his scheming may not be what's best for him in the long run. So we will have to do a bit of scheming on our own."

"What'd you have in mind?"

"A plan. After all, I can't let his cynicism ruin a good thing," she said, clapping her hands together and rubbing, while the mischievousness in her smile climbed a notch. "I'll help you keep your distance from Dev in order to give you both a little time."

"How?" Judith's expression took on an impish quality of its own.

"I'll inform you of his movements in the office. Then you'll know when to visit the site and when to avoid the area. In fact, we can start today. Dev has a meeting this afternoon. That's a perfect time to deliver the signed contract."

Maude stood and picked up her purse, ready to leave. "Remember, this will only work for a short time," she cautioned. "He's a cunning goat. He'll figure out what we're doing eventually and then you'll have to deal with him. At least now you have some breathing room."

Watching her walk out the door, elation surged through Judith. It all sounded so easy.

Their illuminating conversation left her in a more positive frame of mind. Humming, she headed for her office. She could handle Dev McAllister.

~

Her mission completed and armed with more information, Maude marched out of Judith's house, realizing she'd had reason to worry. She'd been Dev's assistant too long not to worry.

In nine years, a true friendship had developed between them and she loved Dev like a son. Oh, she was never a mother figure, because his own mother was still a strong presence. But she was everything else. Conscience, advisor, sounding board, and confidante.

Dev's limo pulled to the curb. She climbed inside. Looking in the rearview mirror, she noticed Mike studying her reflection.

Finally, he spoke. "Well, what'd you learn?"

"You were right. There *is* something between them," Maude said with a resigned sigh.

"I knew it." His face lit with a smile. "Do you think anything'll come of it?"

"I don't know, Mike." Maude sighed again. "She's definitely someone who'd interest him…pretty, intelligent, witty…and she's got grit. I like her. Too bad he's gotten so cynical over the years toward women. I only hope he realizes what she has to offer before he destroys his chance with her."

Mike's smile faded. "You don't think she can bring him around?"

"I hope so."

Mike nodded, his brow furrowing into concern.

Maude understood his concern. She knew all about their friendship, one where Dev came looking for Mike in the evenings for a game of pool or chess and the line between employee and employer was crossed. Dev had become more like an older brother, or mentor, always available for help with school projects or to talk over any problems. Mike attended USF, University of San Francisco, working on his MBA. He lived in the servant's quarters in Dev's big house.

"But whatever he's cooking up, she won't swallow it easily." She offered an encouraging smile. "The next few weeks should be interesting. I'll keep you posted."

"Good. He's the best and he deserves the best."

Maude nodded, agreeing. She had her reasons for wanting the best for Dev McAllister. An hour with Judith Reid was enough to know the younger woman was just that. The best.

In all the years she'd worked for Dev, he'd been nothing but a perfect, generous boss, whose praise and caring went beyond that of a mere employer. Dev became her rock when her husband of thirty-five years had developed prostate cancer three years ago, making it clear that she never had to worry about her job or money. Thankfully, Maude hadn't needed much. Her husband's cancer was caught early and he'd made a full recovery. But Maude never forgot Dev's kindness. The bond it created would last a lifetime.

As Mike pulled away from the curb, Maude prayed that Dev wouldn't do something stupid before realizing what he could have with a woman like Judith.

Chapter 4

Judith entered Mario's Bar and Grille in high spirits. Evading Dev was working, and at those times she couldn't avoid him, work interfered with his efforts to distract.

Her light step increased in speed as she caught sight of Kate Morrison sitting at a table near the window.

"Have you been waiting long?" She gave Kate a hug before pulling out a chair and sitting.

"Just got here. You look good."

"So do you. Love the do. Shorter looks great on you."

"I'm glad you like it." Kate patted her dark brown hair. "Maurice went a little crazy with the scissors."

"So, how's the shop doing?" Judith asked, picking up a menu and glancing at it.

"Sales keep going up." Kate owned and ran an antiques store in Redwood City. "Paul says it's the best investment he ever made."

"I'm not surprised." Paul, a financial planner, had invested heavily when Kate moved her antiques store closer to the new home they'd bought. "Your stock is unique and always changing."

Kate and her husband, Paul, two of her closest friends, got married last year. No one was happier or more surprised than Judith. At one time, Paul had been set on Judith as his one and only, and Kate had been just as crazy about his brother, James. It all worked out in the end, though, when Kate and Paul came to their senses and fell in love with each other, instead. Unfortunately, their new house was forty-five minutes away, so the two had to make plans to see each other for dinner.

"All of which takes time and effort," Kate said. "I'm only too happy to be back from buying so I can now concentrate on selling." She waited until the waitress took their drink orders and left, then updated Judith on her latest trip, the reason this dinner had been postponed. After a moment of silence, Kate prodded.

"Now it's your turn. I've been out of the loop too long. Paul told me you're working with Dev McAllister on your new project, that his company owns the building."

"Yeah, and I'm hoping this job will give me credibility."

"Stop." Kate held up a hand. "Your work already has credibility."

"This will give me more." Judith filled Kate in on what had happened in the past two weeks, including her interview with Dev and the work she'd done since then.

"Small world, isn't it?" Kate said, adding when Judith's eyebrows rose, "That James is working on the same job." Paul's brother was a partner in the architectural firm Morrison, Morgan and Stone, hired in conjunction with Judith's company. "I can't believe you're working with family. They're still best friends, you know."

"Yeah, real amazing." Judith smiled, covering up her ignorance. She figured they knew each other, even recently overcame the small shock about James' involvement, but she didn't realize until Kate's comment that Dev and James were *best* friends. When she and Paul had been hanging out, she didn't dare openly discuss Dev. She'd also steered clear of James and his social scene, never paying attention to him or his friends.

Her focus had been on keeping things friendly with Paul, so she'd skipped as many family get-togethers as she could during those years Kate had dated James.

Her smile dimmed somewhat. "Hopefully, it won't hinder my efforts to avoid Dev."

"Why?" About to take a sip of white wine, Kate glanced up, the glass at her lips. "He's not a man women usually avoid."

"Well, I'm not like them." Judith lowered her menu, deciding on spinach salad and penne pasta, then picked up her red wine the waitress had just delivered. In between sips, she enlightened Kate about her situation, including Maude's visit, without going into specifics.

Kate swallowed another long drink, then asked, "Are you sure you know what you're doing?"

"Of course I do. Dev McAllister's pursuing me, and if I avoid him he can't catch me."

"He's not someone I'd toy with." Kate's face revealed her

concern. "He's always made me nervous, so be careful."

"Don't worry." Judith patted Kate's hand and her smile broadened. "I can handle him."

"Now I *am* worried." She downed the rest and held up her glass as the waitress walked by.

Judith laughed. "You'll see. If I can stay out of his reach, I'll get past this."

"Okay, but don't say I didn't warn you."

Later, as they ordered dessert, the Morrison men showed up unexpectedly at their table, and help for avoiding Dev came from another source, one Judith least expected.

"Hi, honey." Paul bent to give Kate a kiss. "I know we're intruding. After walking by and noticing two beautiful women, we couldn't resist coming in to say hi." He straightened and glanced at Judith, grinning. "Hey, Judith."

Judith smiled. "Hi, Paul." Then she turned to acknowledge James, and was caught off guard at how much he resembled Paul, with the same golden hair and blue eyes, reminding her of a young Robert Redford. It had been a while since she'd last seen them side by side, and from her vantage point they could pass for twins, except Paul was slightly leaner and taller.

"Hello, Judith." James offered her a curt nod, then grinned at Kate and, following Paul, he kissed her cheek.

"I was hoping for a ride so James won't have to drive me home." Paul glanced at Kate with eyebrows slanted. "How about it? Can we crash your party?"

Kate looked to Judith for direction, the question in her eyes.

"Sure," she quickly said. "We were man-bashing. Were your ears burning?"

Paul and James sat amid laughter and more teasing. Within seconds, the waitress handed them menus.

"We were talking about my new job," Judith said once their laughter faded, turning to James. "And what a small world it is that you happen to be the architect on the project."

"It is. No surprise, though. Mac wouldn't use any other architect."

"Mac? I thought he went by Dev now," Judith said, eyeing him warily.

"Old habit. One I can't break." James chuckled. "It annoys

the hell outta him, which is why I don't try." He paused, then said offhandedly, "But I was a little surprised when he chose your company over one of the bigger firms."

"You don't think I can do the work?" Judith's spine straightened as a small sliver of annoyance developed. Despite knowing each other for most of their lives, she and James shared a mutual dislike, only she had more reason, which also played into why she still avoided him. Even though Kate had always defended him, such praise had never swayed her opinion. "My plans are solid."

"You misunderstood," James said sincerely. He offered his signature smile, one so much like Paul's that could be deadly to the opposite sex, excluding her of course. "They *are* solid. I only meant it's odd he'd use an unknown company, no matter how good." His shoulders lifted in a shrug. "Mac's preoccupied with this project and it got me thinking. I've decided his preoccupation may have something to do with you, so I asked Paul to arrange this meeting."

"Me?" Judith's brows knitted together. Why would James suggest something she had suspicions about?

"Yes, you. I'm aware of your history."

She stared, her eyes widening, and he only chuckled, waving off her shock.

"I vaguely remember an incident at our graduation party all those years ago. I also remember him pursuing you and your answer was no." James paused, his attention focused on her face searching for confirmation. When she nodded, he smiled. "Mac's not used to hearing the word no from women. It's damned unnatural that all the man has to do is snap his fingers and *bam*, they're his for the taking. The way I see it, he's pursuing you again and you're still saying no." His eyebrows quirked. "Am I right?"

"He does seem interested. And I have been avoiding him," Judith admitted as a trickle of unease shot into her bloodstream at James' perception. She assessed his face, looking for hidden meaning. Exactly what did he know about that night?

"Even his assistant is helping her," Kate said, interrupting her thoughts with an explanation of her plans for dodging Dev at the site.

47

"I'll help you avoid him during our business functions if you want," James offered as another characteristic smile took over his face.

"It's a nice offer," she said, not entirely comfortable with the idea, but not ready to reject it outright. Her gaze narrowed. "But why would you?"

"To bug Mac, of course. Something's getting under his skin. It's gotta be you," he said, still grinning. "And since it's my life's mission to annoy him, I figure what the hell. What can it hurt to kick it up a bit, increase the volume so to speak, and watch him squirm?"

It sounded plausible. She eyed him leisurely, trying to gauge what he knew.

No! He obviously didn't know much and he *was* offering salvation. "Well, I'd be a fool to refuse help." Her laughter bubbled up, and relief replaced wariness. "I'm a mere amateur where Dev's concerned and need any advantage I can muster in dealing with him."

They all laughed.

"Okay, here's what we'll do." James rubbed his hands together, clearly getting into his role.
"When there are functions, like those stuffy cocktail parties we have to attend because business demands it, I'll keep Mac occupied until you've met your obligations and can leave."

Judith grinned. Another gurgle of amusement escaped. "You know the plan might actually work." She couldn't believe how easy circumventing dealing with Dev suddenly became, and even more amusing? Help came from such close sources.

"I can't wait to see his reaction," James said once they finished strategizing. "I haven't had this much fun since right before Paul got engaged. Now that he's married, he's no fun to razz. At least not like when he was single."

"Morrison sibling rivalry at its best." Kate snorted when Judith sent her a questioning look. "James considers Dev family and subjects him to the same brotherly taunting. This childish rivalry's been going on for years. Male bonding taken to extremes."

Judith looked first to Paul, then to James. The brothers instantly schooled their faces into innocent expressions, clearly

48

having played this game before.

James stood. "Well, I've got a busy day tomorrow and still have a couple of hours of work to do, so I have to cut this short." He shrugged into his leather jacket and placed money on the table before adding, "Just be careful, Judith, and remember. Mac's not long term and he can be brutal with women. I'd hate to see you hurt."

Watching him go, his warning hung in the air, but she ignored it. Things were going her way, and now with James' help, she could continue keeping Dev at a distance.

~

Judith added a touch of mascara, her thoughts on the busy day ahead. After applying lipstick, she smiled.

Weeks had passed since she and her friends had eaten dessert while formulating plans. James' warning was totally forgotten. July was almost over and the project was flowing. If nothing changed, Judith expected to be done by late September or early October. She only needed to keep it together until then.

James had honored his promise. More than that, he had become a friend, once she realized he wasn't the jerk she'd thought him to be for all those years. As co-conspirators, they spent more and more time together, even sharing impromptu lunches because he'd stop by the work site, usually around lunchtime.

This didn't concern her until he pushed for a dinner date. Suspecting he wanted more than the friendship she offered, she accepted mainly to clarify her position.

Their date had ended with a kiss that left her more confused than ever. She enjoyed his company, and told him so, but she also explained that she had to get through the next couple of months and tackle the problem of Dev before even thinking of going in another direction.

James and his interest would just have to wait.

Shaking her head at the memory, she strode briskly toward the kitchen and another cup of coffee. Today she planned to work with the lighting contractor at the site and wore casual capri pants and a short-sleeved sweater. She wasn't worried about bumping into Dev because Maude told her yesterday his schedule was full with meetings.

Humming to herself, she filled her travel mug, grabbed her briefcase, and ran out the door for the bus stop.

~

That same morning, Dev stepped out for an early run. He usually ran every morning, but lately he'd been too swamped with work. Today he ignored work because things with Judith had stalled, and he needed these five miles through the Presidio to think and figure out why.

How could she be avoiding him? Nothing was going as planned.

As he got further into his run, he contemplated the events of the last month. He'd been traveling quite a bit, and he couldn't waste his precious opportunities at the site. Yet Judith had the uncanny ability to disappear whenever he arrived only to show up later, when he was elsewhere.

The first time this happened was the day they'd visited the work site. He spent the afternoon at his office ignoring other business so he would be free to catch Judith when she dropped off the contracts. He knew she had them because Maude had personally delivered them at his request. He'd only left his office for one unavoidable quick meeting, and upon returning, had discovered she'd been there in his absence.

He thought it a coincidence. At first. Until several opportunities ended with the same results. She had to be getting inside help.

Maude Abrams wasn't his primary suspect mainly because she'd been a loyal assistant for the last nine years and one of the few people Dev trusted.

She began working for him when he was a junior executive with Global Products, Inc., a conglomerate he'd started his career with fresh out of grad school. Two years after he completed his rise as Global's CEO, he left to found his own company, and Maude had followed, her skills becoming an integral part of his recent success.

As always, his position as McAllister, Inc.'s CEO demanded a great deal of his most precious commodity, time, and he couldn't waste that precious commodity now or ignore compelling evidence against his assistant. He'd lost too much ground in the past few weeks, and he wasn't about to lose more.

Maude knew his schedule, and somehow Judith had gotten her to defect. How could she? After all these years? He almost felt betrayed. Almost.

That alone made him realize what a strong adversary Judith was. He'd underestimated her. His growing admiration of her spunk and determination escalated. He'd always enjoyed doing battle with a worthy opponent and she'd definitely proven herself.

His strategy would have to change. Maude was a clever lady. Damn her meddling. He could see it clearly now. Maude thought of herself as Judith's avenging angel, with the task of keeping her safe from him. He'd have to take his assistant out of the picture and level the playing field.

Dev smiled as he ran. One problem solved.

Next…his thoughts turned to another niggling puzzle. Why Judith slipped through his fingers to go missing in action when he searched her out at those few social events they attended when Maude had no part in them. Conclusion? Judith had to be getting help from another source, James R. Morrison III, his best friend and now a suspect. He didn't see the connection, though, and had no proof, only intuition. Still, it was too coincidental for him to dismiss outright.

One question ate at him. Why? What would motivate James to help Judith?

He knew Judith and Paul were still close. But James and Judith were mere acquaintances, or at least that was the impression his friend had always conveyed.

He ended his run with a cooldown a block from his house, still pondering what to do. He'd have to dig a little deeper and that would take more time, and right now he had little to spare.

James and his motivation moved to his mind's back burner to stew before he acted.

While taking the stairs two at a time to his apartment to shower, his attention switched to finding a way to rearrange the busy day ahead.

An hour later, Dev strode off the elevator.

"Good morning, Vickie," he said to the receptionist, bestowing a warm smile.

"Good morning, Mr. McAllister."

He stopped outside his assistant's door. "Morning, Maude. Any messages?"

"Morning, Dev. No, things are quiet this morning. Do you need anything else for your nine o'clock?"

Dev grinned. "No. I got it covered."

He started for his office. Once seated behind the huge oak desk, he immediately made a few calls, canceling everything. Hanging up, he leaned back, swiveled around in the black leather chair, and stared out the window, smiling deviously.

His thoughts drifted to Judith and their confrontation when he would catch her at the site. Blood surged through him in anticipation.

But first, he had another mission.

He picked up the phone.

"James? It's Dev."

"Hey, Mac. What's going on?"

"Not much. Well, not much that I want to discuss over the phone. We need to meet."

"How about lunch?"

"No. I'm busy for lunch. I was thinking sooner. In about twenty minutes?"

"Sure. My schedule's free."

After replacing the receiver, Dev stood. Mike was downstairs, waiting to take him to James' office in San Mateo. On his way, he stopped at Maude's door for the second time that morning.

"As you know, I'll be out most of the day. If you need me, call my cell and leave a message." Then, because he couldn't resist, he met and held Maude's gaze. "Oh, and by the way, I think you should change your name to Meddler." He hesitated, then added, "*Et tu, Brute?*"

Her astonished, guilty look told him he'd hit his target. He turned to go and heard her mutter, "Well, the game's up." Then louder, to his back, she said, "It took you long enough to figure it out. You must be getting rusty."

He stopped dead in his tracks, spun around, and glared. "Just be glad you still have a job," he threatened before exiting her office in quick, angry steps.

Chapter 5

James gazed out the picture window behind his big dark mahogany desk, having hung up with Mac. He had an idea of what was coming. In fact, he'd expected a confrontation long before this.

Judith!

His thoughts flew back to that first night he'd played offense for her, at a cocktail party sponsored by Bay Area builders at a hotel banquet room near Fisherman's Wharf.

He was having a bad day where everything that could go wrong did. He took a little time before the party to unwind with a quick drink and was surprised to glance over to see Judith enter the bar.

She walked up and asked, "Is this seat taken?"

"If I said yes, would you leave?" he replied with a grin on his face, not knowing if he wanted company.

"That bad, huh?" She sat and ordered a glass of red wine from the bartender, then turned back to him. "So tell me, what has you drinking this early and right before a cocktail party where the booze is sure to be excellent, not to mention free?"

"Oh, I don't know." He sighed. "I guess I'm a little shot. Business is a killer, leaving no time for my usual outside pursuits. I haven't had a date in two weeks and my mother has issued a command performance for this weekend. Need I go on?" She laughed and he asked, "So why're you so early? I thought you'd arrive late to avoid Mac."

"I'm meeting friends for dinner later. I thought I'd get an early start, put in my time, and then head out, but I don't want to be the first to arrive. Traffic was lighter than I expected, and here I am."

His bad mood was quickly forgotten as he and Judith bantered back and forth. He soon realized she was a great conversationalist, and they discussed all sorts of things. In minutes, she had him laughing over a story about a client's demands. A special friendship bloomed during those enjoyable minutes they spent nursing drinks while waiting to join the party. In fact, her quick wit and easy smile shattered James' original impression of Judith.

How could he have thought of her as an ice queen for all those years? Once he got through her first cool layers, warmth emanated from every cell in her luscious body.

No wonder Paul was smitten for so long. James finally understood her allure.

He couldn't help liking her as he looked into her laughing, intelligent eyes. She intrigued him as no one else had.

He knew Mac and Judith had unfinished business. He knew he shouldn't be thinking about pursuing her and he damned well knew Mac wouldn't like it. But she was worth igniting his friend's temper.

Those thoughts and more ran through his head when they slipped into the party. He left Judith to field Mac's advances, leaving her free to go around the room meeting her business obligations.

An hour later when Dev got caught up in a discussion with one of his builders, James spied Judith heading for the door.

He made a beeline toward her. "Our mission tonight was successful. How about getting together one evening to plan our next attack?"

He spoke in jest and Judith responded in kind, her voice teasing, "Well, my dance card is full right now, but give me a call and maybe I can squeeze you in somewhere."

James had been deadly serious. He went back inside strategizing a way to get Judith to go out with him. He wasn't above using anything at his disposal to achieve his goal, even taking advantage of the current situation.

Over the next few weeks, James made headway with Judith. In addition to the social obligations they had agreed on, she went out with him several times. True, those had been spontaneous lunch dates because James started stopping by the site on the pretext of business, planning it so that he could take her to lunch.

During these impromptu dates, James got to know Judith a little better, which only made him increase his efforts. She was always friendly but aloof, and her natural reserve was a potent draw, too much of a challenge for him to ignore. He couldn't resist breaking through the barrier she erected around herself, because once through her cool reserve, a warm, vibrant woman always emerged.

She wasn't a pushover. He respected her business sense, but most of all, he truly liked her and had full intentions of delving deeper.

James pushed for more, knowing full well Judith only regarded him as a friend.

When she finally agreed to an actual dinner date, he was ecstatic, forgetting all about the problem he was supposed to be helping her with. He simply wanted to be with her. She had an easy way about her; he could relax and be himself. She laughed at his jokes, listened with interest while he talked about his day, and then would share her day with him.

On the night of their dinner date, James knew he was in serious trouble when he walked her to her doorstep. After a wonderful meal and great company, all he could think about was taking their relationship to the next level.

He wiped sweaty palms on his pants, feeling as nervous as a high school kid on his first date, an interesting experience. He couldn't remember any time in his life when he was nervous around a woman.

Slow down, his mind screamed. Judith doesn't see you as anything but an older brother.

He disregarded all signals but one.

He grinned when she turned to him with an outstretched hand. He glanced at it, and ignoring it, he placed his hands on her shoulders, bringing her closer while bending his head.

Then, he kissed her.

The kiss was gentle, loving, sweet…full of promise, speaking of what was beginning to burst inside his heart, yet when he tried to deepen it, she pulled away.

He let her go and looked down into remorseful green eyes that conveyed so much emotion.

His bubble of anticipation deflated instantly. Judith had been nothing but honest and open from the start. He couldn't fault her for his stupidity of allowing his feelings to get out of hand so quickly.

James' phone buzzed. "Mr. Morrison, Mr. McAllister is here to see you," a voice said, yanking him back to more pressing matters. Yep, he thought, as his hand moved over the intercom. He'd rushed Judith and only had himself to blame. "Send him in, Susan, and hold my calls."

He could still hear her brutally honest voice in his head telling him she liked him but she had to sort out whatever was going on with Dev first.

He understood, but it didn't stop his disappointment.

James smiled wistfully. At least he'd accomplished one goal that night. Judith no longer thought of him as brotherly. Lousy compensation, but it *was* something.

~

Dev walked into the office just as James swiveled his chair around and nodded.

"Hey, Mac, you're looking well. What brings you into my neck of the woods?"

He heard the name and cringed. That James continued using the college nickname, even after repeated requests to use his true name, always irritated him. Dev figured it also played a big part as to why the habit never died. His irritation increased a notch and, because he was already annoyed, his reply was caustic.

"You know why."

"No hi back? No social niceties?" Motioning to a plush chair in front of the desk he said, "Sit down, can I get you something to drink?"

"No, I don't want a drink," Dev shot back, practically growling. "Like I said, you know why I'm here."

"To warn me off, right?"

"I didn't expect such an outright admission of your meddling," Dev said, his voice and face registering surprise.

"Well, here's another kicker. It started out as a lark to aggravate you."

"Okay, you've achieved your goal and aggravated me. Now back off."

"No." James lounged back in his chair and grinned.

"I'm warning you. Drop it."

"And I said no. I know Judith means something to you and I know you are playing some kind of game where she's concerned.

All I need to do is figure out what it is."

"Just leave it alone! It's none of your affair."

"I'm changing the rules and making it my affair," James said, bringing his chair forward.

"Why?" Dev's eyes narrowed. Curiosity over his friend's involvement rose. "What's it to you?"

"Judith doesn't deserve to be treated that way."

"What are you, her guardian angel?" Dev asked, rubbing the back of his neck in frustration. "God save me from meddling avenging angels."

"Look, Mac, you've never told me what happened ten years ago, and quite frankly, after so long the memory's a bit hazy. But come on. Ten years is a long time. Most people learn to forget and move on." James peered into his eyes, searching. "Why is this important?"

"You wouldn't understand," Dev whispered, shaking his head.

"Try me." When Dev remained silent, he persisted. "How can you expect me to sit by while you callously rip her to shreds?"

"Why are you so interested in Judith?" Dev's gaze narrowed, suddenly suspicious. "I thought you didn't like her. You've never been interested in my affairs before."

"I don't like to see you hurt women."

"You're a fine one to talk," he scoffed. "I've watched you go through your fair share without being concerned before. So I'll ask again, why Judith, and why now?"

"We've become friends and I don't like to see my friends treated in such a manner."

"Now that's a laugh! *You* friends with Judith."

After a long pause, James finally said, "She's special, Mac, can't you see that?"

Something in James' tone alerted Dev and he could only stare at his friend. "My God," he said under his breath, as realization sunk in. "You're in love with her, aren't you?"

"No! Maybe—hell, I don't know. All I know is she doesn't deserve you and your games, and I am asking you as a friend to leave her alone."

Jealousy roared up in Dev. Deep, dark, green jealousy. No

one was going to take Judith away from him, not when he was so close to victory. She was his right now, and would be until he was finished with her. With an iron will, he clamped down the urge to pound James into the ground. How dare he attempt to stop him?

"I can't do that, James," he said, once he achieved a bit of control. "Not even for you."

"How can you act so callously toward her?" James asked, his tone pleading. "She doesn't deserve you and your treatment."

Still staring, Dev slowly shook his head, not changing his mind. "You don't understand."

"No, but I understand you're a ruthless bastard, Mac." James' voice held controlled fury. He paused as if to give his next words more effect. "Listen and listen well so there'll be no misunderstanding between us. I haven't figured out what you're doing, but I do know that you personally, not your company, bought the building. For one purpose…to bring Judith into your path." When Dev's eyebrows shot up, he added, "I've seen the returned invoices. They were paid with your personal checks, not company checks. And don't think I can't see through all those missed occasions over the years where you might've run into her. Your absences were planned. You couldn't risk seeing her or you'd lose your opportunity to lure her into your net." He broke off, shaking his head. "I know you as no one else does. I can only speculate that whatever is in that cold heart of yours, it's not good. You'll probably shatter Judith's heart to pieces. But you know something?"

After James' painful speech, Dev was done listening and barely holding on to his temper. He growled out through clenched teeth, "What?"

"I'll be there to pick them up." James came out of his chair and leaned toward him, gripping the desk. His face contorted in anger. "Even though I know I'm second choice, I'd grab on to Judith any way I can. You'll just throw her away like you would a piece of trash." He gave a disgusted snort. "I've always admired you and thought of you as a brother, but right now I think you're one goddammed fool. Be warned, Mac, I plan to do everything in my power to keep you from hurting her because she doesn't deserve that. Now, get the hell out of my office before I say or do something we'll both regret."

This wasn't supposed to happen. James, the brother he never had, was beyond angry, but Dev was in no mood to placate. He prayed their friendship could survive this. Not once in fifteen years had they ever fought over a woman.

Dev started for the door. Before he left, he turned and said in a voice full of agony, "For what it's worth, I am sorry. She's an obsession and has been for ten years. I have to exorcize her from my brain in the only way I know how. I never thought it would affect us, though."

~

James sat back down and took deep breaths, working to get his anger under control while staring into the empty space his friend had just occupied. Mac had always treated women as objects, never letting any get close to him. Lately, it seemed he viewed women with more scorn and it was clear this scorn was now directed at Judith.

A slight smile worked its way across his face. No, not scorn. Obsession…or love. Yeah, love. Mac was in love with her. Stupid bastard didn't even realize it.

Leaning back in his chair, James' smile grew. Maybe the earth would shift on its axis and Mac would be the one with the broken heart. If anyone could break through that hard wall he put up, Judith could. Of course, if successful, it meant his own dream of having her would go up in smoke.

But what the hell. His track record with women was shitty. Beyond shitty.

His thoughts strayed to his one and only long-term relationship with Kate, Paul's wife, and his smile stretched into an all-out grin. He had to admit he made a better friend and brother-in-law than committed lover. He'd probably screw it up with Judith too, if he got the chance, so maybe this was better.

James rubbed his hands together. He'd stay in the game a little longer if only to agitate Mac, because agitating Mac was always entertaining.

Chapter 6

Dev's thoughts were not cheerful as his limo sped back to the city. He told Mike to take the long route so he could use the extra time to think and regroup.

Damn. Jealousy ate at him. The foreign emotion had taken him completely by surprise. The cold rage that had swept through him over James' confession to feeling something for *his* Judith still left him shaken.

What had transpired between them to spur James' uncharacteristic protectiveness? While he wasn't cruel, he never got emotionally involved enough with a woman to become her champion. He'd had numerous affairs over the years, but no one held his attention for long, except Kate, Paul's wife. He'd dated her for eight years without committing before Paul fell in love with her.

So where had that protective streak toward Judith come from? Why hadn't Dev seen it coming?

He shook his head, disgusted at the answer.

He'd become a little too sure of himself and his abilities where Judith was concerned.

He shouldn't have kissed her in the car that afternoon. A cocky stunt, but he couldn't help himself. He'd wanted to stir the Judith pot just a bit...rile her. Besides, she'd been too hard to resist.

Now he had a lot of ground to make up, thanks to his meddling friends who'd aided and abetted the enemy. What a hilarious predicament. Usually he could laugh at himself and enjoy the irony, but not today. The longer he took to win his ultimate prize, the riskier it became, especially since he was beginning to see Judith as more than a conquest.

She should've been his by now, or at least well on her way. Instead, she was as elusive as a Dow Jones average over fourteen thousand. She was good. Too damned good. No one else could have breached his loyal friends in such a way.

A surge of pride burst through him when he thought of her ploys to thwart him.

Where to go from here and how best to proceed to gain back his lost advantage?

Good questions.

Mike stopped the limo in front of the site and ran around to open his door.

"Wait here," Dev said, after climbing out. "I'm not sure what my plans are."

He then walked up to the building's entrance, pulled out a card from his wallet, and slid it through the slot near the door handle on the right side. The door unlatched and Dev pushed inside.

A state-of-the-art security system had been installed early on to prevent vandalism and keep out unwanted visitors. Other improvements were now in full swing.

Evidence of that work was more noticeable as he stepped inside. Workmen pounded and drilled everywhere. Despite the fact that the floor looked like an empty shell with building debris strewn about, he saw at a glance how quickly the job had progressed, pressing on him even more that the clock ticked.

He walked over to one of the workmen he recognized, sidestepping a couple of big boards, and said, "Have you seen Ms. Reid?"

Halting his hammer in midair, the burly guy turned and nodded. "She's working with the electrician and lighting contractor, Mr. McAllister. Third floor."

"Thanks." Dev headed for the stairs. While walking up to the second floor, he glanced down at his feet and noticed his Gucci loafers, as well as the cuffs of his Armani suit pants, were covered in sawdust. He'd left his jacket in the limo. Even with rolled-up shirtsleeves, he wasn't dressed for the site. His business attire would provide an edge when he confronted Judith and he needed every advantage he could get.

He landed on the third floor only to find she was up one more flight.

He finally spotted her with the lighting contractor, bent over blueprints and deep in conversation. He heard snippets of her voice discussing the gauge of the electrical wire running through the ceiling.

When she called the man Jack in a familiar tone, Dev's ears and eyes went on full alert.

Standing back and watching, Dev noted frank admiration in the contractor's stance as his gaze kept going to her breasts and legs. All of a sudden, Judith's head came up in a laugh, and the man's satisfied smile told Dev he'd achieved his goal.

Irritation rose up. How dare she flirt with these guys and try to avoid him at the same time? Patience fled. She was his, and he was going to make damned sure she realized it.

Eventually, one of the workmen grabbed the contractor's attention and Judith refocused on the blueprint, unaware of Dev's presence.

Dev sneaked up, put his hands on her shoulder, and gently turned her around. "If I didn't know better, I'd think you were trying to avoid me. Are you, Judith?"

The look of surprise on her face was almost comical. For an instant, he'd cut through her calm reserve as she blinked, totally stunned.

"Dev, what are you doing here?" she finally managed to toss out.

"Now, that's a funny question. Imagine my surprise when I discovered my trusted assistant aiding and abetting the opposition. How do you suppose that happened?"

He watched the change of facial expressions. Oh yeah! He'd caught her off guard as she stared at him in silence, her mind clearly spinning.

"I haven't the slightest idea what you are talking about," she said lamely a moment later.

He leaned closer. "*Tsk...tsk...tsk.* Judith, you've been a very naughty girl evading me." He saw goose bumps on her arms and smiled, having no doubt his sultry whisper in her ear was the cause. "And I can't let your insolence go unpunished. Your sentence is to spend the rest of the day making it up to me."

She laughed nervously and stepped out of his reach. "Surely you're joking, I can't leave here. I have a job to do."

With that she turned and started in the direction the contractor had taken, but his firm hand on her arm stopped her. When she looked up into his eyes, he let her see the seriousness in his stare. No wasn't an option. He held the contact.

When Judith averted her gaze, he said, "I'm beginning to think you don't like me and my feelings are hurt."

She snorted. "That's impossible…you have the hide of a rhinoceros. I think it takes a lot more than my barbs to pierce through it."

"Ouch." He offered his most charming smile. "So, how about it? I promise you'll enjoy it." His smile deepened when he saw indecision in her bright green eyes. "Come on, your chariot awaits. We're off."

His grip on her arm tightened and he turned to go.

"Dev, really, I can't leave just yet," she said, trying to pull free. "I still need to finish—"

"Lover boy Jack can wait or, better yet, let him work without you," he said, cutting her off and dragging her along. "He has your plans and you've already gone through most of the floors. They're all similar. If he has questions, he can wait until you're here again." By then, Dev would have had a little time to work his magic and Jack's flirting would amount to nothing.

"All right, I guess I can take an hour for an early lunch," she finally agreed. "So, where are we going?"

"It's a surprise. You'll know when you get there."

"I love a man of mystery."

"You will, Judith, you will," he murmured under his breath.

"What was that, I didn't catch it?" Judith glanced at him with the question in her eyes.

"I said, you will love my surprise, that's all." Dev smiled inwardly. He'd won this round and mentally geared up for the next.

With purpose, he walked her down the stairs and out of the building.

~

The limo pulled up when Judith and Dev walked out. The driver left the car idling and rushed to open their door.

Judith scooted inside before Dev clambered in next to her. Grinning, the chauffeur slammed the door, then ran around, got in, and started driving.

Judith didn't catch Dev's quiet instructions as he leaned forward.

Her senses went on full alert when he turned back and she noted his expression.

"What are you planning?" She didn't trust that cheshire smile covering his face.

"You'll see." He then sat back, stretched out long, muscular legs, and visibly relaxed with his arm along the backseat. His hand was close enough to play with her hair.

Excitement zinged throughout her system.

Something was definitely going on in that sharp brain of his, she decided after eyeing him for long seconds, but for the life of her, she suddenly didn't care. Judith closed her eyes and leaned into the seat, relishing the feel of his fingers on her hair. In the next few seconds, more of her resolve dissipated, rising like vapor off a warm pond on a cool morning.

She was tired of resisting the magnetic pull that his personality generated whenever they were together. She no longer had the will to hold him at arm's length, mostly because she was tired of fighting her own attraction, especially when all she wanted to do was pull him closer and never let go.

Yeah, right! As if she could possess him once she let him catch her. She had few illusions. This wouldn't be a lasting affair. Instinctively, she sensed Dev viewed her as a trophy to be won. Once attained, he'd put her up on the shelf and never look at her again.

Since she never wanted anything long term either, why not take what she could get and build memories to last the rest of her life. What could be the harm in that? She might get burned, but what a fire they would create.

As the limo headed into Golden Gate Park, they sat, each smiling in contented silence, stealing surreptitious glances at the other, lost in their thoughts.

Finally Dev's voice disturbed the quiet.

"What did you say to my assistant to get her to totally defect?"

Shaking her head to clear her thoughts, she glanced at him. "What are you talking about?"

"In all the years I've known Maude, she's been nothing but a loyal employee…a true friend. In one afternoon, the two of you meeting negated all of that, and I want to know how."

"We talked about a lot of things, but the conversation mainly revolved around you."

"I assumed as much. Can you be more specific?"

Judith shrugged. "Well, Maude did mention how devious you are and what an unconscionable bastard you can be."

His bark of laughter had her grinning.

"She should know. She's privy to most of my dealings."

"You don't let many people know the real you, do you?"

In a heartbeat, his expression closed. "No, I don't." He straightened, cleared his throat, and added, "So don't be getting any ideas."

She sobered but, unwilling to spoil the moment, changed the subject.

"Where are we going? I need to be back no later than two. I have several appointments this afternoon."

"You aren't going back this afternoon." Dev took his cell phone out of his pocket. "If you need to cancel or postpone anything, now is the time to do it."

Incensed, her chin went out and she huffed, "You're just assuming I'll ride along willingly and let you dictate what I do or don't do?"

"That's exactly what I'm doing. Consider yourself kidnapped. But in all fairness, the evening will be your choice. If I can't convince you to spend it with me, then I'll return you to the work site."

Her jaw dropped. "You can't be so bold as to ignore my plans?"

"Didn't Maude fill you in on that aspect of my personality?" Dev asked. He paused before adding with total conviction, "If not, let me assure you…I'm plenty bold. And since you've demonstrated that you're a worthy opponent, I plan to be as bold as I need to in order to spend time with you. So accept it gracefully and enjoy the day."

"All right." She nodded. Imagine that? He considered her a worthy opponent. She swallowed a smile, and sternly conceded, "Just don't get in the habit of making plans for me without my approval or you'll find out exactly how worthy an opponent I can be." She held out her hand. "Give me your phone. I have a couple of calls to make."

"Sure." He slapped it in her hand. "Just so we understand each other, I meant what I said. I was prepared to kidnap you." He nodded. "But it *is* nice to have your consent."

She snorted as she punched in numbers. "At least tell me where we're going."

"Like I said, it's a surprise." His expression turned smug. "We'll be there in a few minutes."

Judith disconnected her last call as the limo pulled to the curb and stopped.

The chauffeur, still grinning, got out of the car and opened Judith's door.

"Watch your step, ma'am." He offered a hand.

"Thank you." Grabbing it, she stepped out.

"Thanks, Mike. I'll call you when we're ready to leave," Dev said, now standing behind her.

"The zoo?" She laughed, looking around. Her gaze sought Dev's. "You brought me to the zoo? I'm seriously starting to doubt your mental stability."

"Don't look so surprised." Dev chuckled. "And yes, I had all my marbles the last time I counted. I always come here when I want to unwind and relax. I figure you've been putting in long hours and could use a little of my therapy. Trust me, it works."

She gaped at him, intrigued. This was so un-Dev-like. "What's so special about the zoo?"

"I love watching the animals. They're natural, have no hidden agendas. They operate on pure instinct for survival and I relate to them. I enjoy observing their honest pursuit of life."

He turned and said something to Mike before grabbing her hand.

"Come on, let's go!" He darted in the direction of the ticket counter, dragging her behind with all the excitement of a kid at a carnival.

Unprepared for this aspect of his personality, she was again swept along with a force that stunned her.

Definitely not the simple guy on the make as she'd pegged him as all those years ago. There were so many facets to his psyche that a new one caught her eye every time they got together.

This boyish eagerness to visit the zoo did more to pierce

through her reserve than all of his other charms put together.

Judith couldn't help thinking she was a lamb going to slaughter, but she no longer cared. In fact, she was now willing to lie on that sacrificial altar, and caution be damned.

She ran after him, laughing at the absurdity of the moment as the rest of her resistance to Dev melted.

Chapter 7

"Here's your ticket," Dev said, as they walked through the entrance.

"Thanks." Judith took it. "So, what do we do now?"

Dev laughed. "What do you mean, what do we do now? We look at animals." Still holding her hand, he walked faster. It was a gorgeous day with temperatures in the low 70s. The early morning fog had lifted enough to let the sun in.

"I knew that."

"When's the last time you visited a zoo?" he asked, nearing the first fenced-in exhibit.

"I can't remember."

"If you can't remember, then it's been too long." He stopped and pointed. "See the lemurs. A couple of different species live there. Watch."

Her eyes followed his hand and she watched for several minutes. "I don't see anything."

"You're not looking hard enough. Their natural camouflage protects them in the wild. The ring-tailed lemur is easier to spot."

Judith's gaze narrowed. She scanned the brush. "I see them," she squealed. She stood on tiptoes and leaned closer, mesmerized as two animals groomed each other and ran around when done. "Now they're playing." She shielded her eyes from the sun and glanced at him. "You know a lot about them."

"I told you, I come here often. This is one of my favorite exhibits. Come on, there's more to see," he said, giving her a tug.

Like a couple of kids seeing the animals for the first time, they rushed through the exhibits, each trying to outdo the other with silly antics. They laughed and joked about stupid things.

"I see a family resemblance," Judith said, outside a black panther's cage.

When he looked at her with questioning eyes, she laughed.

"You mean no one has told you that you have the look of a predatory cat?" Without waiting for his reply she went on, saying,

"With your dark good looks and sleek body, you couldn't be mistaken for anything other than a panther, although the mountain lion comes in a close second."

Though spoken in jest, her assessment sent waves of pleasure through him and his six-foot-two-inch frame stretched taller.

Not to be outdone in their game, when they came to the exhibit of gazelles, he looked at Judith and said in a voice full of taunting innuendo, "If I remind you of the panther, then you remind me of that gazelle out there—feminine, graceful, and all prey—just waiting to be eaten."

Her response was a throaty, tempting laugh that said she knew she was his dinner, but he had to catch her first. She then took off running for the next exhibit, with Dev on her heels laughing along with her.

From then on, he chased after her...totally aware of her allure...occasionally becoming aroused at something she said or did. Thank goodness for his pleated trousers, otherwise it might have been a little embarrassing.

They stopped for lunch and ate in companionable silence that was becoming their norm, gorging themselves with abandoned pleasure as if eating gourmet fare instead of hot dogs, chips, and soft drinks.

"For dessert," Dev said, handing Judith cotton candy.

"I haven't had this stuff since I was a kid."

"You've lived a deprived life. We still have more to see," he said, pulling her along.

Dev couldn't remember a time he'd felt so relaxed with a date. Judith's exuberance was intoxicating and he now wanted her with a longing that ate at him. The more he was with her, the more he wanted her.

By the time they'd walked the zoo's perimeter, both were exhausted and eager to reach the limo.

When Mike pulled up, Dev didn't wait for him to get out. He opened the door and Judith slid inside.

He quickly followed. "Ah, comfort at last. My feet are killing me." Then he glanced at Judith. "Is your car at the site? I can drop you off."

"No, I took the bus today, but I need my briefcase," she

said, with her eyes closed and a serene smile on her face. "I left it at the building. Can you drop me off, wait while I get it, and then take me home?"

"No problem." He tapped on Mike's window and gave him instructions.

The mood in the limo on the ride back to the building was subdued. Neither spoke.

In the few hours he'd spent with Judith, he'd realized one fact. There was no way on God's green earth he would be able to walk out of her life once he tasted her.

Dev sighed, totally disgusted with himself for his lack of resolve. But that didn't stop him from amending his plan to continuing the affair until it ran its course. He'd eventually tire of her. When that happened, he'd have his revenge. Why torture himself?

One thing he wasn't willing to concede. Judith had to come willingly with a need greater than his. *No, that'll take too long. Face it, McAllister, she only has to match your need and it's taking all your endurance to keep it together long enough to achieve that.*

He frowned at the dismal truth as the car slowed. They were already back at the site.

"Do you need me to accompany you?" he asked as she hopped out when Mike opened her door.

"No, I'll just be a minute."

Dev watched her rush inside, deciding he needed to take action and initiate a surprise attack so she'd have dinner with him.

~

Judith hurried up the stairs to her temporary office on the fourth floor. Her thoughts weighed heavily on her mind, growing heavier with every step until she reached the last one.

She grabbed her briefcase as reality hit with full force. She was way past big trouble, tumbling headlong into love. She had no other explanation for the hum of excitement she couldn't quell and it felt wonderful.

Hugging her middle, she stopped at the landing and smiled dreamily, remembering…everything. She was sure Dev had shown her a glimpse of himself he rarely showed others. She could be mistaken, but she didn't think so. The guy kept his inner self under lock and key, unlocking it only for those he trusted.

It warmed her heart to realize that maybe he was coming to trust her just a bit.

Still, she worried. Not about having an affair. Oh, no. Now more than ever, she wanted Dev that way. Her uneasy thoughts rested on her secret. Or rather her virginity. If she hadn't wanted him to know about her inexperience that night in the gazebo ten years ago, she really didn't want him to know it now. Suddenly, her old insecurities surfaced.

How could she be sexy and alluring when in reality she was inexperienced and gauche? That gawky, awkward teenager who was two years younger than all her classmates because of skipped grades pushed forward, haunting her, jeering at her, telling her she was anything but provocative. He couldn't possibly find her sexually attractive once he realized her lack of expertise.

Why in the world hadn't she made love with Paul when they were together? Or why hadn't she found someone else?

She sighed. She knew why. Kissing Paul was like kissing her brother and did nothing for her. Keeping things friendly with him had been hard enough. If she'd given him any indication of interest, he'd have stepped up his efforts to woo her.

And because she measured all men to Dev after that night, no man had ever impressed her enough to grant him a chance to try. She understood that now.

Who knew back then that Paul would be married to her best friend and she would eventually want to make love as an experienced woman?

The past couldn't be rewritten, but maybe she could hold Dev off until she felt more comfortable with his lovemaking. By then, he wouldn't find her gauche or care about her inexperience, and hopefully, he wouldn't laugh at her ineptitude. After all, he'd find out when they did the deed. It wasn't like she could hide it.

She chuckled, having mentally formulated a plan, tossed the anvil of worry off her shoulders, and returned to the limo with a lighter step.

She sat back in the seat and glanced up. When she caught Dev's slow, sensual smile, the air crackled with energy, even as the space surrounding them instantly contracted.

Heat emanating from that stark blue gaze as it met hers

71

scorched her brain, setting off alarm bells. Her breath caught in the back of her throat. Her lungs malfunctioned. She couldn't move. The car pulled away from the curb. His smoldering stare held her in suspended animation, underscoring a hum of sexual awareness bouncing around the small space.

He leaned over. "Have dinner with me tonight." The urgency in his whisper made her insides quiver.

Licking her lips, she started to object. Big mistake, she realized, noting his eyes focused on her mouth. She wasn't prepared for the warmth swamping her system the thought generated nor was she prepared for how that fiery gaze wiped her memory clean. Even though she saw it coming and steeled herself against him, she had a hard time remembering why she was objecting. Oh yeah. It had something to do with slowing him down.

"Umm…I don't think we should." Her words came out in breathy little puffs, and in seconds, all thoughts but him leaning closer evaporated.

"Should what?" he asked before his mouth descended over hers. His soft lips felt warm and she couldn't stop the moan of pleasure as they worked magic for long minutes. Then, his mouth moved over her face kissing its way to her ear, nibbling and gently sucking her lobe. A blast of pure pleasure shot through her as his tongue darted in and out before he whispered, "Kiss or have dinner together?"

"Mmmm." She closed her eyes, enjoying the sensations coursing through her. "Both."

"Why?" He groaned. "I want to be with you. And I love kissing you." His tongue continued teasing her ear, shooting hot sensation into her bloodstream. "I know you feel the same. Say you'll have dinner with me, or so help me, I'll prove it to you, right here, right now."

"Promises, promises," she whispered without thinking.

"Don't toy with me, Judith." His voice was just above a whisper, but definitely a warning.

She smiled into his neck. Why not use this experience? What could happen in broad daylight with a witness in the front seat? Grasping on to courage, she lowered her mouth and touched his skin, mimicking his kisses and nipping at his neck.

His lips' pressure increased, moving at a frenzied pace across her face, until they covered hers. Then he slowed, added his tongue, sucking her willpower and leaving her breathless.

She moaned. A fire of pure need flared within her. He'd been stoking the flames, she realized too late, from the moment she'd climbed inside the car. Unable to stop herself from responding to his mouth's demand, she kissed him back, going with instinct as sensation after sensation rolled over her.

Somehow, the message of self-preservation her brain had flashed since the kiss began seeped into her consciousness. She had to stop or his words would prove true. Her virginity would be lost in the backseat of a car, just like all her other friends, only ten years later. Not a bad way to go, but they did have company.

She broke free. "Okay. Okay. Stop!" she said in a breathless whisper. "You've proven your point. I'll have dinner with you."

When she opened her eyes and focused, he was leaning against the seat cushion breathing heavily, fighting for control considering his fierce expression. She'd obviously skirted closer to the edge than she'd first thought. She swallowed hard, having no idea what to do with all that power once it let loose.

"It seems this is becoming a habit," he managed a moment later.

"You mean kissing?" He didn't respond. She smiled. "Kissing's nice. I like kissing."

His eyes opened and his gaze snared hers. "Figures." The limo slowed to a stop in front of her house. "How much time do you need?"

Straightening her sweater, she cleared her throat, working to bring a calm reserve back into her voice. "How about two hours. Then I can finish a few things I need to do for tomorrow."

She made the mistake of glancing into his eyes, noticing stark desire still lurking. She swallowed, subduing the sheer terror she could taste at the back of her throat.

How in the world had she ever thought she'd know how to handle him when the time came? That awkward, inexperienced teen resurfaced just then, making her feel totally out of her element. How she hated that feeling. A feeling that told her she was different from everyone else. The need to escape enveloped her. She grabbed the handle and opened the door, not waiting for the driver, and said on her way out, "I'll see you then."

"I'll be here at seven," Dev said. "Dress casually."

~

"Am I amusing you, Mike?" Dev asked after catching his chauffeur's grin in the rearview mirror.

Mike's smile died. "No, sir."

"Just drive home, and quit calling me sir," Dev said, pondering Judith's departure. She appeared to be running for her life. "Maybe she is," he added under his breath. "Just like me."

As Mike drove, Dev sighed and stared out the window without seeing the city streets they passed, his thoughts too consuming.

His objective had been to keep things light and fun during the next few weeks and intensify his efforts to put himself in her path, now that the impediments, namely his friends, were out of the way.

Though he'd tried to do exactly that today, he'd failed. Miserably.

He snorted.

The scenario *was* becoming habit.

The desire to master Judith in that age-old, primal way consumed him. It was all he could do to keep himself from flipping her on her back and pumping, emptying all he had into her.

He laughed. Damn! He had more finesse than using such a Me-Tarzan-You-Jane approach.

He recognized and accepted the predatory part of his personality, understood it helped with his rise to the top of his field so quickly. But it bothered him that Judith brought it out so easily.

He couldn't remember a battle he'd fought in the last ten years that meant as much.

Objectivity, his biggest strength, flew out the window when it came to dealing with the sexy woman who challenged him, enticed him, and gave him nothing but trouble, all while making him feel completely alive.

That Judith had stopped things once again, and not him, was a glaring warning.

Since knowing and dealing with any weakness also played a

big role in his successes, he firmly resolved to put a leash on his desires.

With the instinct of the cat Judith thought he resembled, he sensed her wariness. He subdued the urge to rush in, to take her by surprise, to break down her barriers by force because doing so wouldn't give him the satisfaction he craved.

He simply had to slow things, maintain his distance, or he'd squander his chance for revenge.

Damn, what a dilemma!

Chapter 8

Once inside, Judith stood with her back to the door, just breathing.

You can do this. He's only a man.

"Yeah, right," she scoffed, heading toward her office. "The only man who's ever attracted you." Then she stopped. A slow smile spread across her face remembering Dev, his eyes closed and breathing heavily. He'd been just as affected as she…maybe more.

She couldn't not do this.

Humming, she strutted down the hallway to finish a few unavoidable tasks.

With those out of the way, Judith ran a hot bath. Submersing herself in bubbles, she relaxed and sipped wine as Shania Twain belted about love in the background. Thoughts of the afternoon washed over her and no foolish insecurities were allowed to taint the memory.

Dev was there with his smiling taunts, his laughing eyes, and his heated kisses.

If she never saw him after tonight, she had enough memories to keep her heart warm for a lifetime. Why had she closed herself off for so long? The notion made her life seem rather empty. Look at all the joy she'd lost out on by keeping others at a distance. The joy of a kiss, of sharing an adventure, of simply being with someone who made her feel alive.

Not one to indulge in regrets over mistakes made during her twenty-seven years, she did regret not having other memories like today's to look back on. She hadn't thought about what she'd be missing from her life when she chose to lock her inner self away from the world. Now she realized why people had affairs and fell in love. It was such a wonderful sensation. She had already experienced the hurt of betrayal. Had it accompanied this euphoric feeling of well-being, if only for a moment, the painful cost would be well worth the price of admission.

Judith glanced at her watch, then jumped up and quickly dried off with an oversized towel hanging close by. She wrapped it just under her armpits and padded into her bedroom.

After fussing over what to wear, she decided on casual black slacks and a slate-blue sweater that complemented her light coloring. She spent extra time on her makeup.

She swept her hair off her neck, holding it in place with a clip. Despite its simplicity, the effect was elegant.

Dangling earrings, her only jewelry besides her watch, danced when she moved her head. Satisfied with her appearance, she dabbed perfume behind her ears, between her breasts, and on the underside of her wrists.

The buzzer sounded and a slight thrill raced along her spine. Dev had arrived.

Judith opened the door to a magnificent man. Khaki pants and a navy sweater over a white polo shirt showcased his tall, muscular frame to perfection.

Grinning, he offered her a bouquet of wildflowers. "They're so colorful, they reminded me of you."

"Thank you." She smiled warmly, taking the flowers. "How sweet. Let me put them in water. Sit down." She indicated her sofa with her hand, saying over her shoulder on her way to the kitchen, "I'll only be a moment."

She walked into the room and almost jumped when she realized he'd followed right behind.

She stilled an urge to run her fingers through an errant lock of black hair that teased his eyebrow and searched a cupboard for a vase, ignoring the sharp edge of attraction poking at her consciousness. Awareness left her speechless as she filled the vase with water and added the flowers. "Would you like anything?"

"No, we should get going," he said rather brusquely.

She hid her confusion over his curt tone in the task of retrieving her sweater. He seemed detached. Where had the Dev from that afternoon gone? She chanced a glance in his direction and offered her best attempt at a smile. "I'm ready."

He nodded, silently studying her face.

"Where are we going for dinner?" she asked, shooting for normal.

"I hope you like home-cooked food, because tonight you'll sample the best California has to offer," he answered with more levity. Then, he cleared his throat and rubbed the back of his neck, as if searching for the right way to express himself. After a lengthy pause, he added, "Judith, I'm trying to be on my best behavior. But if you keep looking at me with those soulful eyes, we can skip dinner. Get right to the dessert, and I don't mean strawberry shortcake."

Relief washed through her when she caught his teasing expression. She grinned.

"I guess I have a little reprieve then, don't I?"

"For now, but don't push it. You're much too tempting," he warned.

Judith locked the door and noticed his shiny black Lexus parked in front of her house. "What? No limo tonight?" she teased, eyeing him with eyebrows raised.

"My chauffeur, Mike, needed the night off," Dev said. "He's a grad student at USF and quite a character. Knowing what it's like to work and attend college, I accommodate his schedule when I can."

His small kindness impressed her, made him seem much more human. Most in her set wouldn't think twice about someone as lowly as a chauffeur. The hired help was something taken for granted, always there, but never seen as individuals with ambitions and dreams of their own.

Dev opened her door, waited until she was settled, then ran around the car to slip in next to her with cat-like ease. Seconds later, they were off on another adventure.

"You're very nice," Judith said with total sincerity after glancing over at him. "Aren't you?"

"Well, don't let it out, or my competition will kill me." Though spoken in jest, something in his broad smile said more, said he cared about what she thought of him.

"So where are we going?" Judith asked, making a mental note and filing the detail. "I can't think offhand of any restaurant that serves home cooking in the area."

"That's because it isn't a restaurant. We're going to my mom's house. It's a bit of a drive. I promise to have you home by eleven." Dev shrugged. "Hope you don't mind. She gets wacky if

I don't take her up on her dinner offers every once in a while. I already agreed to tonight, so I couldn't get out of it."

"You're taking me home to meet dear old mom?" Laughing, she put her hands on her chest. "I'm touched."

"Yeah?" He snorted. "Well, don't go getting any ideas. I'm only making up for lost time. I wasn't willing to wait another night to be with you. Of course, I've never brought anyone home for dinner before, and I shouldn't tempt her with you. She'll definitely read this all wrong."

"Oh?" Judith's grin widened. "Why?"

Traffic was light. By now, they were driving across the Bay Bridge and out of the city.

"I'm not adhering to her plans for my future. Wedded bliss is all she talks about. That and grandbabies. Problem is, I'm not the marrying type."

"Don't worry about wrong ideas." She rolled her eyes in an exaggerated manner. "I'm not interested in marriage any more than you are. I certainly don't have any burning desire to be Mrs. Dev McAllister. Still, it should be interesting to meet the woman who gave such a paragon life."

"Oh, really?" he asked, giving her a sharp look.

"Yes, really."

"Then we understand each other."

She nodded. Her admission about marriage was honest, but the thought of him totally dismissing her out of hand stung a little. She understood the rules of their game and fully accepted the consequences. Still, a tiny bud of hope that had been blossoming inside withered.

"Tell me about your mom," she asked, steering the conversation off her morose thoughts.

"Not much to tell." Dev shrugged. "She's a great lady. You'll like her. Everyone does. Worked as an executive secretary for the same firm for twenty-five years."

"Really?"

"Yeah, she just retired last year, is into decorating now. Has completely redone the house where I grew up. She loves looking at paint palettes and swatches of fabric."

"She sounds nice."

Dev nodded and didn't say more.

It wasn't long before he signaled to exit the expressway, then veered onto the surface streets of San Leandro, south of Oakland.

"What a charming place," Judith said, looking around when they pulled into the driveway of a small house among a row of similar houses, except several weren't as well maintained. Dev grew up here? A stark difference from the large home of her youth in the Nob Hill area of San Francisco and completely opposite of what she would have expected if she hadn't known of his past. "I love the trees."

"The neighborhood's a little rough, but my mom likes it here. Says her house is easy to take care of and her friends are nearby. I like it because it's far enough away to not interfere with my life, but close enough to keep in contact."

He helped her out of the car. She started up the drive, but Dev's hand on her arm stopped her. She turned and looked into his eyes, searching.

"Thank you for being you and thank you for being here." With that, he kissed her softly. Then, he straightened, and hand in hand, led her up the path.

Judith put one foot in front of the other, feeling slightly unbalanced. He was so good at keeping her there.

At the front door, he rang the bell and opened the door at the same time.

"Come in. Come in," a striking woman greeted with a smile. She wore stylish burgundy slacks and an ivory sweater that emphasized her short dark curly hair and intelligent blue eyes exactly like Dev's. When those eyes took in Judith, her eyebrows shot up. "And who's this?"

"Mom, this is Judith Reid."

"Nice to meet you, Mrs. McAllister." Judith took her outstretched hand.

"*Pfft*," she said, waving her other hand. "Call me Maggie." Her smile was engaging, but there was a calculated gleam in her eyes as her gaze assessed. "It's not every day Dev brings a woman home to dinner."

Maggie had the same coloring as Dev, but where her son was tall and muscular, she was compact. Her eyes crinkled when she smiled, revealing a few wrinkles. However, there were no other hints to betray her age. Judith just assumed she'd be meeting a much older woman.

"I know what you're thinking. Don't even go there," Dev warned, shaking his head. "She's just a friend." He caught Judith's attention and snorted. "See what I mean?"

"Yeah! Only friends. I got it." Maggie laughed and winked at Judith, then led them further into the living room. "Still, it's odd. I can't remember this momentous occasion ever happening before."

"There's a reason for that."

"What a lovely place you have, Maggie," Judith intentionally cut in, looking around and noticing with an experienced eye the tasteful and inviting space.

"You like it?" A smile lit Maggie's face. "I've had fun piecing it together."

Judith nodded. The colors were done in subtle greens and golds, sage being the most prominent because it was used on the walls as background. The carpet was a neutral cream color, and throw rugs scattered throughout added more color and texture to an already interesting room. Beyond, she spied another less formal dining room, also tastefully done.

"Dinner's almost ready. Just waiting on yams. Go ahead and sit." Maggie indicated her glass, resting on the coffee table. "I'm drinking gin and tonic. What can I get you? I have red wine, beer, gin, and vodka."

Judith sat. "Red wine's fine."

"I'll have beer, Mom. I'll get drinks."

As soon as Dev was out earshot, Maggie turned to her. "So, Judith, how do you know Dev?"

"I'm the commercial designer on his latest project."

"Ah, you're working together?"

"Yes, we're colleagues." Judith spent a moment telling Maggie about her background.

Maggie's gaze flew to the empty hallway Dev had taken. "Well, there goes my wishful thinking." She sighed. Judith shot her a questioning look and she laughed. "Don't mind me. I like you and to be honest, I was hoping you were a date." She hesitated, then offered in a more conspiratorial tone, "I'd love grandbabies, but Dev's not cooperating. He thinks love's an emotion for fools."

"Mom," Dev warned, appearing in the hallway, obviously overhearing her last sentence. He handed Judith a healthy glass of wine and then sat on the arm of her chair.

"What? I'm behaving." With an innocent expression on her face, Maggie shrugged, but her steady gaze remained on them. "Judith was filling me in about your project and how you're working together." She smiled, saying under her breath, "Just friends and colleagues, my ass," holding the glass to her lips.

"What was that?"

"I said, it's nice that you're friends and colleagues." Her smile broadened, daring him to disagree.

Dev snorted. "Yeah, right."

She ignored him, asking instead, "So, how's Maude? James?"

Dev just sighed, shaking his head. They'd obviously played this game before, Judith thought, as he said, "Maude's fine and so's James. He's in a tizzy because his mother's driving him nuts with her charity ball for breast cancer in a few weeks. You're going, right? I'm supposed to ensure your attendance."

"Marked on my calendar." Maggie twirled her gin and tonic so the ice and liquid swirled, and studied the results. "Wouldn't dream of missing it. No way I'm incurring Alicia Morrison's wrath." Still eyeing the couple, she asked nonchalantly, "So, how's business?"

"Hectic as usual. There's always a crisis to handle. The building's progressing. Probably be finished by October."

Chitchat went back and forth until a loud ding came from the kitchen.

"That's my cue." Maggie stood. "Dinner's almost ready. You two go in and sit."

"Why don't you go ahead?" Dev said. "I'll be right back."

"Do you need any help?" Judith offered, once Dev was down the hall. She followed Maggie into the kitchen.

"There's not much left to do. Besides, my kitchen, my rules. When you invite me to your house, I'll let you do it all."

"So, Dev tells me you're a single mom." Judith leaned against the counter as Maggie grabbed hot pads. "You did a great job. He's very nice."

"I think so, but then I'm prejudiced."

Knowing she was being nosy, yet unable to contain her curiosity, she said, "Must've been hard raising a child on your own."

Maggie opened the oven. "I've had my ups and downs, the biggest down being Dev's father." The scent of pineapples and brown sugar floated out in a puff of steam, adding to the mouthwatering sight of a pan of ham and several yams she set on a trivet.

"I've never regretted marrying him, though. How can I regret something that produced my Dev? Such a wonderful son, a ray of sunshine brightening my darkest days, he's more than made up for my ex's faults." She moved to place the food onto a serving tray. She sighed and her smile turned wistful. "I do regret my choice of men to love. He was such a lousy father and husband. But what did I know? I was young and stupid. All water under the bridge. Here, grab this and go sit down."

With dish in hand, Judith obeyed the order. In the dining room, Dev, already at the table, first relieved her of her burden then Maggie's, who'd barged through the door in exuberant efficiency.

"You might've been young, Mom, but you were never stupid." He placed the dishes on the table, then helped both women sit. "Not from my vantage point."

"Maybe." Maggie scooted in her chair. "I know my time for marriage and love is past. You, on the other hand, are young, have your whole life ahead of you, yet you're shutting yourself off from love."

Dev shot her a warning glance. "This is not the time or place for this discussion." He turned to Judith and grinned. "Told you she's trying to marry me off. Now you see why I never bring women here."

"Oh, hush." Maggie waved dismissively. "You can't tell me my choice of husbands hasn't tainted your view of life and love."

"Will you stop?" Dev laughed and shook his head. "You gave me a wonderful life and I've told you over and over I'm happy. So, drop it."

"Humph. I'll drop it. For now. But I'm telling you, life's empty without love."

Dev groaned and put his head in his hands.

Judith smiled, struck by their closeness, their easy and open relationship, and the definite bond that they shared. Suddenly, she felt a stab of envy. She loved her parents, and they loved her, but she didn't have all that.

Such silly thoughts. She had everything anyone could want, great friends, a job she had passion for, money. While she and her parents weren't close, they loved her and would stand by her if she needed them.

Yet throughout the meal, similar thoughts persisted. While Maggie chatted on about a cooking class she was taking, Judith reflected on their earlier conversation. She didn't want regrets twenty years from now, and if she continued keeping herself from experiencing life, that in itself would be something to regret.

Instantly, she was glad Dev had brought her tonight. A simple dinner like this was one of those memory-making events she was thinking of earlier to bring more joy into her life. She felt the joy between Dev and Maggie, their connection. Maggie was right; life without love was empty and she was tired of an empty life. It was time to let joy inside.

Joyful! The word described exactly how she felt.

Something wonderful happened to her during that informal gathering around a table where thoughts and bread were shared. She consciously took the risk and opened herself completely to life.

All too soon the evening was over and the three made their way to the front door.

Dev bent to kiss Maggie. "I can't remember an evening where I enjoyed the company and food so much. Thanks, Mom, I love you."

Maggie grinned. "I love you too, son. Take care and don't forget to call me."

"Ha! As if you'd let me," he teased, his voice full of love and laughter. He waited for Judith to go ahead of him.

"I had a wonderful time. Thanks, Maggie," she said, finding herself engulfed in Maggie's exuberant hug. "I'd love to reciprocate and have you to my house for dinner, except I don't cook. Maybe we can meet at a restaurant sometime?"

"Anytime, just let me know. And social niceties aside, I mean it when I say I'd love to see you again, Judith." All smiles, Maggie winked and added, "Maybe Dev'll get smart and see what's right in front of his face. Good night."

~

The door shut behind them and Dev sighed, rolling his eyes. Judith laughed.

They walked to his car in silence. In no time, she was tucked into his Lexus with him in the driver's seat. He shifted into reverse.

"I meant what I said, too," he said, as he backed out. "I can't remember an evening where I've enjoyed myself more."

He glanced at her after long seconds passed with no response, and smiled at her reclined position and closed eyes. "Judith, you are starting to concern me."

"Umm hmmm." She offered a serene smile. "It *was* a nice evening. I like your mom. You're lucky to have her. And face it, Dev." She paused. "I've caused you concern ever since we met all those years ago. You've just never admitted it to yourself before." Another pause. "You know what you need to do?"

"And what would that be, Ms. Reid?" he asked, her confidence completely throwing him off balance.

"Enjoy. Simply enjoy!"

When her soft snore hit his ears, Dev realized she'd fallen asleep. He drove across the Bay Bridge with his thoughts centered on his sleeping beauty.

Enjoy? What did she mean by enjoy?

His mind spun, replaying several scenes. Her calm, cool smile, her laughing taunts, her heated kisses, every detail that led them to this point.

And what point is that? Where are we? What game are we playing?

What the hell was happening to him?

During dinner, Dev's instincts had picked up on a slight change in Judith. Before his eyes, she'd somehow become more vibrant as if she'd shed an invisible outer skin to reveal what was underneath. The memory left him raw and shaken.

While the old Judith fascinated and attracted, this new Judith terrified.

He needed to retreat.

This quest for revenge was taking a path he'd never

anticipated. Uncertain wasn't a word that portrayed him. He'd always had an absolutely clear picture of his goals and method of achievement. Yet, for the first time in memory, he wasn't quite sure how to proceed or even if he was doing the right thing.

Dev felt like didn't know anything anymore. His thoughts were all jumbled and confused. He should get as far away from her as he could and stay away. The moment the thought was out, he discarded it. He had no desire to be rid of her, and there was the rub. She'd been an obsession for so long. He was starting to think he would never get her out from under his skin.

What to do? What to do? What...to...do?

Good question, one he still hadn't answered when he turned onto Judith's street and pulled into her driveway. Leaving the motor running, he went around to the other side, opened her door, and bending himself into the car, he woke Judith with a soft kiss.

"Come on, sweet thing, it's time to get you into bed," he whispered, running the back of his hand down her cheek.

Judith woke gradually and smiled. Then stretched.

"Oh, Dev, promises, promises," she murmured in a silky voice hard to ignore.

He chuckled. "Someday, Judith, those words will be your undoing, but not tonight. Come on, out you go." He straightened, grabbed her arm, and helped her out of the car. He then placed his arm around her waist and together they walked to her door.

"Key?" he asked.

Judith dug into her purse, pulled it out, and placed it in his outstretched hand.

Dev opened her door before handing the key back. He then placed his thumb and forefinger under her chin, raising it so she had to look into his eyes. His stare held hers while his lips moved lower in a gentle, soul-searing kiss that left him wanting.

"Sleep well, Judith," he murmured. "I'll pick you up tomorrow night at seven. Dress casually. We'll do pizza, okay?"

"Okay, Dev. I'm only agreeing because I'm too sleepy to argue."

"I know." He grinned. "Why do you think I'm pressing now? I need the added advantage."

He placed his hands on her shoulders, turned her, and gently pushed her inside. Resisting an urge to yank her to him, he walked slowly to his car, marveling over how easily he let her go. His entire world had tilted on its axis. All because of one sexy, intriguing woman. He needed a break from her to regroup and decide how to handle this new revelation.

Chapter 9

The next morning Judith woke with a smile and stretched. Her dreams had been of Dev.

Her ear-to-ear grin never faded as she hurriedly showered and dressed. She was in love with Dev McAllister. Nothing could take away from her joy, not even the hectic day ahead.

The staccato tap of her shoes echoed on her way down the hall. She entered her kitchen for breakfast in a different state of mind, despite an insurmountable task. Dev protected his heart. Let few in.

She now thought in terms of 'before yesterday' and 'after yesterday.' Yesterday, she expected the worst. That once Dev got what he wanted, he'd leave and she'd accept. Today, however, she realized she could have his love, something she wanted desperately. She was willing to risk everything to get it.

Rejection and ridicule no longer mattered. If the worst happened, she'd survive.

Her excitement built as she wolfed down a bowl of store-brand raisin bran.

Now energized, she grabbed her travel cup of coffee, purse, and briefcase and practically skipped to the bus stop.

"I heard you've been seeing James," Kate said, drawing Judith's attention later that day at her favorite restaurant. The waiter approached with their salads. The second he was out of earshot, she added, "So what's up with that?"

"What?" Confused, Judith's forehead furrowed.

"Paul let it slip that you and James had a dinner date," Kate said.

Judith cleared her throat and hesitated. "We went out."

"I heard there's more." Kate let out a disgusted snort and rolled her eyes. "I'm your best friend and I'm the last to know the latest scoop."

"Outside of a few lunches and a friendly dinner, there is no more. Translation? No scoop. We're friends." She shrugged.

"Period."

"Am I missing something? Paul seems to think James is pursuing you."

"It's complicated." Judith twisted her paper napkin, not meeting Kate's gaze. "Since I've gotten to know James, I realize he's not the jerk I thought he was all those years he made you miserable. I do like him, but only as a friend."

"Okay, now I am curious." Kate grinned and pierced her with a stare that didn't miss much. "Long before my heart picked Paul, I'd have given anything to have James chase after me wanting more. He's not a fish women usually throw back, at least not without taking a bite first. What gives?"

"Devon McAllister." She cleared her throat, and tucked blonde strands behind her ear. Not quite sure of how to drop her bombshell, she just blurted out, "I'm seeing him now. I had dinner with him last night, and will again tonight. And he's kissed me, so I guess that constitutes seeing someone, but I'm not sure, since I'm not up on my dating etiquette."

"Are you sure that's wise?" Kate asked, after too many seconds of dead silence. "I thought you were avoiding him. Man, I've really been out of the loop. First James and now Dev? Come on! Fess up. What the hell is going on?"

Judith's feelings were too new. She wanted to savor them without outside interference for a while longer, so she gave Kate a brief update on what had happened in the last twenty-four hours, leaving out the part about her newfound love for Dev.

"I don't know, Judith, the man has ice water for blood." Kate swigged half her wine, then sighed. "Are you sure you can handle him?"

"Probably not." She smiled. "But I can't ignore the attraction between us anymore."

"He's always intimidated me, not an easy feat, as you know." Kate's silence lengthened before she advised cautiously, "I hope you don't have any grand illusions about reeling him in. I've watched the best try and fail. When James and I dated, eons ago, we'd sometimes get together with Dev and the flavor of the month, an apt term, given the variety. So sad how the woman he was with always seemed more interested in him than he in her. Of course, he traveled a lot back then. Never had time for much of anything, but even if he had, I doubt he grasped the concept of a long-term relationship. He's worse than James. At least James tried."

Nodding, Judith remembered James' lack of commitment had given Kate years of grief. She should probably take her own advice and steer clear of Dev like she'd cautioned Kate to steer clear of James when he'd disappear into his job. Her opinion had always caused conflict between the two friends, and Kate kept her distance when she and James were doing well because of Judith's negative feelings toward him.

"I might get hurt." The picture of what her life could be seemed bleak if Dev didn't return her love. "I need to see where this leads. Until then, no one else will do, including James." She smiled too brightly and asked, "Are you going to Alicia Morrison's charity ball?"

"Need you ask? Paul's helping his mom with the planning," Kate said, taking her hint. The subject was closed. "James'll be there too. She usually guilts Dev and his mom into attending. What about you? I know that's not your thing, but now that you and Dev are an item, is he taking you?"

"He hasn't asked. I was thinking of going alone, but I was hoping to sit with you and Paul."

"I can't see why not. It may prove a little awkward." She paused. "You know, with both James and Dev there. We usually all sit at the same table with Paul's parents."

"Maybe." Judith shrugged. "I've been pretty up front with James. If Dev and I are together, even for a little while, I'm going to have to face the two of them together sometime. They're best friends, after all."

"Yeah! But I'm glad it's not me. I've had my share of riding the emotional roller coaster." Kate's grin grew. "Do you remember when you were dating Paul and I was still dating James? All four of us were just plodding along...for years with the wrong person. It's amazing we came out of it unscathed and still friends."

"How could I forget?" Judith smiled. It boggled the mind how her two best friends, sworn enemies for years, had somehow found each other. And now they were married. "Paul and I were never meant to be. Neither were you and James." She toyed with a bite of Caesar salad before spearing a mouthful. She chewed, then swallowed. "It's just a pity we wasted so much energy and time figuring it out. We were all coasting." She took a deep breath and said with conviction, stabbing another bite, "I'm done coasting through life. I want more."

"Oh, Jude." Kate reached for her hand and squeezed. "I hope you get it."

The conversation turned to other topics. It wasn't long before Judith looked up the see their waiter coming their way.

"Would you like anything else?" he asked.

"No, just the check please." Kate aimed her gaze on Judith. "Before I forget, are we still on for your birthday bash?"

"Don't call it that. It's merely a simple dinner with friends. Not a big deal, got it? And yes, I have it marked...the Sunday after the ball, right?"

"I meant dinner." Kate grinned. "So I guess this means I can't invite the forty people on my list?"

"I'm not laughing. I mean it! I don't want a big affair." Judith looked at her watch. "Oh, darn. Gotta run. I'm meeting a contractor in ten minutes. Can you get the check? Next time's on me."

At Kate's, "No problem," she jumped up to give Kate a quick kiss on the cheek. She tossed over her shoulder, "See ya! Love ya! Bye!" then hustled out the door.

With three blocks to go, she hit the street running. Thankfully, the afternoon sped by and it was time to head for home.

The bus ride took forever. At her stop, she charged off the bus, impatient to see Dev again. She practically ran down the street while dodging tourists, and took the porch steps two at a time.

She unlocked the front door. Glancing at the clock, she kicked off her shoes.

"Okay, five fifty-five. One hour and five minutes till Mr. Wonderful arrives," she murmured, rushing through the house to start a bath.

The buzzer sounded an hour later and Judith, dressed in jeans and a sweater, was ready for pizza. She opened the door, her apprehensions from lunch, as well as Kate's warning, all but forgotten. Kate and James weren't meant to be. She and Dev had a different relationship from theirs. She did have a relationship...of sorts. What kind, she had no clue, but she prayed it would be lasting.

"Hey, handsome." She noted Dev's casual, too-attractive-for-his-own-good appearance. His jeans weren't old, only slightly faded, and fit him well enough to show off his assets. The leather jacket gave him a rugged look. Imagine. All that masculinity. Hers for the taking.

She grinned. "You look prepared for a fun evening."

"Hello, beautiful." He tugged her into his arms. "And you look good enough to eat."

Dev bent to kiss her. She tasted peppermint when his tongue slid into her mouth, then caught a whiff of spicy aftershave. His hands slid the length of her arms. Goose bumps formed, adding to the thrill of his mouth moving across her neck as he nipped little kisses to her ear. "You definitely taste good enough to eat," he whispered, the sexy sound traveling in waves straight to her core along with the other sensations.

When his hands grazed her breasts, she flinched. Dev pulled away and grabbed her hand, as if nothing had happened. "Come on before I lose what little self-control I have."

Judith could tell he'd noticed her reaction. She locked fingers with his and let him lead her out into the night, wishing she wasn't so inexperienced and jumpy.

He took her to Pier 39 and they played tourist. They ate in a restaurant overlooking the bay. It was one of the most romantic nights of her life because Dev's attention was riveted to her. Even as they walked off dinner, he acted as if everything she said held importance.

Later, after an evening Judith swore she'd never forget, they stood on her front porch.

"This is habit forming," Dev whispered. Just before his lips found hers, he added, "I could kiss you all night."

Familiar sensations coursed through her and she opened herself more. She loved kissing him. When his hands slid around her back and started kneading, she luxuriated in the feel until his thumbs caressed the undersides of her breasts. The unexpected bursts of pleasure shocked her...then petrified her into reality.

She wasn't ready to make love with him. Not yet. And judging by the hardness of his obvious erection, he was more than ready.

She broke the kiss and cleared her throat.

"I guess that means you're not going to invite me in."

"Not tonight," she said softly, shaking her head, as heat rushed up her face. She closed her eyes. She opened them to his intent gaze focused directly on her.

"Okay, beautiful. I can wait." Dev gave her a quick peck on the cheek and pushed her inside. "I'll pick you up tomorrow at seven. Dress for dinner. I'm bringing out the big guns and romancing you."

Judith shut the door and leaned against it, wishing she'd had the guts to go further. Why oh why did she have to be so inexperienced? She headed for her bedroom with one thought. She'd have to work on bravery.

Chapter 10

Judith looked in the mirror for one final check just as the buzzer sounded the next evening. Dressed in every woman's secret weapon, her little black dress, she was satisfied with the results and started down the hallway to answer Dev's summons.

She laughed as she opened the door. "You're early."

Dev stood staring. His smile died, transformed into an open mouth, before he closed it.

Then, she saw an appreciative, smoldering gaze sweep over her, sending a thrill of exhilaration through her.

"Turn around," he said, sounding strained.

She pivoted slowly, beaming. "Well, do I pass?"

He swallowed hard, then grabbed her hands, and pulled her closer.

"If your score was any higher I'd need resuscitation. Judith, you are absolutely breathtaking."

"You aren't so bad yourself, Mr. McAllister." Judith prayed he couldn't tell how fast her heart raced. Another gurgle of laughter escaped as she gave him a thorough examination.

Dev's starched white shirt with stylish tie complemented the navy suit that fit him to perfection. The deep color made his eyes appear bluer. He looked dashing and distinguished, like he'd stepped off the cover of *GQ* magazine.

"You do clean up rather nicely," she said. "Would you like a drink before we go?"

"No. We shouldn't linger." His voice was teasing, but something in his expression and tone told her he wasn't joking. "If we don't leave now, we'll never make it out." He led her to the door. "Do you need a jacket?"

She grabbed a black matching wrap. Dev took it from her and placed it over her shoulders. Keeping his warm hands there, he turned her. Drew her closer.

"I shouldn't do this, but I can't resist just one kiss," he whispered as his soft lips hovered above hers. He moved his head back and forth and grazed, not quite connecting, as intense sensations shot through her. His almost kisses had her on edge, anticipating more. Unfortunately, the more was too fleeting. His full lips made the connection for only a moment before he broke it. Disappointment flared instantly when he stepped back.

"Let's go while we still can," he said in a strangled voice, and steered her out the door.

"Promises, promises," Judith teased, enjoying his obvious distress. Tonight she felt more in control, more sure of herself, bolder. Tonight, she didn't want to be the inexperienced virgin. Tonight, she decided to flex her femininity.

~

Dev waited for her to lock the door and disregarded her taunt, not sure of his control at the moment. Hell, he was still reeling from the stunning vision of Judith in a sexy black sheath of a dress. Sleeveless and backless, the kind that hugged every curve and accentuated those long, never-ending legs that first attracted him ten years ago. The earthy, sensual scent he got a whiff of every time she moved had the blood pumping through his body and pooling south.

His chest tightened with every step he took, guiding her.

He angled his head for a side glimpse, then sucked in a breath when she smiled and briefly snared his gaze. Emerald earrings dangled at her ears, emphasizing the green in her eyes, which stood out even more due to makeup, artfully applied.

He broke the connection and focused on the ground in front of him. He had to get out of here.

Keep moving.

"Why, Dev, you seem to be in a big hurry," she said.

Holding his gaze straight ahead took discipline, especially since all he heard was tormenting amusement in her laughter.

He kept walking, gently pushing her along.

"I believe you're flushed."

Dev ignored her.

Judith tossed out another throaty laugh. She was definitely enjoying herself at his expense. He continued letting her little jibes pass and urged her forward with his hand on the small of her back.

"What's the matter?" she goaded. "Are you afraid of me?"

She laughed again before adding, "Well, you should be!"

Thankfully, they neared his car. He slowed his steps and thought he was home free until Judith ran her hand up and down his chest.

"Ignoring me, Dev?" she asked, almost purring. Another throaty laugh, this one sexy as hell, rang out, further weakening his resistance. He had to do something to make her realize the consequences and fast. If he didn't, he wasn't sure how long he'd be able to withstand her taunts without losing control of the situation. He had no intention of letting that happen.

Dev stopped suddenly and maneuvered Judith up against the Lexus so quickly she never saw it coming. His head lowered, locking lips.

In seconds, her moan filled his ears and he felt her hands grip his arms, telling him she was aroused as he. Using an expert mouth, his tongue prodded, seeking entrance to her closed lips.

She moaned louder, opened her mouth, and gave in to his silent demands. He leaned into her, situating her against the fender to make sure she felt what he couldn't hide. The scene was so similar to the morning in her living room, but this time Judith didn't back off. One hand shoved into his hair, while the other wrapped around his neck, drawing him even closer. For a moment Dev couldn't think. Could only feel. His hands found her breasts and he stroked through the silky material.

When she flinched slightly, the movement registered, enough to pull him out of his erotic haze. Dev pulled back, shaking with need and holding on to his control by a thread.

"Let me assure you," he growled. "You're playing with fire. I don't know why I'm prolonging the inevitable, but for some reason, I get this feeling you're still not ready. And God only knows why I care, because I am more than ready now. So heed my warning, you are walking a fine line, lady."

Then he jerked the door open, waiting until Judith was inside before slamming it shut and working his way around to the driver's side.

~

Subdued, Judith remained silent as he started the car, completely at a loss for words. She felt both elated and worried. Elated because she knew Dev was on the verge of losing control and she was the reason. Worried because she had no clue what to do next.

She couldn't pretend to be a femme fatale and seduce him.

She did want to go to bed with him, but she didn't want it to be so easy for him.

That thought brought out a self-deprecating laugh. All she'd ever done with Dev was make it easy.

"What's so funny?"

"Nothing," Judith said too quickly, a guilty look spreading across her face.

"You might as well tell me. I need a good laugh about now."

Watching him, his mannerisms seemed humble, so unlike the arrogant man she thought she knew.

"Okay," she said, reaching for honesty. "I was having such fun teasing you. Actually, I felt pretty full of myself and forgot I'm no match for you. At this point, I feel pretty stupid, so I guess you could say I'm laughing at myself."

Dev slowed and pulled to the curb. After shifting into park, he reached across the seat and cupped her face in his hand, forcing eye contact. He paused.

"That's the problem…we are well matched. And I still haven't figured out what I want to do about it. I'm not used to plunging in—no pun intended." He grinned. "Without knowing what the outcome will be."

"I thought seduction was always your plan."

"Maybe." He shrugged. "Somehow, it's gotten more complicated."

"Complicated?"

"Let's just say my original plans have veered off track. I have no idea which road I'm following now."

"Really?"

"You sound shocked."

"No." She offered a wan smile. "Sorry to be so difficult."

He grunted. "Like hell, you are." He shifted the car in gear. "I should've planned better once I found out about Maude's defection. You're no pushover."

Her smile stretched. She was warmed by his sincerity as well as by the heat emanating from his eyes. Maybe he felt the same way about her as she felt about him, but needed time to accept it.

"Where are we going?" she asked as her confidence returned.

"Max's," he answered, slowing for a red light.

She'd never been to the trendy restaurant. "Is the food good? I heard they have a dance floor and live music. I love to dance. Are you a good dancer?"

"Yes, the food should be good. They have a four-star rating. And I think I can keep up with you on the dance floor. You'll have to judge for yourself," he said, chuckling. A moment later he added, "How goes the project? Did you and lover-boy Jack get the lights figured out?"

"Why, Dev, if I didn't know better, I'd say you were jealous."

"You wish!" he snorted. The smile on his face told her he was enjoying the exchange as much as she.

~

The valet rushed up to open Judith's door, once they stopped in front of the restaurant.

Dev handed him a ten-dollar bill, saying, "Take care of her, she's a little touchy," then grabbed Judith's hand, intertwining fingers. Together they walked into Max's.

The mood inside was festive, despite low lighting. Sounds of music drifted to the outer room where the hostess was busy seating several couples.

"I'll be with you in just one moment," she said, giving Dev a nod.

He nodded back and turned to Judith. "We shouldn't have to wait. I have reservations."

Judith glanced around. "This is nice. I'm impressed."

Dev's gaze followed hers. The décor did speak of an understated elegance. He was glad he brought her here, since he found he liked impressing her.

The hostess returned, and grabbed two menus and a wine list. "This way, Mr. McAllister."

Dev caught Judith's raised eyebrows.

He shrugged. "I eat here frequently."

He started off by ordering a bottle of expensive, aged cabernet once they were seated.

They'd barely ordered their entrées when a voice interrupted.

"Hey, Judith! Mac! Fancy meeting you two here."

Both looked up simultaneously to see James and a woman.

"Would you mind if we joined you?" he asked, clasping Dev's shoulder.

"No problem," Judith said at the same time Dev said, "Yes, this is private."

"Ladies always have first right of refusal, so you're out of luck, Mac," James said laughingly. Indicating his partner, he added, "Stacy, this is Dev McAllister, a good friend, though you wouldn't know it by his greeting. And Judith Reid, another good friend. This is Stacy Johnson, she's in advertising."

Dev stood and nodded in the direction of the empty chairs. "Please have a seat," he said more graciously than he felt, and shook her offered hand. "Nice to meet you, Stacy."

"Any friend of James is a friend of mine." Judith took Stacy's hand and put up her cheek for James' kiss.

Dev scowled as Judith quickly lowered her head, obviously trying to hide her smile.

"Please bring two more menus and give us a few more minutes," he said to the waiter who had stepped back at the new arrivals. Then Dev turned to James. "I'm surprised to see you here. Didn't you cross this off your list of places to go? As a matter of fact, that's why I'm here. I was hoping to avoid running into people I know."

James laughed, clearly unperturbed. "I'm here because I knew you two might be. Face it, Mac. I like being a thorn in your side. It's my life's ambition."

Dev snorted, then sighed and accepted his teasing good-naturedly, sensing Judith was somewhat relieved with the interruption.

"Well, I for one am glad you stopped by," she chimed in. "It's nice to have company."

"What am I? Chopped liver?" Dev asked with a grin. "Am I such poor company you need others to run interference?" He put his hand to his chest. "I'm crushed. And here I thought you were starting to like me."

"I wasn't implying any such thing," Judith said, as her face reddened. "And you know it." Then refocusing on James, she added, "I'm only glad you felt comfortable enough to scout us out, that's all."

Dev caught the knowing glance that passed between them

and his jealousy ignited. What was that all about? The fact that Judith wasn't immune to James bothered him.

He stewed for all of five minutes because no one could remain in a funk with so much joking going on around them. Soon he was laughing along with the others.

Halfway through the meal, James brought up the charity ball his mother was chairing that would take place in two weeks. "Are you taking Judith?" he asked.

Dev stopped eating and swore under his breath. He hadn't had a chance to ask her.

He gave James a 'butt out' look and said, "We haven't discussed it yet, but yes." He then turned to Judith with raised eyebrows. "I know this isn't the most romantic way to invite you, but would you like to go?"

"I'd love to." She placed her hand on his and squeezed reassuringly. "I'd already planned on going. It's even better to have a date. We're all sitting together, I presume?"

"Yeah, my mom will love it," James answered. "The more the merrier." Without missing a beat, he turned to her. "Okay, Judith, what about your birthday bash?"

Judith put her head in her hands and groaned. "I can't believe Kate told *you* about it. She'd better not be inviting the whole world."

"Oh? Birthday?" This was something new. Dev glanced at Judith, eyebrows quirked. "Am I invited?"

"I don't know, it's Kate's affair." Her voice was full of laughter. "You haven't done something to offend her, have you?" Then, shaking her head, she said, "You'll have to talk to her for specifics. She's letting me know the time and place a couple of days before. It's for the Sunday after the ball."

Just then the bill came. Both James and Dev dove for it. Dev won by inches. He put his credit card in the folder without looking and handed it to the waiter.

James rose from the table and turned to Stacy. "Quick…let's make our getaway before he changes his mind and makes me pay."

Dev grinned. "I owed you one, so think of us as square, okay?" He was only too glad to use this dinner as an apology to end their skirmish about Judith. The fact that James was here goading him meant he'd forgiven and forgotten.

"I don't know! I hate giving up my guilt leverage so easily. But thanks for dinner." James shook Dev's outstretched hand. "I'll be in touch. See you, Judith."

"Good-bye, James. It was nice meeting you, Stacy," Judith said.

"I enjoyed dinner." Stacy smiled. "Thanks for letting us crash your party."

Dev stood after they'd gone and tugged Judith out of her chair and into a hug.

"Finally, I have you to myself," he whispered in her ear. "Let's dance. And then we'll have a nightcap. I don't want the night to end."

"Okay." Judith nodded.

Out on the dance floor, he wrapped his arms around her and pulled her close. It was heaven, holding her. He contentedly swayed as the band played a slow ballad.

They danced several numbers, laughed, and drank some more, until Judith glanced at her watch. "Oh, good grief. It's after midnight. I have an eight o'clock appointment with an inspector to complete the lighting permit, after which, I have a full horrendous day scheduled."

"I have a busy day ahead, too." Sighing, he stood. "Come on, let's get you home."

He took her arm and slid it behind him. With his hand resting on the small of her back, he led her toward the double glass doors.

The valet was quick as few cars were left in the lot.

They drove in comfortable silence. At her house, Dev turned off the ignition. "I did mean to ask you to go with me to Alicia's event," he said in a low voice. "It's in Palo Alto, so I'm spending the night. I've reserved a suite at the same hotel. I'd like you to stay with me. Will you consider it?"

Dev knew he could seduce her and take what he wanted. That hadn't changed. Yet, he wanted more than easy submission. Now that his quest for revenge had become a foggy dream, almost forgotten, he didn't know why he was hesitating. He only knew he was, and his intuition, always zoned in, told him Judith was holding back. When they finally did make love, he wanted her to do it with total abandonment. His patience was wearing thin, and this invitation would accomplish two things.

First, he'd have more time to work on her reticence, and second he'd set a time limit on his endurance. If he achieved his goal before then, well, he'd be perfectly happy. If not, he could deal with two more weeks of torture.

"I'd love to, Dev."

"Good." He smiled and shoved out of the car.

While leading her up the porch stairs, his smile never waned.

He took her key, opened her door, and pulled her close for another scorching kiss that left both of them shaking.

"Good night, Judith." He had to make a getaway while he still could. "Dream of me."

Chapter 11

Dev carved out time for Judith over the next ten days, despite a demanding schedule. He would drop by the site to escort her to lunch or pick her up most nights to take her to dinner and dancing, to a play, or to a movie.

Every evening ended with heated kisses, yet each night he would go further. Deepen the kiss, until it was all he could do to hold on. Then, he would sense her hesitation and pull back.

After too many days of the same torture, Dev had finally hit his limit.

Though he'd deliberately set out to seduce, the side effect was a double-edged sword. He was the one being seduced. The one left with an aching need. He craved release, for both of them. He couldn't take more of the same without it.

On the Thursday before the ball, Dev wove through Judith's neighborhood on his way to her house after a long business trip. His thoughts were on their last heated encounter, just five days earlier.

Pressing business had left only Sunday to be with Judith, which started out with a wonderful breakfast at Dev's favorite spot. Next, they bicycled to Sausalito and on to Tiburon, lazed the afternoon away riding, shopping, and eating. After a romantic dinner in Tiburon, they took the last ferry home.

In order to free up time for the charity ball and the events leading up to it, he'd had to leave early that Monday morning, so he'd planned to use the night wisely. The entire day he'd thought of one thing. Returning to her place and making love to her.

When that time came, he'd taken her into his arms. She'd responded in kind, had reached her hands around his neck, and had drawn him closer, causing his need to veer out of control. Starved from weeks of only having small portions of Judith, his mouth grew hot and demanding…fast. He'd restrained himself far too long. He had no intentions of leaving without release.

Complete the act.

His hands roamed everywhere. When he lifted her top, she flinched.

The movement penetrated his brain. Her hesitation registered, but his body screamed *no*! Why it mattered, he had no idea, just that it did, and the effort to pull back was unimaginable. The only open road at that point, besides a cold shower? Retreat. Retreat quickly.

He snorted, remembering his lame excuse.

"I should go, I have an early flight. I'll call you. I'll be back on Friday. Then I'll have more time," he'd said, rushing out the door before he could change his mind.

Why had he left? Why hadn't he forged ahead? What the hell was wrong with him?

Dev shook his head and eased the car into a parking spot. How he'd been able to leave at all was still a mystery. He damned well didn't understand Judith's hesitation. Her hesitation no longer concerned him. His endurance was at an end.

~

Her doorbell buzzed and Judith glanced at her watch. Kate was early.

Thoughts of Dev, or rather their last evening together, weighed heavily on her mind as she strode to answer the door. Judith couldn't imagine what she'd done wrong, but something had made him leave early. His schedule was so hectic, she hadn't heard from him in two days. Right now, she felt like an overtightened bow ready to snap. If only the string would break.

She couldn't sleep. She couldn't eat. All she could do was dream of Dev, who'd be home tomorrow, which was why Kate was at the door. If she didn't stay busy, she found herself wanting him. Wanting him did no good, because he wasn't there.

The insistent buzzing continued.

"Why are you laying on the bell?" she yelled from the hallway. "Use your key."

Judith jerked the door open. Her jaw dropped and she could only gape, speechless, as Dev leaned negligently against the jamb, flashing a white smile.

Her shock faded as she watched him step inside, shut the door, and lock the chain. Then he spun around and caught her gaze, offering a candy bar.

"For my lady. Sweets for the sweet."

"Dev! I'm charmed!" she finally blurted out. Though corny, she couldn't resist falling for it or him, not with that endearing grin. "What are you doing here? You were supposed to call."

"I finished as soon as I could and rushed over, unable to wait another moment to take you in my arms and do this."

He bent till his lips met hers, wrapped his arms around her and started walking, pushing her backward all the way to the sofa. When she couldn't go any further, he deftly managed to get them both down on it without breaking their connection.

Judith sank. Let sensation overtake her. She loved his kisses.

"Damn, Judith, I need you!" he whispered into her ear after kissing his way there. "I can't stop thinking about you. All I want is to be inside you!"

She moaned, melting at his fervent voice…at the feel of him. With all the love she felt, she poured her heart and soul into kissing him, using her mouth and hands with his same urgency, meeting his thrusting tongue, demanding everything.

His hands roamed, touching her…everywhere. Pleasure rolled over her, wiping out all unconscious resistance, like waves washing footprints off the sand.

She had no idea when he'd managed to unbutton her blouse, but suddenly she was naked from the waist up, the warmth of his fingers adding to the sensations bursting inside of her.

His lips left her mouth, traveled lower, rested at her breasts. When he tugged on her nipple with his teeth, she moaned.

His fingers kneaded their way to her center. Need drove Judith as she moved her body in rhythm with his hands. Suddenly, flames shot through her and burst into an orgasm so powerful, yet filling her with need. The need to have Dev inside her.

She met his gaze. Her same desire was mirrored in those intense eyes saying all he wanted, all he could think about, was to be inside her.

She smiled and reached for him.

Neither heard the buzzer at first. When the noise finally registered, she was jarred back to reality.

"Oh, good grief…Kate!" Judith said, pulling away just as the reality of their interruption hit Dev. The buzzer grew more urgent. "I forgot she was coming by."

"Get rid of her." Dev's voice was low and dangerous; his expression fierce.

"We're supposed to be going to dinner."

Kate used her key and pushed the door open, but the safety chain hampered her efforts. She called out, unfazed, "Come on, Judith. Open up."

"I don't care how you do it, just get rid of her."

"Be reasonable, Dev." Judith refastened her bra. "I invited her and she drove forty-five minutes. I can't ask her to turn around and leave. It's your fault anyway," she hissed, quickly shrugging into her shirt. Then, she called, "Just a minute, Kate, I'll be right there."

"Well, hurry. I've got my hands full," Kate replied.

"And how is it my fault?" Spots of anger dotted Dev's cheeks as he shoved a hand through his hair. "We wouldn't be in this position if you'd have told me you were expecting company."

"Oh, like you gave me a chance when you waltzed in here and started your macho moves?" She rapidly buttoned her blouse. "I had no idea you were coming. I wasn't in the mood to sit around and wait for you like a lovesick fool. So I invited Kate up to spend the evening because Paul's out of town tonight. You can tag along if you'd like, but I'm not changing my plans."

"Judith," he barked, his patience clearly snapping. "After what just happened here, you can't expect me to sit idly by while you two chitchat. That'd be torture." Then, as if realizing his hopes of finishing what he'd started were dissipating, he practically begged, "For God's sake, can't you do something to get rid of her? I'm dying here."

"I can't, Dev, I'm sorry," Judith said, on her way to the door.

She unfastened the chain and Kate stormed in.

"Took you long enough, what were you doing?" Then spotting Dev on the sofa and rapidly evaluating the situation correctly, she said, "Oh! Oops!" She grinned. "Hi, Dev. You back so soon?" She dropped her packages on the sofa table and walked further into the room.

He smiled, showing all teeth. "Yeah, I flew in early and thought I'd surprise Judith. But hey, I guess I'm the one who's surprised. I should've called. Only I couldn't because I was out of cell phone range most of the time. I just didn't think. So I'll disappear. Wish I could say it's been a pleasure, but I'd be lying." He grabbed Judith by the arm and dragged her with him. "Can I have a private word with you before I leave?"

"Sure." Judith raised her eyebrows at Kate while he pulled her along. "I'll be right back."

Once out of sight, Dev hauled Judith closer and bent. Their mouths connected in a punishing kiss that spoke of his frustrations. Then, his lips suddenly softened.

He exhaled heavily when he finally let go and almost growled. "This is not over. I'll be here tomorrow night to pick you up for dinner. Or better yet, you can fix me dinner and we can take up where we left off."

"Oh, Dev, I'd love to." Laughter rose up and she kissed him again. "Dream of me, will you? I'll be dreaming of you," she murmured, right before she shut the door. More glee erupted over his stunned, disbelieving expression. It was priceless.

"Well, that was interesting." Kate sat on the same off-white sofa Dev had vacated. Her voice filled the silence as Judith approached. "Judging from what I interrupted, I assume things are going well?"

"Let's just say if you'd come five minutes later, you'd still be standing outside ringing the buzzer."

"That close, huh?" Kate's smirk and raised eyebrow made Judith chuckle.

"Yeah, saved by the bell, literally. I'm glad you came when you did, though. It won't hurt Dev to wait a little longer, suffer a little more. I make it too easy for him as it is."

"You think it's wise to toy with him like that? I would've understood. All you had to do was give me a sign."

"I know." Judith shrugged. "And wise or not, my emotions are out of whack. This gives me a chance to catch up with them."

"I can't help thinking you're pulling the tail of a tiger. And I'm afraid that particular tiger's going to give you one hell of a ride."

"He's already doing that. He's a cyclone of energy and much too good at sweeping me with him."

"You must be doing a bit of sweeping of your own. I've

never seen him put so much time and energy into an affair before."

"I hope so, I'd hate to think these strong feelings I have are only one-sided. He may not love me, but he's definitely not immune to me." She paced. "I'm going crazy, up one minute and down the next. I feel like I've been on a roller coaster the last few weeks." Sighing, Judith spun around and headed for the kitchen. "Come on, let's quit talking about men and fix something to eat."

~

"Damn," Dev said, opening his car door. What the hell just happened?

Shaking his head, he slid inside and started the ignition. While driving, his grip on the steering wheel tightened. He forced himself to breathe…to relax.

He felt like a ticking time bomb waiting to explode at the slightest provocation.

What he really needed was a drink. He rarely drank unless it was wine or beer during dinner, and certainly never when bothered by problems, but this was an extreme occasion.

Dev entered his club, a place where movers and shakers in business gathered to see and be seen, and noticed several acquaintances.

He veered straight for the bar, in no mood for small talk.

"Thanks," he said to the bartender who placed a drink in front of him.

He turned around and swore under his breath. James was heading right for him.

"Hey, Mac, never expected to see you tonight. Where's Judith? Has the war been won, or are you two still dueling it out?" James joked, not realizing how close his remarks hit.

"I don't want to talk about it." Dev headed for an empty, out-of-the-way corner table.

"Ugh! That bad, huh?" he said, dogging his heels. "Come on, sit and tell Uncle James what happened. Maybe I can offer some advice."

"I sincerely doubt it. Just go away." He pulled out a chair, sat down, and took a gulp of his drink. When James plopped down next to him, Dev quirked an eyebrow. "You're still here. Why is that?"

"Man, you have it bad!" He grinned.

"Okay, I'll bite. What is it I have?"

"You've fallen for Judith." James put up his hand and waved it. "Ah, ah, ah. Don't deny it. It's written all over your face."

"I don't want to discuss it," he said, annoyed that his face showed his thoughts and that his friend was so perceptive. He swigged another healthy swallow and added, "So, take the hint and go away."

"You might as well talk because I'm not leaving." James leaned back in his chair, his expression clearly revealing he was enjoying Dev's misery.

Dev ignored him and drummed his fingers on the table, thinking. Maybe getting another viewpoint would put all this into perspective.

"If you're staying," he said, after downing the remaining contents in his glass, "make yourself useful and buy me another bourbon. Booker's on the rocks."

James could be the perfect sounding board. They had always shared problems. Except none of their problems had ever involved the opposite sex before, and Dev wasn't sure he wanted to share this problem now. He mulled it over in his head while James ordered a round at the bar. She was obviously willing. Why should he care whether she was hesitant or not? It never stopped him before. He would just redouble his efforts. In the end, everyone would be happy.

The alcohol must have loosened his tongue, because once James placed their drinks on the table before sitting across from him, Dev decided he really did want to talk.

Without going into detail, he divulged just enough information for James to get the gist of his problem, ending his tirade with, "I haven't seen her in almost a week. And I really was hoping to be with her tonight." Dev swallowed, then met James' gaze. "You want to know the worst part?" When James kept silent, he continued. "I'd planned it all so carefully, and things were going great until Kate showed up. Then she slid through my fingers, more slippery than mercury."

"Come on, Mac, face it. You're in love with her."

Dev's gaze moved to his drink. He studied it intently. Shit! Maybe he was. He sure as hell wasn't about to admit it to James.

"No." He shook his head. "You got it wrong."

"Like hell I do." James chortled. That was the only word to describe his laugh. "You're in tune with her feelings. She's important to you."

"What makes you such an authority on love and women?"

"I've been watching Dr. Phil reruns on cable, and the guy makes sense."

"I don't believe this." Dev shoved both hands through his hair.

"What?" James appeared baffled. "He's not that bad. I watch him when I work out."

Dev threw out a disgusted grunt.

"I'm serious," James said. "You're in love. I know you. No woman, except Judith ten years ago, has ever caused you a second thought. If one became complicated, you'd move on." Dev's eyebrow rose and James put up his hands. "Hey, I have my own issues, so I don't judge. Maybe you should think about settling down. You're not getting any younger. You've obviously found someone who's worth changing your usual habits, so you should just give in to it. Face it, Mac, she has you hook, line, and sinker."

He stared at his drink, wishing what James said didn't ring so true.

"I don't want this. I don't want to love her. I don't want or need the complications. This wasn't supposed to happen. Damn, what am I going to do?"

"My mom would say to just quit fighting it and marry her." He grinned. "Come to think of it, she's probably right. Marrying her will solve all your problems!"

"Listen to you. Talk about the blind leading the blind. Like I should consider advice from you?"

"Hey, just because my own life's in shambles, doesn't mean I can't give good advice. Mark my words, Mac. You'll finally come to the same conclusion. I'm trying to save you time and energy."

"Yeah?" he said, feeling much better, even though a little toasted. "I'll think on it." And because his mood was suddenly lighter, he added, "I'm hungry. How about grabbing something to eat?"

"Sounds good," James agreed. "I always say, if you can't

satisfy one craving, at least there's always food to satisfy the other."

"There's only one thing that'll take away that craving, and food's not even a poor substitute, but it's something to do. Come on, I'll buy you a burger."

Chapter 12

"Tell me you're joking," Dev said to Judith over the phone the next day.

"I'm sorry. What could I do?" she asked, after dropping another obstacle to sexual fulfillment in his path.

His mood couldn't sink any lower.

Her parents, retired and now living in Santa Barbara, had flown into town a day earlier than expected and were staying with her.

Since the Morrisons and the Reids were old family friends, they'd initially intended to spend one night in Palo Alto to attend Alicia Morrison's big fundraiser and then head home.

Their plans changed, Judith explained, because they decided to spend time with their daughter.

"Can't they stay in a hotel?"

"You know I can't let them, so don't suggest it. Anyway, as I was saying, we could all get together for dinner. That way you could meet them. I'm sure you'll get along fine," she said.

Dev picked up on her tone and smiled. Obviously, she had her doubts.

"Okay, sounds like a plan," he readily agreed in order to prove her wrong. "But since I can't spend the night with you, can't you spend the night with me?" he asked, giving it a last ditch effort to salvage something of the evening.

"No, I'd feel funny, leaving them to go off. Besides, they don't come up very often, and I rarely see them."

"But they just showed up without notice. How can they do that without at least finding out if you were free or not?"

"You're being childish. You didn't ask either. Last night you just told me you would be here tonight and I would fix dinner. Accept it gracefully. So we're not spending tonight together? We'll have tomorrow night. What's one more day?"

"Hell, I feel like a kid who's had his candy taken away," he said, almost pouting. "I don't like it but I'll accept it. You owe me one, Judith, and I always collect my debts."

"I know, Dev." Judith sighed. "Where do you want to meet for dinner and when?"

"Let me call around and make reservations. Mike'll pick you up at seven. He doesn't have class on Fridays. Okay?"

"Okay."

"Damn," he said under his breath as he hung up the phone. Thoughts of spending the evening wrapped in her arms, slowly moving in and out of her, were all that had kept him sane these past hours. He expelled a long sigh, releasing a sharp pang of disappointment.

His need for Judith had already overwhelmed him before tasting her passion last night. Now, he could barely contain it. He hadn't slept worth a damn and tonight would be no better.

James' advice filtered into his brain. *Just marry her. That will solve all of your problems.*

Definitely something to consider.

~

Dev walked up to Judith's door at seven sharp and rang the buzzer.

When she answered, Dev quickly pulled her out of the house and tugged her into his arms.

"This is cruel and inhumane, Judith," he whispered, his head an inch above hers. "All I can think of is to be wrapped with your naked legs around me, with me moving inside you, fulfilling both our needs. And I want you to know that whenever you look at me tonight, those will be my thoughts."

His mouth connected with hers. The second she melted against him, he pulled away.

His gaze swept her confused features and he smiled. Mission accomplished. Judith was off balance.

"Just wanted to fan the flames for tomorrow," he said softly. "Wreak the same havoc on your senses that tonight'll be doing to mine." Then he led her back inside.

The look on her face kept his grin in place. Judith cleared her throat and stumbled through introductions, clearly working to maintain her dignity.

Kenneth and Miriam Reid were exactly as he'd pictured them, late fifties, polished, and reeking of money.

Trailing after them, he mentally rubbed his hands together. The evening might be more entertaining than he thought.

The group reached the street and the limo inched forward.

Dev observed the Reids' reaction and swallowed a smile. He'd never been one to boast of his achievements. In fact, sometimes having a limo and driver warred with his middle-class background. Though need facilitated the use, deep down, he still thought it pretentious. Yet, noting the look of acceptance in Judith's parents' eyes as Mike raced around opening doors, he felt like pounding his chest.

Suddenly their approval mattered, mainly because he knew it would please Judith. And, as he was coming to understand, pleasing Judith also pleased him.

He'd have to think about that later. Now, he simply wanted to get through the evening without embarrassing himself.

He shook his head at the direction his mind traveled and gave directions to Mike, who seemed to be grinning a lot lately.

"Am I amusing you?" he asked, noting another smile.

"No, sir." Mike met his gaze, his grin not fading one bit. "Just doing my job."

"You seem awfully happy. Why?"

"School's going well."

He accepted the explanation as the Reids seated themselves.

Dev followed Judith and sat next to her. During the ten-minute ride, he couldn't resist taunting her. Just a little. Every chance he got, his hand would land on her thigh. He'd give a slight squeeze and watch her face redden. Several times, he reached across under the pretext of pointing something out, intentionally brushing his elbow or the back of his fingers over her breasts. Then he would lean in, whispering low enough so only she could hear, "Do you know what I'm thinking, Judith?"

"Will you stop," she whispered, climbing out while Dev held the door after Mike had pulled to the curb. "You've proven your point. They should've found a hotel. Are you satisfied?"

Dev grinned deviously. "Not at all, sweetheart. You haven't seen anything yet."

Judith snorted, as they walked single file into the trendy and noisy Marina District restaurant.

"It's always crowded. We'll probably have to wait, but the

food's excellent," he explained to Kenneth before giving the hostess his name.

"It'll be about twenty minutes, Mr. McAllister."

"Thanks." He looked expectantly at the group. "It's a nice night. We can walk."

All agreed and headed up Chestnut Street in two groups, Dev and Kenneth several steps in front of Judith and her mother.

"So, what do you do, Dev?" Kenneth asked after half a block.

"Started out in computers. Designed websites. Now I scout companies to invest in. How about you?"

"Safety pins. Business changed when Velcro took off. Wasn't any fun after that, so I sold everything and moved south. Got tired of the fog."

"Santa Barbara, right?"

"Yes. Play golf in perpetual sunshine now. I keep my mind busy managing my assets."

Dev nodded. He didn't add to this, but almost choked when he heard Kenneth's next question.

"So, what're your intentions toward my daughter?"

"Excuse me?"

"Only a dead man could miss the electricity sizzling in the air when the two of you look at each other. I'm old, not dead."

"Oh?" Dev stared at him, too speechless to say more.

Kenneth chuckled. "I didn't miss the bit on the ride over, either."

"Really?" How had he overlooked those shrewd eyes? Dev definitely underestimated the man, which immediately snapped his admiration up a notch.

"She's a diamond in the rough, my Judith. A rare jewel. Takes an exceptional man to see that and I'm thinking you might be one."

"You have a point. She does sparkle," he said noncommittally.

"That she does." He clapped Dev on the shoulder. "You've obviously done some polishing. She shines when she's with you, my boy." Kenneth sighed and shook his head. "Never understood her. Always been off in a world all her own. Her mother and I had lost hope in her finding someone who would interest her enough to venture out. You *are* more than friends, am I right?"

Dev cleared his throat. "You could say that."

"Humph. Could and do. Don't try to deny it. I'll be honest and straightforward here, because that's my way. I like you. I can tell Miriam likes you. Nothing would please us more than to see her settled with someone like you. But don't hurt her, or you'll have me to deal with."

Dev stiffened. "You've been blunt, so I'll be honest as well. I understand your concern. I have no intention of hurting Judith, but our relationship's between the two of us and none of your business."

"Good answer," Kenneth grunted, chuckling. "I knew there was a reason I liked you."

It was time to turn around.

"So what did you and my dad talk about?" Judith asked after they split off into couples.

"You," Dev said, nuzzling, unwilling to let Kenneth Reid's warning stop his fun. "He thinks you're a diamond in the rough...that I've been polishing you."

"He did not," she huffed.

He nodded and grinned, noting her blush. "Didn't want to spoil his fun and tell him I haven't quite finished...that tomorrow night I get to buff the top layer."

"Shush. They'll hear you."

"Cat's outta the bag. They know we're attracted to each other."

"What'd you say to him?" She viewed him warily.

"Nothing. He's got eyes and he keeps them on you. He's a shrewd son of a bitch." Dev nuzzled her neck again and whispered, "Yet he has no idea how much I want you. But you do. Don't you?"

"You're not letting up, are you?"

"No." Judith was still blushing. His grin widened. "I like melting that cool layer of calm reserve you throw off. Can't resist the woman underneath," he murmured, circling her ear with his tongue before biting the lobe. When Judith shuddered, he pulled away. No sense embarrassing himself in front of the wily older man a few steps ahead of them.

They eventually made it back to the noisy restaurant. Minutes later, the foursome was seated and the waiter handed out menus.

Conversation flowed freely, helped as much by their easy camaraderie as the wine, also flowing freely. Dev sat next to Miriam and across from Judith. His position at the table limited his attempts at catching Judith's eyes and sending her smoldering looks. Eventually, he tired of the game, relaxed, and enjoyed the rest of the meal.

Judith and Miriam laughed when both men grabbed for the check. Since Kenneth was sitting closest to where the waiter placed it, he emerged the winner.

"Thanks for dinner," Dev said graciously, rising from the table. He usually didn't like being on the receiving end, especially with men of means and power. It implied a debt owed, no matter how small, another throwback to his humble upbringing. Now, however, he didn't care. He turned to help Miriam with a small thought niggling at the back of his mind. Being around Judith Reid was changing him. In fact, he was starting to realize he had a tainted view of wealthy people and had become a reverse snob. Despite having money and being a traditional family, the Reids appeared no different from Dev and his mom. They loved their daughter like Maggie loved him. Their challenges in life were just different.

The return ride to Judith's was made in companionable silence.

When the limo halted in front of her driveway, Dev sighed, wishing the evening didn't have to end. Unfortunately, he saw no way to extend it.

Mike came around and opened the door. The Reids scooted out, scurrying up the walk and into the house with amazing speed for an older couple.

Dev took advantage of their hasty departure to prolong his own. He emerged and tendered a hand to help Judith.

Slowly, they ambled up the walk. Someone had turned out the porch light, giving them privacy. Using it wisely, he wrapped his arms around Judith, pulled her closer, and just held her for a moment with her head against his shoulder. He then placed his chin on her head and sighed.

Finally, he spoke. "What am I going to do with you?"

Judith leaned away. With searching eyes, she placed her hand on his mouth, silencing him. "Let's focus on what we'll have tomorrow night and not on what we're missing, okay? I'm sorry your plans for tonight got mucked up, Dev. But at the same time I *am so* happy you had an opportunity to meet my parents. I enjoyed the evening. Thank you!" She then stretched on tiptoes, reached a hand around his neck, and pulled his head lower.

Her lips touched his.

Dev needed no further invitation to taste her. Usually his kisses were hot and demanding, but tonight they were gentle and accepting. He didn't want to let her go, so he prolonged the kiss. She held him captive with her mouth and his need for her increased exponentially in those long seconds. Soon, he had to break the connection. His control was shot.

With regret, Dev kissed the top of her head. Then he spun her around and opened the door.

"Try to get some sleep, Judith. You're going to be busy tomorrow night, and sleep will be the last item on the agenda."

"Promises, promises," she said before she closed the door.

He grinned and started walking down the path. No doubt about it, he was in love with her. He'd have to figure out a way to get her to marry him as nothing less would do.

Chapter 13

"We need a break. While we're gone, decide where you want these columns." Dev worked to keep annoyance out of his tone. Relegated to helping Alicia Morrison with last-minute chores for the big event being hosted at a hotel across from Stanford University, he and James had spent the last ninety minutes attempting to appease her, with little luck. The woman was crazy when it came to details. "When we return, we're only moving them one more time. Come on, James."

Yearly growth in popularity made this ball the "must-do event." Two banquet rooms, along with the lush courtyard including four fountains, were needed to accommodate ticket holders.

"I know I'm being difficult," Alicia said, a little too contritely to be believed. "But it needs to be perfect and no one sets the stage like my boys."

Dev snorted. He was on to the slave driver. Even though there were plenty of workmen to *set the stage*, she always used *her boys* because she could and did get her pound of flesh.

"It looked perfect the first five times we moved them, Mom," James said, before stalking off with Dev.

"Your mom can sure be a pain. Next year I'm going to be out of the country when this comes up," Dev complained as they reached a soft drink machine.

He checked his watch. The day wasn't going fast enough. He still had two hours to go until Judith arrived. Kenneth and Miriam were treating her to lunch to celebrate her birthday before driving south to Palo Alto.

Dev shoved in correct change and pushed the button. He snatched the Pepsi that dropped from the chute, popped the top, and guzzled.

"So, Mac, how goes the love life?" James wiped off his can.

"My, we're nosy." Dev leaned onto a table, crossed his legs, and swigged more cola.

"Yeah, I guess I am." He grinned. "So? Don't keep me in suspense."

"You're a good friend and all, but that I don't share."

"Still not getting any?" James snorted, slapping his thigh. "That's my Judith—a challenge to the end."

"She's not *your* Judith." He fought to keep his jealousy at James' possessive tone from sliding out in his voice. Nor could he mention his true thoughts about Judith and marriage. That would only provide more ammunition for razzing. "Speaking of Judith, I assume you'll be at her dinner with Kate and Paul tomorrow night?"

"Okay, I can take a hint." James laughed. "I wouldn't miss her twenty-eighth birthday, but I'll probably go alone. It's only been a couple of months and Stacy's already dropping hints about marriage. Why do women jump to that stage so quickly?"

Something about James' comment bothered Dev. "Judith has to be older than twenty-eight. Paul and Kate are both thirty and she went to school with them." He frowned. "Are you sure?"

James shrugged. "No. I overheard Kate and Paul talking, so I probably misunderstood."

"Hmmm." He would have to ask Judith about it later. "So, you're thinking of giving Stacy the boot, huh?" he asked, shelving the thoughts. "You know, James, maybe you should think about settling down. We're not getting any younger."

"Hell, Mac!" James snorted, scrunching his nose in disgust. "You sound like my mother. You used to be more fun and understanding before you got all starry-eyed with Judith."

"I'm not starry-eyed, and don't knock it if you've never tried it." He broke off. "Damn! Listen to me. Now I sound like *my* mother," Dev said, horrified by the thought.

"God save me from reformed womanizers. They think they can save the world."

Dev laughed. "Yeah, well you just wait. Someday you'll meet someone who'll knock your world upside down, and when that happens, I want to be there to gloat."

"Don't hold your breath. Women like Judith don't come along every day and I'm not willing to settle for second best. Let's get back to work. I hate talking about relationships. I especially hate the word relationship. It ruins my appetite."

Dev grinned as James stormed off. Hell, he was happy and wanted everyone to feel the same way. He gulped the rest of his Pepsi, then tossed the can in the trash and followed James.

~

"Dev seems nice," Miriam said, as Kenneth made a left turn onto Nineteenth Avenue, driving south to I-280 for the trip to Palo Alto. Her eyebrows rose, as she angled her head to make eye contact with Judith, who was sitting in the backseat. "Will he be staying at the same hotel?"

Judith nodded, noting her speculative look. Since all the general, safe topics had been covered during lunch, Miriam was now digging. Worse, she was drawing conclusions.

"I liked him. Man's got character. He obviously knows quality when he sees it," Kenneth said, cheerfully. He caught her attention in the rearview mirror. "And he's obviously taken with you."

Judith groaned inwardly. Her father's smug smile meant he'd drawn the same conclusions. Her parents probably wouldn't be so understanding or pleased if they knew of her plans. In fact, she knew exactly what they wanted for their daughter. Marriage.

She had no idea where the relationship with Dev would lead and, judging by what he'd told her, marriage wasn't the main item on his agenda. No! Tonight, seduction was. She smiled. It was definitely the main item on her agenda.

She wasn't about to divulge her thoughts, and rather than remaining silent, as she often did with them, she diverted their attention with, "I love Alicia's theme. *A Taste of Italy* sounds so romantic."

"I can't wait to see what she's done this year," Miriam said. "Her parties are always fun. She really knows how to squeeze the most out of these affairs."

"I like them because the booze is always good," Kenneth joked.

"Really, Kenneth," Miriam chided. "This is for charity." She turned around to face Judith. "It's nice to see you going out more and enjoying life. You spend too much time alone."

"What time does your plane leave?" Reviewing her social calendar wasn't high on her to-do list, either. "Do you think you can get in a round of golf in the morning before you leave, Dad?" Thank goodness he loved the game and never failed to yak about it when asked. He spent the next thirty miles doing just that.

Eventually her tortuous journey ended when Kenneth slowed the rental car and pulled up to the hotel's busy entrance, full of vehicles and several attendants issuing orders.

Judith scrambled out. She loved her parents. But they could be suffocating at times, like now. A bellboy with a luggage cart met her. She pointed out her things and discreetly asked if they could be stored for a bit. No need to advertise that she planned to room with Dev. She was meeting Kate in the ballroom. If she couldn't find Dev, she would use Kate and Paul's room for storage.

Judith turned to see her parents were out of the car, and her father handing the key to the valet.

"I'll see you later." Eager to break away, Judith gave her mother a quick hug, and then her dad. "I love you."

"Aren't you checking in?" Miriam asked, clearly bewildered. "Why not come with us?"

"I'm helping Kate. I told her I'd be here at two and it's ten after now. You two go ahead and get settled." She waved and hurried away.

~

"Okay." A frown settled over Miriam's face. "I guess we'll see you later."

"You can't push her." Kenneth scowled, then softened his tone and affectionately patted his wife's hand. "She knows her own mind. She always has and always will. All you'll do is put up barriers. Let her work it out with her young man. And, if nothing comes of it, for God's sake don't let her see our disappointment."

"I know, Ken, but I can't help it. I want the best for her. I don't want to see her all alone when we're no longer here."

"Well, I'd like to see more of her before you have me buried, so try harder. I enjoyed last night, and the only way we're going to get more evenings like that is to accept her the way she is. She's a grown woman who deserves our respect for her choices," he said gruffly. Then in a softer tone, he added, "Come on, let's go check in." He took her arm and led her into the hotel with the bellboy shuffling after them.

~

In the ballroom, Judith spotted Kate and Alicia, both with arms full of sheer fabric.

"Let's try it this way." Alicia draped her end over another column.

"Can I help?" Judith asked, nearing them.

"Oh good, another body to help." Alicia climbed down the ladder and nodded. "Here, take over. I'll tell you when it's perfect."

"Finally, the cavalry has arrived." Kate heaved a heavy sigh, as Judith started climbing, then followed Alicia's terse orders.

"Hold it there. No, drop it another inch."

"This is it," Kate said with annoyance, while hanging up her end. "This is the best way to drape it, and you know it." Her look dared her mother-in-law to object. She tacked her end and then helped Judith with hers. "If it's not good enough, find someone else to bully." Kate moved the stepladder, then snatched another pile of fabric and stormed to the next pillar.

Judith followed.

Alicia remained silent, as if sensing the mutiny about to take place.

"Perfect! I think this scene is set." Alicia beamed and clapped her hands an hour later.

Kate stretched. "Thank God. I was beginning to think we'd never get it right."

"It looks so romantic," Judith said. "I can't wait till tonight."

"I'm ready for my massage. I've earned it." Kate grabbed Judith's hand. "Come on."

As they turned to leave, Judith caught Dev and James out of her peripheral vision right as he saw her. Both men were dressed for work detail in body-hugging jeans and t-shirts that traced every feature of their muscular, well-built frames. Judith only had eyes for Dev's fine form, now heading her way.

"Hi, beautiful!" He reached out to grab her hands and hauled her closer for a kiss. He nuzzled his way along her neck to her ear and whispered, "Did you miss me? I missed you!"

"You know I did." Smiling into his chest, she tried to keep

her voice from sounding too breathless.

"Ahem, don't mind me, I'll just stand over here while you two finish." Kate backed up in an exaggerated step.

Judith laughed and pulled away.

"Not so fast." Dev gripped her hand tighter and halted her progress. "What's going on? I still have another hour left with Paul and James." He leaned in, lowered his voice, and said, "Then I'm going up for a *nap*," with the emphasis on nap.

Kate seized Judith's arm and tugged. "We've got plans, bucko, so go take your nap. Alone."

Ignoring Kate, he pulled out a key card. "We're in room five fourteen. Why don't you come on up when you're done with your *plans*?"

"Will you two stop." Judith smiled, shaking her head. "Dev, Kate and I are having a manicure and a massage. I'll take my stuff up to your room then return as soon as I can."

Judith grasped his t-shirt in a fist and brought him an inch from her lips. She gave him a sloppy kiss and spoke so only he could hear. "Since you told me to rest up, I find I'm not the least bit sleepy for a *nap*."

She snatched the card from his hand, scooted out of his range, and hurried out with Kate. She giggled as Dev called after them, "You know, Judith, I give great massages."

~

Dev stood, watching them leave and unable to stop grinning. Damn, she fascinated him.

James' voice startled him from behind. "So, what's up? What's taking so long?"

"Sorry." Dev spun around. "I was giving Judith a key."

"Come on, Mac, I just want to finish. I swear, next year I'm following you out of the country. My mother is driving me crazy!"

"She's not that bad. But I agree. Let's finish."

"That's it, right there!" Alicia Morrison said, nearly an hour later. "Perfect. Thank you so much." Alicia's smile could only be called satisfied. "I knew I could count on my boys."

"Finally," Dev huffed out a long sigh. "I'm outta here." He left the two before she changed her mind.

In the elevator, he leaned against the wall and rubbed his

neck, totally exhausted and ready for a nap. He'd logged long hours over the past two weeks without much sleep. Even when he'd tried to sleep, more often than not, thoughts of Judith kept him awake.

He smiled. He'd have an hour of shut-eye, then he'd take a 'nap' with her.

Outside his suite, he ran the key card through the slot, made his way through the living room to the plush bedroom, then spied Judith's dress hanging on the closet door. Her bags were off to the side.

Dev shed his clothes and headed for the bathroom. First a shower; then he'd doze. He reached for the faucet and saw her toiletries mixed with his on the counter. A feeling of contentment shot through him. Her things were there, which meant soon she would be too.

He stepped under the hot water and soaped up. Tension eased from his shoulders as heat relaxed his body. Minutes later, he sat on the bed wrapped in a towel. Yawning, he stretched out, wishing Judith would hurry.

Chapter 14

"This is worth all the work we did," Kate said.

"I agree." Judith sighed, unable to move a muscle once the masseuse finished. There *was* something decadent in receiving all the amenities the hotel offered.

Twenty minutes later, she signed the bill, using Dev's room number. Hopefully, he wouldn't mind. She would reimburse him later.

"Now that I've been pampered, I'm ready to tackle tonight," Kate said, as they walked in the direction of the elevators.

"My sentiments exactly." She did feel totally revived and ready for the evening ahead. Nervous energy hummed through her system, yet she wasn't in such a big hurry to rush upstairs.

"What room are you guys in?" Kate pushed the Up button.

Judith fingered the key card. "Five fourteen." The elevator door opened. "What about you?" She stepped inside and pressed five.

"Five twenty-seven, so we're on the same floor, not that it makes much difference for all we'll be in them." Kate checked her watch and grimaced. "Wow, we barely have time to get showered, dressed, and made up for tonight...and I'm starving. I missed lunch. I might just have to break down and grab a snack from the room, but I hate paying five dollars for a fifty-cent candy bar."

When the doors reopened both stepped out. Pausing, Judith poked through her bag. "Here, have a breakfast bar. I carry them to work in case I can't go out to lunch when it gets hectic."

"What a lifesaver." Flashing a relieved smile, Kate tore off the foil. "Thanks, Judith, this is perfect."

Outside Dev's room, Judith slid the card through the slot and took deep breaths to quell the swarm of butterfly wings fluttering inside her stomach. "Wish me luck."

"You don't need luck," Kate said, laughing. "I have eyes and I know the *L* word when I see it. Just have fun. See ya downstairs in a bit."

Judith nodded, then slipped inside. When the door closed behind her, she glanced around.

"Dev?" she called softly. "I'm back." She stopped short, catching a glimpse of him through the adjoining room double door, spread out, face up on the bed, naked except for the towel around him.

Sound asleep.

She stomped around, trying to make enough noise to wake him, yet soon realized he was out cold. Feeling curious, she kicked off her shoes, snuck closer to the bed, and stood, simply gazing at his toned body.

"Dev, wake up." She bent over and shook his shoulder. "Dev...we have to get ready."

When that didn't work, she lifted his arm, then released it to flop on the bed, which did nothing to wake him. That was when the towel came loose, drawing her focus to what hid underneath—naked perfection.

He's gorgeous. Such a beautiful male specimen, and he's all mine. At least for a while.

Her eyes glued to his form, she sat next to him and gave his shoulder another shake.

She didn't take her hand off his shoulder. Instead, her curiosity got the better of her, and she leaned closer. Eventually, she let her hand roam up and down his chest. His sprinkled wisps of black hair felt soft under her fingertips. One nipple hardened when her hand grazed it.

Her gaze flew to his face, but he was still out. Growing bolder, she straddled him to position herself for easier access.

She loved looking at his splendid body and wanted to discover it. She had to touch him. Checking his face periodically, she realized he wasn't likely to wake up anytime soon without an alarm, so she felt safe enough to continue her explorations.

At first, she tentatively stroked up and down his torso, staying above the waist. For lingering minutes, that's all she did. But her hands naturally worked their way south, below the V of black hair. Before she knew it, her hands grazed his penis and the organ jumped to attention.

Then, he moaned.

She stopped, not daring to breathe. When nothing happened and the erection remained, she couldn't resist kissing it. Her heartbeat quickened. Unable to stop, she wrapped her mouth around the tip and began gently sucking.

Dev moaned again and whispered, "You feel so good."

Judith raised her head to glance at his face, expecting him to be awake. She exhaled a relieved sigh. He was still sleeping soundly. Becoming bolder, mostly because he seemed comatose, she wrapped her hands around him. Her curiosity increased, compelled her to continue. It was so thrilling...and...so unlike her. He felt so warm in her hands, so sinful, so exciting. She started stroking. Her excitement spiked when his erection expanded. Seconds later, he began moving in her hands. The ferocity of his motions shocked her. So much so that she tightened her grip.

"Please, Judith," he whispered more fervently, moaning louder. "I've waited so long. Let me love you. I need you."

Oh my God, she thought. This had gotten totally out of control. What now?

She couldn't stop...could only watch, mesmerized, reveling in the power she felt. After a few more strokes, he climaxed.

Too stunned to move, she held her breath. Her behavior shocked her. She'd never been so bold in her life. Having taken advantage of the situation, she panicked. Dev might not be too happy. She scurried off the bed and into the bathroom, grabbed a washcloth, and wet it with warm water before returning to wash away the effects, praying he wouldn't notice.

She checked his face. Relief swept through her when she noted his closed eyes and even breathing.

Carefully, she dabbed at his skin and wiped up the evidence.

~

Dev was experiencing the most erotic dream of Judith. Never far from his thoughts, she weaved a spell over him, mesmerizing him with her touch. He'd wanted her for too long. Where she was concerned, he had no control. His dream, fueled with desire, took on a life of its own. Judith was naked in his arms. Damn, she felt good...so real...he had to be inside her.

Finally, he was there, moving in and out. He'd died and gone to heaven. He didn't dare wake up, afraid that if he did, she'd disappear. So he continued until he succumbed to the pleasure and exploded, before falling back into oblivion.

Dev, not fully awake yet, but sensing her nearness, grabbed Judith's arm and stopped her movements.

"It wasn't a dream, was it?" he whispered. With half-closed eyes, he took in her mortified expression, as frozen in place, she stared at him with eyes that had doubled in size.

Judith swallowed hard. Shaking her head, she closed her eyes.

"Why, Judith?" He remained silent, watching. Finally he asked, his voice barely above a whisper, "Why didn't you join me?"

"I don't know." She focused on her hands. "You were there and so beautiful. I just had to touch you. And then one thing led to another."

Dev's gaze never faltered. When he saw her risk a glance, he smiled.

"You're not angry?" she asked, visibly relaxing her shoulders.

"No," he murmured, sensing her dismay. He sat up and patted the bed next to him. "Come here, Judith."

She still didn't move.

"Come on, I won't bite." Chuckling, he added, "Well, maybe a little nibble here and there."

She expelled a large breath and scooted to the edge of the bed where he'd indicated.

With one arm around her, Dev pulled her close and kissed the side of her face.

"That dream was one hell of an erotic experience and we haven't even begun to make love," he said. "What have you done to me, Judith?"

The phone on the bedside table rang. Dev glanced at the clock and swore. He reached to pick up the receiver and growled, "What now?"

"I didn't interrupt anything, did I?" James' laughing voice shot through the line.

"What the hell do you want?"

"To see if you two would like to join us downstairs for a quick drink before the bash begins, but I think I have my answer."

"You got that right. Good-bye, James." He hung up and

Sandy Loyd

glanced at Judith. "We should get ready, they're expecting us downstairs. What I want to do will take more than a few minutes. I need all night." He maneuvered her onto his lap with his feet on the floor. "But we have time for a kiss." Nuzzling, his lips found hers while he lost himself in her mouth, a mouth that molded to his. When her tongue tentatively touched his, his erection poked her. He nibbled his way to her ear. "Let's skip the ball…take up where you left off," he whispered. "Only this time, we'll both fully participate." Then, working to persuade her with kisses, he captured her lips between his and gently sucked.

Judith moaned, but broke free.

"Please, we have to go down." Her request came out in breathy little wisps that only made him want to kiss her more. But he released her, set her aside, and stood, as she added, "Otherwise they'll know what we're doing."

Dev's bark of laughter rang through the room. He stalked naked to the bathroom, still laughing.

"What's so funny?" Haughty annoyance was laced in the three words.

"You! What do you think they think we were doing right now? Considering my sharp retorts, James has more than a better idea. I guarantee they're all downstairs right now drinking and wondering if we're having a good time."

"Oh." Judith offered him a sheepish, embarrassed smile that did nothing to ease the urge to take her into his arms again.

"Come on. Get moving," he said, focusing on washing his face instead. "Otherwise I'll think you've changed your mind about going downstairs."

He had an electric razor in his hand, ready to turn it on, when she appeared at the door holding all her stuff. "Hurry up, because I need the bathroom."

"I hope you're not one of those women who take forever. We need to be out of here in thirty minutes to be fashionably late. Forty-five, and we'll border on being rude."

"You just worry about you. I'll be ready in plenty of time," she countered, moving past him. She placed her items about the small room. Then she nudged him away from the doorjamb he leaned against while shaving, still watching her. She waved. "But I need the bathroom, so shave out there."

130

He moved and she quickly closed and locked the door.

Dev stood at the window and stared out fifteen minutes later when the bathroom door opened. He turned. She emerged in a slip and stockings all made up, looking like a Grecian goddess. The sight of her padding to the closet where her dress hung left him breathless and he couldn't stop gawking.

Judith took the dress off the hanger, quickly donned the navy silk creation, and stepped into her shoes.

Dress and shoes finally on, she straightened and floated in his direction. She came up to him, presenting her back. "Could you?"

Could I what? Take you in my arms and never let you go? Yeah, I could do that. He shook himself, realizing she meant for him to do up the zipper. He kissed the top of her shoulder near her neck.

"Wouldn't you rather stay here?" His broken voice was filled with emotion.

He raised his head and tugged at the zipper before turning her around, his gaze feasting on her beauty and poise, as regal as any queen's in her confection of navy blue. The gown showed off her figure to perfection. The capped sleeves off the shoulder connected to snug material that hugged her breasts and met the gown at the waist, where it gathered to flow the rest of the way to the ground.

The rich color dramatically highlighted her pale features. Her skin glowed. The makeup she'd sparingly used brought out eyes that sparkled blue-green, like Caribbean waters. Sapphire earrings and a matching necklace completed her look, an exclamation point of jewels directing attention to her bare neck and shoulders.

His mouth met hers, melded, and worked to convince her with kisses to remain here with him. To hell with the rest of the world.

"Please, Dev." She pulled away. "My parents will notice if we don't go downstairs. Please?" She met his gaze with pleading eyes. "What's a couple of hours of mingling? Then, the rest of the night will be ours, I promise."

Her soft voice wafted past his ears. Dev melted. He'd do anything within his power to please her, he realized. If a few more hours give or take was something important to her, what could he do but agree?

"Promises, promises, Judith. I'll hold you to yours."

He brought her hands to his lips and said, letting the adoration he felt show in his eyes while looking into hers, "You're a vision to behold tonight. I'm going to have trouble keeping my hands to myself, keeping lewd and lascivious thoughts at bay."

Judith beamed. "I do feel like a fairy princess." She gave him an appraising scan and grinned. "Come on, my handsome prince, we have a ball to attend."

"Lead the way." Dev bowed. "I'm yours to command, my princess."

Chapter 15

"Hurry. We're already late." Judith grabbed Dev's hand and pulled him off the elevator.

"And whose fault is that?" Dev asked, chuckling.

She saw heat in his eyes when they connected with hers. She felt beautiful.

Of course, he was just as beautiful. She was used to seeing formally dressed men. It pleased her to note that his tuxedo fit him as if created specifically for him. She admired the distinguished and dashing figure he made walking next to her. She felt proud to be the woman at his side tonight.

The two entered the courtyard. Judith stopped and looked around.

The mid-August night air was dry and cool, perfect for dancing under the cloudless, star-filled sky. As they walked further into one of the ballrooms, she smiled, sending silent kudos to Alicia.

The room was magical. She certainly knew how to stage a production. And that is exactly what this was, a major five-star production. The theme, *A Taste of Italy*, came out in every detail from banquet rooms made to resemble Italian palazzos to the courtyard, with its many fountains. The orchestra played soft dinner music as guests milled about, talking and finding their tables in the act of seeing and being seen. There were several tables outside, but most were inside.

The Breast Cancer Awareness Charity Ball appeared to be a huge success. The hefty price of admission—$1,000 per ticket—didn't stop anyone from attending. The amount of money earned made it one of the biggest fundraisers of the year, and it was so well attended because Alicia Morrison obviously put on a great party.

As Dev led her through the packed room, Judith tried not to gawk. She hated functions like this where an air of boredom typically permeated. No one appeared bored tonight.

They approached a large group just as James stepped up to Dev and the two shook hands.

"You remember Stacy, don't you?" After introductions, James said, "Keep your eyes open. I can only stand here and chat until I see my mom and then we have to break up. She's spouting a notion about me circulating to make sure everyone is having a good time." He grinned. "Don't be surprised if you're both recruited. I hate playing the role, so I only do it when I see her."

A waiter approached with a tray full of drinks.

"Red wine, right?" Dev reached for a glass and handed it to her before grabbing another.

"Yes, thank you," Judith murmured, glad to have the wine to hide behind.

She sipped and continued her silent observation of the event unfolding, enjoying the show.

In one circle, an annoyed woman was trying her best to recapture a man's attention. His interest had wandered to another man chatting next to him. In a group to her left, someone was obviously working to curry favor from another, while he talked nonstop. The man he was trying to impress seemed anything but. There were those couples that had eyes only for each other and other couples that had eyes for everyone else except their partner. That these different scenes played out within a stone's throw from where she stood caused a laugh to break free.

Dev, about to say something to Stacy, turned to her with raised eyebrows and a question lighting his eyes.

"Nothing, I'm just enjoying myself," she said. "I feel lucky to be here with the most handsome and debonair man in the room."

"A compliment deserves a compliment." He smiled warmly. "You are by far the most beautiful woman present." He then turned to respond to something James had said, but not before encircling an arm around her waist and hauling her closer in a proprietary move.

Judith's smile inched a little wider. Sipping wine, she surreptitiously observed Dev. So polished and sure of himself, a dominating presence even while surrounded by leaders, he was completely in his element. In a room where the best and the brightest from the Bay Area mingled, he stood out. Judith could only marvel that he was the one to break through her wall of reserve she'd put up all those years ago. Happiness welled up inside her when they all advanced toward their table because dinner was about to be served.

"You remember my mother, Maggie," Dev said, just before helping Judith into her seat.

"Nice to see you again, Judith." Maggie grinned, then introduced her date, and the evening progressed as waiters hurried around to serve the first course.

Judith picked up a fork and knife to cut her steak. Even though it was typical banquet fare, there was nothing typical in the food's preparation or delicious taste as wine and liquor flowed. While eating, too caught up in the many different conversations going on around her, she was amazed at how everyone seemed to be enjoying themselves.

The orchestra began playing a livelier tune.

Dev stood.

"Would you like to dance?"

"Yes, thank you." She set her napkin aside.

"If you will excuse us," he said to the group before helping Judith out of her chair. "It's time to work off the meal."

He led her out to the courtyard before pulling her into his arms. "This is what I've wanted to do for the past hour, simply hold you in my arms."

Warmed by the sentiment, Judith looked into his smoldering eyes and could only agree.

The music eventually faded and another man quickly cut in.

Judith smiled at Dev's polite, "I think this is a good time to follow Alicia's edict and dance with a wallflower." Yet his expression, as he stepped away, said he didn't like seeing her in another man's arms. He was clearly handling it with more grace than he felt.

This happened too many times to count during the next hour. By then, Judith was dancing with a gentleman she'd never met, Bob Hemings, one of the directors on McAllister, Inc.'s board. Since he seemed important to Dev's business, she remained courteous, despite his annoying habit of brushing against her breast every chance he got. She leaned as far away as possible from him without insulting him.

"Dev sure pulled a fast one, snapping up the building on Hyde Street without telling anyone." Having gone beyond irritated minutes earlier, she was about to yank out of his reach, yet stopped when he added, "McAllister's board members aren't happy about his leaving the company out of a deal that's doubled in value, and the work isn't even done yet."

"What are you saying?" Her gaze searched his. "McAllister, Inc. bought the building."

"We all wish." He snorted. "Dev didn't go through his company, he bought it himself."

"That's impossible. My contract's with McAllister, Inc.," she said.

He shrugged. "It shouldn't matter for you. You'll be paid no matter what. However, the corporation is out the profits that only McAllister himself will now reap. Of course, there's not much we can do about it. He was perfectly within his rights to take on such a risk."

She wasn't worried. Not about being paid. But the idea of Dev misleading her niggled inside her brain. She'd have to ask him about it.

When the jerk brushed against her, using her distraction to his advantage, she swallowed a nasty retort. If he did that once more, she'd stomp on his instep. She breathed a sigh of relief when the music died, quickly stepped away, and thanked him politely.

She turned, almost bumping into Dev. She offered a welcoming smile yet, when their gazes locked, the anger blazing in his eyes caused her to retreat another step.

"Bob, go and play your games elsewhere," he said in a menacing growl. "And stay away from Judith."

Without a word, Bob skulked away as fast as a rat deserts a sinking ship.

"I'm sorry, Judith. I should have known better than to let that man get close to you."

Judith smiled. She'd never viewed this chivalrous side of Dev.

The music started up again as James appeared.

He clapped Dev on the back. "It's my turn."

When Dev's look turned mutinous, James laughed.

"Come on, Mac. What's one more dance?"

Judith threw Dev an apologetic look while James led her away.

"Looks like things are going well. I'm happy for both of you, Judith." His grin spread, reaching ear to ear. "Of course, you picked the wrong man."

Judith's grin matched his. "You're a good friend." Then, remembering what Bob Hemings had said, she frowned. "James, who owns the building we're working on?"

"What?" James' startled expression told her he hadn't expected the question.

Watching his expression morph into guilt, her eyes narrowed. "Does McAllister, Inc. own it, or does Dev own it outright?"

James hesitated. "Dev owns it. Why're you asking?"

"Curiosity." She shrugged. "Dev's always given me the impression that his company owns it. I was just wondering why he would buy it and then keep it a secret. Do you know?"

"You'd better ask Dev that question," James said, clearly uncomfortable with the subject. "So, have you solved the problem with the dye lot variations in the wood flooring?"

"I know you really don't want to get into the flooring problems on the project right now. I'll drop it."

James sighed. "I'm that obvious?"

Judith laughed. Still, his unease was unsettling. While the dance continued, her mind spun.

When the music died, James returned her to an impatient Dev.

"Thanks for the dance." He bent and kissed her cheek before turning to Dev. "She's all yours." Then he sauntered off.

She felt Dev's strong arms wrap around her.

Chills ran down her spine when she heard him say seductively, "Time's up, I can't wait anymore. I've lost my patience watching too many men ogle and grope you. James was the last straw. It's my turn." He danced them toward the entrance of the courtyard. His arms tightened and he pulled her closer, nestling her head in the crook of his shoulder. She could feel his desire between them.

Before Judith forgot what she'd learned about his company,

she leaned away. "Dev, I need to talk to you before we go upstairs."

Slowly, he shook his head as his fiery gaze heated her insides. "Later. The time for talking is over."

His lips found hers and all thought fled, replaced with sensation as he continued his dance of seduction. As his mouth moved over hers, she wanted nothing more than to return his kisses. She could stay this way all night—he felt so good.

When the music stopped, Dev released her lips. Then, taking her hand in his, he brought it to his mouth, forcing Judith to look into his heated eyes. Warmth enveloped her.

"We've done our duty to Alicia. Come on," he whispered. "Let's go up to the room."

~

James found Stacy and stood a few feet away observing Dev and Judith's last dance. As Dev led Judith out the door, and probably to sexual ecstasy, he couldn't help but feel a stab of envy. After fifteen years of friendship, he'd never been in this position. He'd always been the one with everything Dev didn't have. The tables had somehow turned and his friend had something he may never have. It was obvious to anyone watching, they were in love. Turning to Stacy, he sighed. Why couldn't she be the one to hold his interest? For an ephemeral moment, he felt lonely. Shaking it off, he took Stacy into his arms for a dance, charming her, forgetting his maudlin thoughts.

Chapter 16

"Come here," Dev murmured, pulling her closer, when the elevator doors closed and gave them temporary privacy. His hands traveled up and down her back. He bent to take her mouth with his. Judith's arms wrapped around his neck and she moaned softly. Blood rushed south. His patience for finesse was nonexistent, his resistance shot to hell, and even though he knew the short ride would last mere seconds, he had to get as close to her as possible.

When the doors opened, Dev didn't notice right away.

The doors closed as he lifted his head. It took a full moment before coherent thought returned.

Damn! He never should have touched her until he got her to the room. He quickly pushed the button, grabbed Judith's hand before the now opened doors closed again, and practically dragged her behind in a rush to get to their suite.

He ran the key through the slot and, once inside, wasted no time in spinning her around and hurriedly unzipping her dress. The sleeves slid down her arms, and he pushed them down even faster. When free of her hands, he picked her up and carried her into the bedroom, leaving the dress in a pile of blue on the floor along with her shoes.

He'd already undone his tie, so he quickly shrugged out of his jacket. Sitting on the edge of the bed, he pulled off his shoes. He stood up, undid his cummerbund and pants, and let them slide to the floor.

"What?" He paused before stepping out of them and caught Judith watching his movements. She laughed. He grinned and joined in. "Just getting rid of the impediments. Come here."

In one fluid motion, he had her pinned beneath him while his hands stroked. He used a gentle touch along with his mouth to both soothe and stimulate. She had the most velvety body. All softness with exactly the right amount of curves. He'd never get enough of touching her. He'd never tire of kissing her. He'd never have his fill of her.

His head moved higher until their mouths were almost touching. He grazed, softened his lips to match hers. When she protested aloud and he felt her fingers shoving through his hair, yanking him closer, his mouth became more insistent, more urgent.

He broke contact and nipped his way along her chin to her ear, while his hands continued leisurely caressing. He spent a moment on her lobe, using wet sloppy kisses to drive her wild, knowing he was succeeding considering the low sounds of satisfaction coming from her lips.

"See what you do to me, Judith," he whispered. He moved so his full erection covered her heat, accentuating his meaning, allowing her to feel what he felt. "I've been hard, watching you all night long as other men danced with you, and I've thought of nothing but this."

"Don't stop," she said, writhing beneath him, exciting him further. He stilled...so close to the edge of the erotic precipice. The need to drive into her overwhelmed him. He pushed up on his elbows, closed his eyes, and reached for control. He didn't dare move.

Judith began unbuttoning the studs on his shirt. In three impatient moves, Dev was naked.

"Your turn," he said, pulling Judith's slip over her head. After divesting her of bra and panties, he trailed kisses where the undergarments had been, his hands following with sure strokes.

Dev gently pushed her into the pillows. Her eyes burned with an intensity he'd never noticed before, drawing him closer. For long seconds, he couldn't tear his gaze from hers, not wanting to lose that mental connection.

"You are so beautiful," he murmured an inch above her. His lips brushed her kissable, puffy mouth, not quite kissing. He was sinking fast. "I'm dying to be inside you!"

"And I need you inside me." Her soft plea surrounded him with a pull that reached into his soul and he almost exploded. Her voice became stronger, almost a growl, as she demanded, "Now." Then her hand went around his neck, pulling him closer, clearly not satisfied with his almost kisses. Her demanding mouth sucked the last bit of restraint right out of him.

His touch went lower and, hoping to prolong her pleasure, he caressed inside her, almost losing his resolve when the sounds of her orgasm roared past his ears.

At that point, he couldn't contain his own hunger. For ten long years he'd waited and he couldn't wait another second. He positioned himself above her and thrust. Meeting the barrier he least expected, he stopped. Dev fought the pleasure, but was lured back into the vortex of her sexual spell. Judith wouldn't let him retreat.

His control snapped. The woman was too tempting. She was his life, his salvation, and finally, she was his!

All he could do was move with her increasing the speed and intensity.

As Judith came apart underneath him, he joined her, pouring himself into her in an earth-shattering climax.

When Dev could think again, he rose up on his forearms. His gaze locked on her serene expression as she lay with her eyes closed.

"Judith, you have some explaining to do," he said.

She opened her eyes to answer, but Dev brought a finger to her pouty, swollen lips, moving it slowly back and forth, stilling her response. "But not tonight. We'll sort it out in the morning. Tonight is mine, you promised." He captured her mouth for another heated kiss. Leisurely, his lips explored, even as his tongue stroked the inside of her mouth, keeping his pace slower this time.

Dev was in no hurry...wanted to thoroughly discover her secrets with his hands and mouth. Eventually, his lips wandered tenderly over her, his hands shoved into her hair giving him access to her lovely face, her elegant neck, and her enticing breasts, all the while he continued stroking her insides with a slow, sensual rhythm.

When she moaned in ecstasy, Dev's resolve melted. He couldn't keep to his slow pace.

"Feel what you do to me, Judith," he whispered urgently, brushing moist lips across her neck to her ears. "I can't get enough of you."

Waves of pleasure washed over him, as the words and the thrust sent Judith into another crashing orgasm. Only this release was much more powerful than her others and her contractions grabbed him. He struggled for control, pulled away to go deeper, but he couldn't hold on, exploding with a violence he'd never experienced before. The orgasm seemed to go on forever, the pleasure so fierce. When it finally ebbed, he collapsed on top of her, unable to move. She had taken everything. He had nothing left to give.

It took infinite moments before he could think again. Knowing he was a heavy weight, he turned to his side, moving with her because he couldn't stand the thought of pulling away. His breath caught at the back of his throat, held by emotion, when he opened his eyes and noticed tears streaming down her face.

His hand touched the moisture before he kissed the wetness, tasting it. "Why the tears? No regrets, I hope?"

"Oh, Dev." Her tears flowed faster. "It was beautiful. Thank you."

"Ah, Judith, what did I ever do to deserve you?" he said, disturbed by her sincerity.

He placed a kiss on her forehead and his hold tightened.

Finally, he released her and climbed out of bed. He padded into the bathroom where he found a washcloth. After rinsing it with warm water, he returned to gently wash proof of her virginity from her.

His humble act of servitude seemed to bring on more of Judith's tears. Emotions swirled through him as he finished, leaving him raw and shaken. He tossed the cloth behind him, climbed into bed, pulled her to him, and held her close.

"Try to get some sleep, princess," he whispered before kissing her cheek.

She closed her eyes and drifted off to sleep.

Dev lay awake for a long while, thinking. The puzzle of Judith was starting to make sense but he had many more questions, and she was going to answer them. But he wouldn't get his answers tonight.

~

Sunlight cascaded through the opening in the drapes when Dev woke up next to Judith's sleeping form. He watched her in awe for endless seconds before hopping out of bed and heading to the bathroom for a quick shower.

He let her sleep. After all, he'd kept her pretty busy during the night.

Just the thought of the time spent in her arms had him hard and ready to go at it again.

Damn! He hadn't been this horny since high school. He laughed over his randy thoughts and turned on the shower.

He didn't need more right now. He needed to talk. And to talk, he needed a break from her to clear his mind.

Judith a virgin? He'd been astounded. He hadn't dealt with one since his junior prom with Patty Sue Henderson, a hot little cheerleader he'd dated. He hadn't been much more experienced. It was one of those memories that never faded with time, and the thought still brought a smile to his face after all these years.

She was married now with two kids, living only blocks from where he grew up. He knew this because she kept in touch with Maggie. Maggie always brought her up, in an attempt to make him feel guilty about not doing his part in giving her grandkids.

He stepped into the shower and his mind switched to Judith. A significant question came to mind. How was it possible that she'd never had sex when she'd dated Paul for so long? While his friendship with Paul wasn't on the same level as James' friendship, he knew the guy well enough to know he was a normal heterosexual male. Sex usually followed after dating a certain period of time. So how had Judith kept Paul at arm's length?

If it had been him, there was no way she'd have held him off all those years. He was too much the predator. True, Judith had given him one hell of a run, but he would never have stopped chasing until he got his prey. Last night was proof. Though it took him ten years, he finally caught her.

Hot, steamy water sluiced over him as he thought about their time in the gazebo, another memory that had never faded. His interest in Judith had never abated. Even after a decade, he still desired her.

If he was going to be completely honest with himself, desire wasn't the real reason he took on his quest for revenge. He simply couldn't accept the fact that she hadn't been as affected as he. And now, all of his notions of what happened ten years ago came apart in his mind, reshaped with what actually may have happened. He closed his eyes and put his head against the tile. A hollow sinking feeling grew as reality hit him like the water pouring onto his shoulders. He'd totally misread Judith back then. She'd been a virgin. How could he not have known? All the signs had been there. He'd just ignored them.

Hell, he'd misread her hesitation in his current seduction. Her actions all fell into place and made sense to him now. Suddenly he felt totally and completely unworthy of her. He vowed to find a way to make it up to her because he could not, would not live without her. Not now, especially after last night. Last night only increased his resolve to marry her.

Cold water brought him back to the present. He turned it off and grabbed a towel.

Naked, he padded into the bedroom. Judith was still dead to the world, so he tried to be quiet. He rummaged through his bags for a pair of boxers and a t-shirt. After donning them, he went about the room picking up the pieces from last night, putting his suit on its hanger and stashing his studs and cuff links in his shaving kit. He then went into the outer room and laid Judith's dress over a chair.

He snatched up the phone to order coffee and requested breakfast for two be served ten minutes after the coffee arrived.

Dev let Judith sleep until room service delivered the coffee. He headed for the bedroom and put the cup he poured for her on the bedside table. Sitting down on the edge of the bed, he kissed her into wakefulness.

"Rise and shine, beautiful, the day's growing old," he said, once he released her lips.

Judith smiled, took her time stretching, and after lying with her eyes closed, she finally sniffed.

"Is that coffee?" She opened her eyes and sat up. "Good morning." She stretched again before picking up the coffee and taking a sip. "Did you sleep well? I sure did."

Dev stood. "Good enough. Come on, breakfast will be here in ten minutes. Get a move on. Shower's free. I'll wait for you out there."

"My, aren't we grumpy today," Judith said over her shoulder on the way to the bathroom with her cup.

"Please hurry, we need to talk."

"Okay, I'll hurry. Thanks so much for the coffee. That's a sure way into my heart," she said as she shut the door.

Fifteen minutes later, the bathroom door opened. Naked, Judith walked over to her bags. She grabbed a ribbed t-shirt with spaghetti straps, panties, and skimpy athletic shorts. She wasn't wearing a bra.

Dev sat at a table laden with food and watched her get dressed from the other room. He swallowed hard and swore under his breath. Keeping his mind on the conversation they needed to have would be a challenge.

He thought briefly about asking her to wear something a little less distracting, but quickly changed his mind. It would be much easier to get her naked with no bra after their talk.

She jumped at the sound of his voice when reaching for her socks and tennis shoes.

"Don't bother with those…they'll just be one more thing to take off later."

She looked over and their gazes locked through the doorway. He watched a slight pink rise on her cheeks.

Damn, she's beautiful!

Dev kept his focus on her as she walked barefoot toward him, her face flushed from obvious embarrassment at having been unknowingly spied upon while dressing. He probably should feel guilty, but he didn't. She fascinated him. He planned to notice everything she did from now on.

Visibly maintaining her usual calm reserve, she veered around him to the other chair.

His hand shot out and caught her.

The movement unbalanced her and she landed in his lap. He nuzzled her neck.

"Judith, don't be embarrassed about anything we do together, especially after last night. You're going to have to get used to it, because I like looking at you," he said, right before his lips met hers.

She wriggled to get away, but his hold tightened. Her body stiffened when his erection poked out from his boxers, prodding her soft buttocks. She stopped squirming. Dev smiled into her mouth, wondering how she could be so shy when she turned him on so easily.

His thoughts dissipated when tentative fingers wrapped around his neck as her mouth opened, inviting him in for more.

The kiss lasted until he felt his control weaken. He pulled away before he lost all restraint.

He was breathing a little heavier and he quickly set her back on the floor.

"Go sit down, and try not to distract me," he said grinning. "We really do need to talk. First, have some breakfast and more coffee."

Judith sat as he lifted the lid off one of the plates in front of him and handed it to her.

"I hope you like scrambled eggs and I ordered croissants instead of toast."

"You remembered," she said, giving Dev a pleased look. "It looks and smells heavenly, thank you. I find I'm very hungry this morning."

Watching her, he shook his head. His grin returned as he picked up his fork and dug in.

They ate in silence, each lost in thought.

Finally, Dev couldn't contain his curiosity anymore and he blurted out, "How, Judith?"

She cleared her throat and glanced at her plate, stirring her food, clearly stalling. "How what?"

"You know damn well what I'm asking." His eyes pierced hers when she looked up. "And I should add, why didn't you tell me?"

Judith was silent for too many minutes. "Well, it's kind of hard to explain."

Dev lounged in a deceptively calm manner. "We've got nothing but time, and I'm listening."

"I don't know how." She shrugged. "I guess you could say I just closed myself off to things and never allowed it to happen."

"But, what about Paul? How did you keep your relationship together for so long without sex? I'd never let you get away with it."

"Well, you're right there," she countered, grinning. "You didn't."

He smiled. "You still haven't answered my question. How?"

146

"I don't know." Judith sighed. "All I know is I kept putting up obstacles and he kept accepting them. We kissed but it never got out of control. He never did and neither did I. Then we became good friends and enjoyed each other's company."

Her hand went to her coffee cup and she fingered the rim. "Our relationship got comfortable. He became my shield, so I could keep others away. Finally, it ended before we made a terrible mistake and married. I love Paul and always will, but like a brother. I know by the time it ended, he thought of me as only a good friend." She took a sip of coffee while keeping her gaze on her food. "I wasn't very proud of the way I used him. He was my shield for so long, I think I kept him from finding what he wanted."

"And in ten years there was no one else?" Dev could only stare at her with a skeptical look on his face. He shook his head and said, "If I didn't know better, I would find that very hard to believe. You're an attractive woman."

"It's true, so believe it. Now I have a question for you."

He put up his hand. "In a minute, I'm not through."

"What do you mean? What more is there? It's pretty simple. No one else could ever compare to you. I never wanted to be hurt again, so I blocked everyone out. End of story."

"You never wanted to be hurt again?" he asked. "How were you hurt?"

"I naïvely trusted you when I followed you into that gazebo. But it's all in the past. Now answer me this."

"One more question," he said, flinching at hearing how his actions had affected her. He never imagined he had hurt her. This was going from bad to worse. "And then it's your turn. How old are you?"

"Why?" Her eyes narrowed in suspicion.

"Today's your birthday, and I have a present for you, but I don't know how old you are."

"I'm twenty-eight," she replied cautiously. "Okay, my turn to ask questions."

He quickly did the math in his head. More truth hit him as he said, "Ask away."

He'd nearly taken a seventeen-year-old virgin all those years ago and the thought sickened him. He closed his eyes...let guilt wash over him. Then, he heard her question, and groaned. He certainly wasn't expecting it.

"Do you own the building on Hyde Street or does your company own it?"

"What do you mean?" He was caught and dread exploded in the pit of his stomach.

"To coin your phrase, you know damn well what I mean. It is a simple question. Do you own the building or not? I'd like a simple answer," she said, her voice rising.

"Yes, I own it." He let out a long, remorseful sigh.

"But why?"

"Does it matter? It's in the past."

"There has to be a reason."

"I misread things ten years ago. I leased with the option to buy the building to please you, hoping we could work on it together." He shrugged. "When that didn't work out, I ended up buying it, to lure you. For revenge at your slight." He could lie, and smooth it over. Yet, he loathed the idea of starting a life together with a lie.

"I don't understand. You did it to get back at me?" She glanced into his eyes and he knew she saw everything in them. The guilt, the shame, and the sorrow. "It was a ruse from the very beginning?"

"Please, Judith, I can explain—"

"I was so easy, wasn't I?" she said, cutting him off. "I just fell right into your plans. I can't believe how stupid I was. And here I thought somehow fate brought us back together. But it wasn't fate, was it? It was you. You planned it all. You bastard."

She jumped up and ran to her bags. She quickly put on her shoes without socks, then grabbed her purse and bag.

"I'll get the rest later," she said, on her way past Dev.

"Judith, wait! You can't leave." He moved to block her from charging for the door once he realized she was leaving. "Please, let me explain."

He grabbed her shoulders to stop her.

"Don't touch me." She kneed him in the groin then shouted, on her way out of the room, "Just keep away from me!"

"Goddamn it all," Dev spit out, bowled over in pain.

As soon as he could finally move, he ran to the door and

yanked it open, but Judith had disappeared. He slammed his fist against the wall as realization hit. She'd run out on him *again*. Only this time she wouldn't get away.

Chapter 17

Judith pounded on Kate's door, praying she'd hurry. She glanced toward Dev's room to make sure he hadn't followed.

Agonizing moments went by before Kate, looking like she'd been dragged out of bed, opened the door.

"Kate, I need you," Judith said, her voice frantic. She brushed at the tears running down her face. Her gaze kept darting to the hallway. "Can we go somewhere and talk?"

"What's wrong?" Kate didn't hesitate. "Come in." She pulled Judith into the room and shut the door.

"I don't want to bother you and Paul."

"Hey, what are friends for? Besides, Paul's still out cold. He drank way too much last night, and we danced until the wee hours." She stopped and eyed Judith critically. "But enough about me, what's going on?"

"I need someone to talk to. I feel so horrible." Her trickling dam of tears broke and she started sobbing, unable to control herself.

"I've never seen you so upset."

Kate wrapped an arm around her shoulders and let Judith cry. When her sobs ebbed, Kate took Judith's purse and bag and dropped them on the floor. She then tugged on her hand.

Judith followed her to the sofa. Kate moved to the double doors leading into the bedroom and closed them quietly before sitting next to Judith.

"Feel better?"

"Yes, thank you." Judith nodded, realizing she did.

"Want a cup of coffee? I can order room service."

"No thanks, I've had enough." Seconds ticked by as she sat, trying to figure out what to say. Finally, she blurted out, "Oh, Kate, I don't know what to do."

"Well, I always say, just plunge in. You know anything you say to me is sacred. Maybe I can help. What happened?" Her expression turned questioning. "I can't believe you and Dev are fighting, not after seeing you together last night. So, what gives?"

"Appearances can be deceiving. We're not really an item. He just wanted me to think we were, so I'd sleep with him."

"Wait a minute, you lost me. What do you mean, appearances can be deceiving?"

"Dev was only pretending to be interested in me to get revenge for something that happened back in college."

"Oh, come on, Judith," Kate scoffed, totally dismissing her suspicions with the wave of her hand. "Dev's not that good an actor. And revenge? For what?"

Judith sighed. Damn! Did she sound like a crazy person? Of course she did. She put her head in her hands, thinking. "I should tell you the whole story so you'll finally understand."

She proceeded to tell Kate everything, from the moment she'd met Dev until the scene just minutes before. She told her about Dev's near seduction the night of the party, which led to Dev's current pursuit, the building and the part he played in bringing them together. She finally closed her story telling Judith all about last night, how she'd still been a virgin when they finally slept together, about their conversation this morning and the assumptions she'd made based on the guilty look on his face.

Kate sat against the cushion totally dumbfounded. "I can't believe this. Until last night, you were a virgin?" She looked to Judith for confirmation. When she nodded, Kate snorted. "Why did I never know? I thought I knew everything about you."

"Some things are too personal and private to talk about. I've never told anyone. It was easier to pretend I wasn't, especially with Paul in the picture. People just assumed we were intimate."

"It's a shock. Hell, it's more than a shock. It's incredible." A grin slid over her face. "You had to be the only twenty-seven-year-old virgin in California."

What could Judith say? Yeah, she probably was. The thought didn't make her feel any better. Her virginity always made her feel different. Like an outcast.

"You and Paul were a couple for so long," Kate said. "I'm one of those who always assumed you slept together. Paul and I never discussed it. I figured if he could forget about James sleeping with me, I could forget him sleeping with you." She leaned her head against the sofa. "How could I be so wrong?"

"It's true." Judith sighed, relieved to have finally unburdened her secret. Emotionally drained, she closed her eyes. "I don't know what to do, or what to think anymore. I've lost all objectivity. Since meeting Dev again, my life has been one long roller coaster ride."

Kate appeared to have no idea of what to say, so quiet prevailed.

Both sat lost in thought, until Kate's laughter broke the silence. "Damn, I wish it was later than ten in the morning. I need a drink."

Judith laughed. She was a total mess and needed much more than a single drink. She needed a whole bottle...twenty bottles...to drown her misery.

When their laughter died, Kate gave Judith an assessing look. "You want to know something? You've given me a gift and you don't even realize it."

"What do you mean?"

"Well, since we are both being honest here, I have to tell you something. I've been so envious of you."

"Why?"

"Because Paul loved you first."

"It's a different kind of love with us. You have to know that."

"No," Kate said, shaking her head. "You don't know him like I do, Judith. He loved you a lot more than you realize. I've always felt a little insecure about your relationship. Since there was nothing I could do about it, I accepted it. I certainly never questioned it because I love him so much."

"We've never been more than good friends."

"I see that now. Paul told me he grew up loving you and couldn't change the fact, and he's always said his heart was free when he chose me. He loved you as a boy and loves me as a man. But, you were always there. I'm so relieved to know you never slept with him. Does that make me a bitch or what?"

"There was never any attraction or chemistry between us. Why do you think it was always so easy to keep throwing up obstacles? My lack of interest in him was a challenge to overcome, something he thought he always wanted and couldn't have, which simply made him want it more, even after he realized his idea of us as a couple had flaws."

Kate mulled it over for a moment, then nodded. "Makes sense. And it sounds like a Morrison male."

"If what I'd felt for Paul was one-tenth as strong as what I feel for Dev, maybe you'd have something to feel insecure about. But it wasn't there. On either side."

"I think I know what you're saying," Kate said, offering a sheepish grin. "Do you remember the time we were all meeting in Tahoe to go skiing? You and James got snowed out and couldn't join us?" Judith's eyes narrowed. "Remember?" When she nodded, Kate added, "Paul and I kissed each other. Several times."

"No? Really?" Judith stared open-mouthed at Kate. "You and Paul? In Tahoe? You hated each other then. I always had to play referee."

Kate laughed. "Well, there's the attraction thing you're talking about. When it's there, it's there. Go figure. I was wildly, unexpectedly attracted to Paul. And judging by the results of the weekend, he was too."

"See! We never had wild attraction. I always wondered what changed his mind so quickly when he broke it off for good. I wasn't into Paul then and so I wasn't paying much attention." She grabbed Kate's hand. "I can't believe we were all just coasting through life."

"How true. If not for that weekend, I'd probably still be chasing James. Oh, the mistakes we make," Kate said, sighing.

"I'm glad the weekend in Tahoe created a change. Funny, how life's experiences force us to change."

"I thought it was the worst thing to ever happen to me," Kate admitted, shaking her head. "I felt so guilty…like such a pariah…for taking Paul away from you. I even went out with another guy to try and get over Paul. That almost broke us up before we even got together. Somehow, we managed. But it was one hell of a ride while I was going through it." Kate heaved a heavy sigh. "Now you know my horrible secret."

"It sure has been a day for truths." Judith leaned into the sofa. Her head fell back. "But those truths don't help me decide what to do."

"I don't know what to tell you, except follow your heart.

After watching you two yesterday and last night, I could have sworn Dev was smitten. Gave me a warm feeling just seeing you two together." Kate's expression turned thoughtful. "I don't know if he's cruel enough to be so devious and calculating. He's always been aloof and unreachable, but since you guys have been dating, he seemed more human."

"My heart feels a little bruised right now." Judith's forehead rested in her hand, until she pulled the hand through her hair. "I feel raw. I need to think."

"What about the party tonight?" Kate asked, frowning with concern.

She groaned. "I forgot about that."

"He'll probably be there. His assistant called and got the specifics last week when he was out of town."

"I'm not sure if I can face him. I just want to go home right now. I'll call you later at around four or five to let you know if I can make it."

"How are you getting home? It's your birthday. You shouldn't be alone. I'll drive you."

"Thanks, but I'm fine. I'll take a taxi. It'll be worth the money."

"No! You are *not* taking a taxi. Let me leave a note for Paul."

"Kate, you don't have to. I'll be okay."

"No, just wait." After writing a quick note, she grabbed Judith's things, handing Judith her purse. "Okay, let's go," she said, snatching her own purse and ushering her out the door.

"You're the best. Thanks, I owe you."

"Get out. It's the least I could do for someone who didn't sleep with my husband," she joked as they headed toward the elevator.

Judith had to laugh. "When you put it like that, it puts a whole new spin on it. I like it." It was certainly better than crying.

~

Dev paced, wondering where in the hell Judith had gone. He didn't want to let the world in on his business or have to answer nosy questions about why she left in the first place, so he didn't pursue her. He packed up everything, including her dress, shoes, and other items left behind after her mad dash, checked out, and intended to drive straight home.

He accelerated and merged onto I-280, unable to keep his morose thoughts away. He wished he hadn't screwed things up. He understood her dismay. At the same time, his anger simmered. She hadn't listened to him, hadn't even given him a chance to explain before jumping to conclusions.

Hell, he was angrier with himself more for being such a jerk in the first place. He should've told her he loved her...and had loved her for ten years.

He glanced at Judith's personal effects and knew it would only be a matter of time before he saw her again. When he did, he'd make sure she understood what was in his heart.

Dev didn't want to admit that he couldn't fix what he'd broken. He couldn't risk failure. He needed her and couldn't imagine a life without her. He felt like his soul would die, so fixing this became a matter of life and death.

Somehow, some way, he'd make her see what she meant to him, but at the moment he was stuck on how.

The thought made him realize how much he'd changed since he'd fallen in love. And because of this, he didn't think the tactics he usually employed would work...would in fact do more harm.

Pulling into his garage, his thoughts turned to the present and Judith's birthday dinner. Should he attend? If he did, would Judith even be there?

He was still deciding when he grabbed his bags and started inside.

He put everything away, then noticed he had several messages on his cell phone. He'd silenced it last night and had never turned the volume up. He hit the voicemail button and walked into his bedroom, listening as people he knew, but had no interest in, droned on. Then a message from Kate Morrison caught his attention. He pressed Repeat.

"Dev, this is Kate Morrison," the message said. "Judith will be at her party tonight. She knows you're aware of the time and place, so I thought the news might interest you."

How strange. He replayed it a handful of times. What was Kate getting at? Nothing in the message even hinted at it. No, she's willing to talk...no, she hates you...no, she doesn't want you there.

He determined the call was meant to inform him of Judith's

actions, to use or not use at his discretion. Nothing more.

Okay! He'd go to the party to personally give Judith his birthday gift, but he wouldn't stay long. After Judith opened her gift, maybe she'd give him a chance to explain his actions. Hopefully she'd forgive him for thinking she was a snob in the first place. He was the true snob for judging her.

He strode into his bedroom to unpack and change for a long run, feeling more optimistic.

~

Judith walked into the Union Street restaurant later that evening wishing she'd cancelled. She wasn't in the mood to celebrate, was only here for Kate, who'd gone to a lot of trouble and had arrived earlier to ensure things were ready.

A waiter pointed to the private room. Even though Judith had wanted a small affair, eleven, if Dev showed up, was ten more people than she had the energy to deal with.

She entered and groaned. Streamers and balloons hung from the ceiling. A big banner spanned the room. The rear table held a square cake sporting the same birthday message as the banner. Next to the cake were several gifts and plenty of space for more.

She spied Kate, who excused herself from a waiter and rushed over to give her a quick hug.

"I am so glad you decided to come." Kate grabbed her hand and squeezed. "You'll have fun."

"Yeah, I will." Judith smiled and worked to shake her moodiness. For Kate's sake. "I doubt I could sit at home wondering, especially knowing you couldn't cancel the dinner." Then she added more soberly, "Do you think he'll come?"

"Who knows? Maybe we'll get lucky," Kate said, fully aware she meant Dev.

Judith nodded. Her sentiments exactly, but she wasn't sure if she was hoping he'd be there or hoping he wouldn't.

She had no more time for speculation because the room soon filled with bodies and noisy chatter.

"There's the birthday girl," said one friend who'd rushed over and had her in a bear hug.

Worry about Dev's presence faded as she got caught up in answering a barrage of questions. She laughed good-naturedly over jokes about her old age. No one had a clue her heart ached.

In fact, most didn't know she and Dev were even together.

Someone shouted, "Here, the guest of honor should sit at the head of the table." A chair appeared and she sat.

Judith was in the middle of answering a question about her work when a disturbance at the door captured her attention. She looked up and caught Dev's glance just as he walked into the room. He wore a sport coat, an open-necked shirt, and casual slacks with loafers, looking so handsome, he took her breath away. Annoyed at her reaction, she tore her gaze from his and smiled at the person she was talking to.

Despite her best efforts her gaze kept returning to Dev, who found an empty seat in the middle of the table. She tried to ignore her disappointment when he made no effort to join her. It hurt.

A moment later, James and Paul strolled in. After going up and giving Judith a quick hello and a birthday greeting, they made their way to the two vacant seats next to Dev.

"Hey, Mac, how come you're here and Judith's way over there?" James said as he sat down. "Trouble in paradise already?"

"I got here a little late, and everyone was already seated." Dev said nonchalantly.

"Well, go over and ask one of them to move."

"It's no big deal. Most of Judith's friends don't know about us yet. So I'm going by her cues."

Judith swallowed hard. Dev was going by her cues? What was wrong with her? Why couldn't she just smile at him… let everything go? She didn't understand her motives. Didn't understand why she sat there and pretended to ignore him while surreptitiously watching him. She felt so totally out of her element and wished she could just disappear.

"My mom's on cloud nine," James joked, pulling Judith's attention to the conversation about the ball and what a success it had been going on around the table. "Now that it's over, I can finally get a little peace for the next nine months."

Everyone laughed.

She spent the rest of the dinner in misery.

Thankfully, dessert came and she was relieved when Kate tapped her wineglass with a fork and said, "Time to open presents."

Judith, more confused than ever, was having trouble keeping her eyes off Dev when he wasn't looking. All she wanted to do was run and jump in his arms, to pretend as if nothing had happened, but she hurt inside. Felt bruised and raw and didn't know why. Everything hit at once. She should have called and left a message, asking him to please stay away.

She was finishing her dessert after opening the last of her gifts, and looked up to see the object of her thoughts walking straight for her.

"Happy birthday, Judith," he said. "I'd stay longer, only my presence isn't helping matters. But I did want to give you my gift."

He held out a beautifully wrapped box.

"Thank you, Dev." She took it. "I appreciate your thoughtfulness." Judith looked into his eyes, and seeing the torment in them, she glanced at the present in her lap.

"Please, Judith, give me a chance to explain. Have dinner with me."

"Let me think about it, okay?" she asked, clearly torn. Why didn't she jump at the chance? What was wrong with her?

"Sure. Well, happy birthday. Maybe when you open your gift, you'll know how I feel."

Then Dev turned and slowly walked out.

Viewing his retreating back, she felt bereft. Tears threatened. How could she be crying again? She thought she was all cried out. She glanced at the gift and placed it on the table to open later.

Judith caught James' concerned look and smiled. "James, I'm so glad you came tonight."

"I wouldn't miss it." He hesitated. "Is everything okay?"

"Everything's fine."

He nodded, but didn't seem convinced. "I'm afraid I have an early morning tomorrow. Thanks for having me." He grinned. "I hope you like my gift."

"It's much too extravagant and you shouldn't have done it, but thank you," Judith said, her smile brightening. "I love the wine country and can't wait to make use of your gift certificate."

"I got it with you and Dev in mind. If you change your mind about him, you can always use it with me. Just say the word and

I'm yours to command," he joked, before turning to walk out.

"I should be so lucky." She laughed and shouted after him, "Drive carefully."

The group eventually whittled down to just Paul, Kate, and Judith.

Kate let out a huge sigh. "Wow! Thank goodness it's over. What a weekend. I'm glad I don't have to drive home."

"What, you're not driving?" Paul teased.

"No, I'm not." Giggling, she slapped at his shoulder. "And don't even joke about it. I'm exhausted."

He smiled. "Poor baby, you need some TLC and I know just who'll give it to you." Then, turning to Judith, he asked, "Can she spend the night with you?"

Judith laughed, as Kate tried to elbow him. Kate glowed when he grabbed her elbow and bent his head to capture her lips with his in a quick kiss.

"Okay, you drive a hard bargain," he said after releasing her lips. He kissed her neck. "I'll drive home, but only for a wild night in bed."

Laughing, Kate replied, "On second thought, maybe I will spend the night with Judith."

"Help me carry this to my car," Judith said, ignoring their bantering, wanting to wrap things up. "Then, you guys can continue sparring."

"I can help in just a minute." Kate pulled away from Paul and nodded. "Help her while I go and square things with the bill, then I'll be out to help, too."

"Yes, ma'am." Paul snapped to attention and saluted as she left the room. Then, he looked at Judith and asked in a concerned voice, "Is everything all right, Judith? You seem a little preoccupied."

"I'm fine, Paul. I guess I'm tired. I didn't get much sleep."

"I saw you with Dev last night. Kate tells me you two are more than friends. He's a good man. I hope it works out."

Warmed by his heartfelt tone, she smiled. "Thanks, Paul, so do I."

"You deserve love, Judith," he said, taking her hands in his. He gave her a kiss on the cheek. "Happy birthday." He released her hands as Kate walked into the room, and quipped while reaching for the stacked gifts, "You women sure are slave drivers."

"Paul, you know you'll do anything to have your way with me, so stop complaining and get moving," Kate said.

Used to their teasing, Judith rolled her eyes. They each gathered armfuls and walked out to her car.

Once everything was loaded, Judith hugged Kate and Paul good-bye. Minutes later, alone and heading for her house, only one thing preyed on her mind. Dev. What was she going to do about him? Back and forth, her mind replayed the events of the past couple of months. By the time she parked, unloaded her car, and climbed the stairs to get ready for bed, she'd come to no conclusions.

She sat on the edge of her bed, eyeing Dev's wrapped box in the pile of gifts. She hesitated. Stared at it for a while. Soon, curiosity filled her. She grabbed the box, tore the wrapping, and opened it.

Judith was shocked to see an official-looking piece of paper. Damn. Tears threatened as she read the card. It was a deed to the office building on Hyde Street along with a promissory note. Dev had signed ownership of the building over to her along with agreeing to pay for the full cost of the renovations.

"Oh, Dev," she whispered, her tears flowing freely when she realized what this meant. "You always know how to touch my soul." Emotionally drained, she placed the deed in the box and set it on the floor beside the bed.

She couldn't think…couldn't react. How did one react to someone so overwhelming as Devon McAllister and his gift?

She wasn't about to make any decisions tonight. She was too tired to be objective. She'd sleep on it, and think about things tomorrow.

Problems were always easier to handle in bright sunlight.

~

Dev drove home with thoughts of Judith uppermost in his mind.

The evening had been a total bust.

Her outright dismissal once he'd arrived had hurt. Still, she hadn't told him to leave, so that was something. Though he'd really wanted to be next to her, he'd sat at the empty spot, accepting it graciously and tried to remember he'd been lucky to have a seat at all. He'd known from the beginning how hard it might be to make amends, but his impatience kept resurfacing during the meal.

The desire to snatch her up, to take her somewhere and to force her to listen to him, all but overwhelmed him too many times. He'd tamped the feelings down because the stakes were too high. He couldn't risk losing.

Dev laughed. There was no amusement in the brittle sound. He'd already lost his edge in dealing with Judith and had no control where she was concerned.

Why had he stayed? Instead of annoying her as he'd hoped after being so curtly dismissed when he first got there, all he'd done was torture himself. All evening, Dev had pretended nothing was wrong, but the effort almost killed him. He should have stayed home. Judith hadn't glanced at him once. Damn, how could she not even acknowledge him? He'd had her naked in his arms just hours ago, and she acted as if she'd never seen him before. Unable to keep up the charade, he'd finally given up and left. Defeat left a putrid taste in his mouth.

Dev parked in his garage. Mike was out for the evening and the thought of going inside alone sounded unappealing. He decided on a walk to clear his head. He headed to the marina, then ambled along the water's edge for a mile or so, up and back. It was a beautiful night with a light breeze, the fog rolling in, curling around the Golden Gate Bridge and the lonely moan of foghorns resonating in the background. The desolate sound matched his mood.

Right then, he felt utterly, completely, immensely alone.

Damn it all! She had to forgive him. While he walked, the scenes of the last few months played over and over in his head. Judith. That's all he saw.

How could she be so upset as to treat him with such indifference?

True, he'd originally been motivated by revenge. She'd been an obsession for so long. Yet after spending one evening with her, his plans had crumbled. He hadn't stood an ice cube's chance in hell of going through with his original plans. She'd held his heart from the very beginning as a seventeen-year-old innocent. He knew without a doubt that if he'd finished what he'd started so long ago, he and Judith would now be married with a couple of kids. She was his better half. He must have recognized it instinctively back then.

Why was she running now and not giving them a chance? Those questions tore him in two as he let himself into his house.

Chapter 18

Judith stirred early the next morning. Well rested, she reviewed the events of the last few days more objectively. Memories filled her mind, of Dev and how their relationship had evolved. She groaned, placing an arm over her eyes. She'd simply overreacted. Sometime during the course of the past two months, his motives had changed. Maybe he'd intended full revenge in the beginning, but revenge played no part in their lovemaking.

How could she have believed otherwise? If her heart hadn't told her so, the deed to the building shouted the news.

She loved Dev, but she began to realize her feelings weren't just about him. Everything was jumbled together inside her brain. She needed to think things out. Ponder why she overreacted.

She groaned louder. Knowing Dev as she did, she had to be prepared for his onslaught. He wouldn't give up until he got what he wanted. His gift told her he wanted her. And even if he hadn't told her he loved her, she felt his love.

Two days ago, she might have acted differently. Now she wanted to be sure she'd be going to Dev without baggage. Love was hard enough to keep alive without the past interfering.

She smiled as images of Dev and what he'd do filled her mind. The picture of him making plans to lay siege in an attempt to mow down any obstacles blocking his objective bounced around her brain. There was no way he would sit patiently on the sidelines until she figured it all out.

If she didn't act soon, Dev would be beating on her door within hours. Of that, she was sure. She was vulnerable where he was concerned. She wanted to come to terms with things on her own, without pressure. The magnetic pull of his personality influenced her too much.

What she needed, she realized, was breathing room.

Judith climbed out of bed, feeling lighthearted and pleased with the plan she'd formulated to give herself space. She knew where she'd go. A place where Dev would never find her.

She quickly made a few calls and packed a bag.

~

Dev woke up refreshed, eager to begin his day. After stewing for hours, he'd decided his best approach would be to confront Judith, to wipe out her indifference and force her to deal with him. After all, they'd be setting precedence for the rest of their lives. Indifference had no place in a marriage…and marriage was his ultimate goal. He'd settle for nothing less. If he left Judith to simmer, gave her time to build up her wall, it could become habit, and he had no intention of letting her build walls he'd have to break down every time she got upset.

He would stop by the site at lunchtime and waylay her. He'd done it before; he could do it again. With his plans in place, he pushed them to the back of his mind while he finished dressing. Soon, he headed out the door.

"Morning, Vickie," Dev said to the receptionist on his way to Maude's office.

He stopped at her door. "Morning, Maude." He couldn't keep the grin off his face. He felt like dancing.

"Somebody must've had a good weekend." Maude grinned in response.

"As a matter of fact, I did." He cleared his throat. "I have several things I need to do this afternoon. Can you clear my schedule?"

"I'll get right on it."

"Thanks." He turned toward his office, intending to take care of last-minute details.

When ready to leave, he once again stopped outside Maude's office.

"I'm available on my cell if you need me, but only if it's important," he said. "Anything else can wait until tomorrow, got it?"

"Got it." With eyebrows raised, she asked, "Hot date?"

"Maybe." His assistant was the only person in the office who could get away with such a question. "If it works out, you'll be the first person besides my mother who'll get an invitation to my wedding."

"Well, it's about time." Maude offered a knowing smile.

Ignoring it, he swung around and waltzed out of her office.

Dev's great mood quickly deteriorated when he learned Judith wasn't at the site.

He searched for over an hour before he finally found someone who knew something.

"She's taking time off?" Dev said to the contractor. "How could she be taking time off?"

"Said she needed personal time."

"You're sure?"

"Yeah. No big deal. I know what needs to be done. She gave me a detailed list of things to do and I told her I'd keep track of the work."

Dev questioned him for several minutes before he realized she wasn't coming back to work—not for days.

He promptly left the site and rushed to her house, only to find Judith wasn't there either. The house seemed deserted. He didn't have a key and he walked around the perimeter, peering into windows. He was heading to the front when he saw her next-door neighbor walking a dog.

Dev walked swiftly over to her.

"Excuse me." He put out his hand and put on his warmest smile. "My name is Dev McAllister, and I was wondering if you could help me."

"Hello, I'm Mrs. Kaminski." The woman stopped and offered him a limp handshake. "It's nice to meet you. Have I seen you before, young man?" She eyed him warily, then nodded. "I know you. You and Judith are dating, right?"

"Yes, we are," he replied, amused at her nosiness. "She wasn't at work today, and we had plans. I'm worried about her. Have you seen her?"

"Well, yes. I saw her leave around nine. She opened the garage and then put a suitcase in her car. It looked like she was leaving for a few days, but since she usually asks me to water her plants, I'm not sure."

"Thanks, I guess I'll have to check my messages." Not wanting the busybody to know he had no idea where Judith was, he added, "We were supposed to meet. Maybe our signals got crossed."

"I'm sure she left you a message. She's not flighty like most young people today." The elderly woman shook her head with a frown and clucked her disapproval.

Wanna bet, Dev thought to himself. He thanked her for her time and started for to his car, becoming more annoyed by the minute.

He drove away from the curb and it began to dawn on him that Judith had thrown up another hurdle. How dare she do this? *Damn her!* She wasn't going to get away with it. His patience had snapped. He was tired of the chase. He'd hunt her down. Then he'd take her to Reno and they'd get married right away.

~

On Thursday evening, Dev stalked into his club to meet James for a drink, thoroughly convinced he was going to have to wait for Judith to return home on her own.

He'd spent days trying to track her down, calling friends and co-workers who might know where she'd gone. There was nothing more he could do but wait and the wait was driving him insane.

Recalling his conversation with Kate, he had to believe she was just as clueless as he was to Judith's whereabouts. It was like she'd just disappeared. Dev had started to worry.

His nights had been unbearable; sleep elusive. He'd tossed and turned during those hours of darkness until he fell into a fitful sleep, only to awake an hour or so later with thoughts of Judith roaring through his brain. It was those same thoughts that kept him from falling back to sleep.

By Wednesday, when he'd finally received word, he'd been frantic. Maude had informed him of Judith's response to his many anxious calls to her cell phone. If not for that phone call, he would have had the police put out an all-points bulletin for her.

And her message? Judith called to say she'd be in touch when she was ready.

What the hell had she meant? When she was ready? Her message merely pushed him closer to the edge.

He'd been furious to learn she'd called while he was out.

"You'd better not be in league with Judith's scheme or you can find yourself another job," he'd ranted to Maude.

"I tried to get Judith to call your cell," Maude had said with genuine concern mixed with horror. "I told Judith you were really worried about her, but she was still adamant about only leaving a message."

Maude's sincerity had mollified Dev, but did nothing to keep him from leaving a few more heated messages on Judith's cell phone. Eventually, one fact became clear. He had no choice but to accept her decision. She wouldn't be back until she was ready.

Though her message had calmed his worst fears, his temper tonight was at the boiling point. As he nursed a beer while waiting for James to arrive, Dev decided it was just as well she was out of his range right now.

He wasn't used to waiting. Not being able to take charge to work the situation to his benefit took its toll. He looked as haggard as he felt from lack of sleep. His mood was surly.

This was how James found him as he walked up to the table.

"Hey, Mac." He pulled out a chair and sat. His gaze took in Dev's appearance and quickly divined his mood. "Are you okay? You look like shit."

"Yeah? Well, nice to see you too," Dev said belligerently. He guzzled his beer, glaring at James, daring him to say more.

"Cheer up! I'm on your side. I'm here to help."

"What? You mean you no longer wish I'd screw it up with Judith so you can sweep in and take over, 'pick up the pieces' when I'm done, if I remember right." He sneered as jealousy overcame him. He knew he was being churlish but he couldn't help it. He had to lash out at someone.

"Hell, Mac." James sighed. "I never had a chance with her and you know it. Besides, your relationship gives me hope."

"Right! Some relationship I have. My partner is absent. Has been for the last five days. To make matters worse, it appears I'm responsible for her departure." And because he wanted to think of something other than his own problems, he asked, "I'm curious, though. How can my relationship give you hope?"

"Hope that I'll find someone someday."

He snorted. "And what is it about my wonderful relationship that makes you think so?"

"Well, here's my theory," James said, grinning and rubbing his hands together. "I'm sure there's someone out there for me. After all, I'm not nearly as cynical or as hard to please as you. Besides, if Judith can bring the mighty Dev McAllister to his knees, there's hope for me."

Dev winced. James' description was closer to the truth than he realized. The memory of him on his knees, bowled over in pain, flashed through his mind. He smiled for the first time in several days and said, "Be careful what you wish for, James. Sometimes love hurts."

"If I had someone like Judith, I'd have to say, bring on the pain because it'd be worth it."

Dev burst out laughing.

"What?" James looked up with eyebrows raised. "It wasn't that funny."

"Trust me, there are some kinds of pain you don't want." He stood, feeling revived, and asked, "You want a beer? I'm heading up to the bar for a refill."

James nodded. "Sure. Whatever they have on tap would be fine. When you get back, I'll tell you my news."

Dev headed to the bar. He returned carrying two longnecks. He set one in front of James, the other in front of his chair, and took his seat.

"Okay, what's your news?" he demanded.

"Well, I think I may know where Judith is." James took a swig, then set his bottle on the table and grinned.

"What, and you didn't tell me the minute you sat down?"

"Hey, I just got here, and I just got my beer. Man, I'll be glad when Judith returns and you're back to normal!" James laughed good-naturedly, shaking his head.

"Where is she?" Dev's impatience was ready to burst. "Get on with it."

James slowly brought his beer to his lips and spent another long moment drinking.

"Well?" Dev urged.

Finally, as if figuring he'd tortured him enough, James grinned and said, "I think she may be at the house in Tahoe."

"Why do you think that?" *Tahoe?* Dev's brain spun.

"My mom. I called to tell her I was going up this weekend, and she told me I couldn't. Said it was being used."

"Don't other people use it? I'm not driving four hours on a hunch."

"Yeah, but usually she tells me who's using it. Most times, I can still go up and stay in the guesthouse without disturbing anyone." He paused to take a long swig.

"Don't stop now," Dev said. "Finish telling me your reasons."

"Mom wouldn't give me a clue as to who's up there and she was very evasive when I tried to pry a name out of her. Finally, she said it was one of Dad's business associates and they were staying in the guesthouse as well."

"Sounds logical."

"Yes, but Detective Morrison, here," he said, tapping his own chest, "thought her explanation was too pat. So I called Dad. But I didn't want him to know I already talked to Mom." He winked. "Spying can be tricky, you know."

Dev glared and waited.

"Okay...okay. No patience," he said, shaking his head. "I asked him if I could use the lake house. Do you want to know what he said?" He stopped and looked at Dev. At his impatient nod, James said, "He said, 'Fine.' Can you believe it? He had no clue. When I asked about someone from his company staying there, he seemed puzzled. Said no one from the company was using the house." James laughed. "I told Dad what Mom said. It was pretty funny, he got all flustered and tried to cover it up by saying, 'She should know, so I guess she's right.' And not wanting to alert Mom, I told him that was good enough for me and I wouldn't go up. I quickly ended the conversation. Then I called you. So what do you think? Am I better than Inspector Clouseau or what?" James asked, obviously pleased with his detective work.

"I don't know." Dev stared into the amber beer bottle as elation burst inside him. "You might be on to something. Did you call the house?"

"No. We don't want to tip her off."

"Good point. Let me think." Dev sat forward, silent for a moment, wondering if he'd found Judith. "Is the key still in the same place you guys always keep it?" At James' raised eyebrows, he said, "You know, the one you use in case you lock yourself out."

"Yeah, my parents would have said something if they'd moved it."

Dev grinned. "Well then, I'll make a trip to Tahoe and bring this whole episode to an end."

He took a big swallow of beer and wiped his mouth with the back of his hand. Finally, this nightmare encompassing the worst days of his life would be over. Anticipation replaced negative thoughts. Just thinking of what he'd do once he had Judith in his arms again had his heart racing.

"I've got to admit, Mac." James offered a relieved smile. "I've been worried about you."

"You're a good friend, James." Dev stood and clapped him on the shoulder. "It's good to know someone like you is watching my back. You know I feel the same about you. I've got yours covered."

"Hey, how about a game of pool? Winner picks up the tab for tonight, dinner included," he joked, shrugging off Dev's praise.

Dev laughed. Both knew he was the better pool player. "You're on." He owed James more than the evening. "And, since it's a no-brainer that I'll be the winner, I'll buy you another beer before we begin."

They walked over to the bar. Dev gave an order for another round to be delivered to the pool table, before both men headed in that direction.

As the evening advanced, Dev's mood lightened. In between his shots, he formulated a plan, happy to have concrete information with which to work. He'd head up to Tahoe the next afternoon, using the morning for work to be done in the office. He smiled deviously and aimed his pool cue. Tomorrow he'd surprise his wayward princess.

"I'm happy for you, Mac." James flashed a grin.

Dev only grunted as his ball rolled into the pocket.

Later, after several games and a hearty dinner, the two walked out of the club to pick up their cars.

"It's funny, I never think about romance much," James said. "I mean, Paul found Kate and he's happy. But hey, that's Paul, the stable one. It's something you expect from him. Still, I have to tell you. Just watching you and Judith together gave me a warm fuzzy feeling and restored my faith in love. I hope you find her in Tahoe."

"Thanks, James. I hope so too. And thanks for tonight. I needed it." Dev handed his stub to the valet. "I'll let you know what happens."

Chapter 19

Friday afternoon Judith walked through the house with its huge wall of windows, taking in the awe-inspiring view of the Sierra Nevada Mountains surrounding Lake Tahoe on her way to the tree-lined deck with a book to read while sunbathing. She loved the setting, especially this time of year. The weather was perfect, not too hot and not too cold. The contrasting verdant shades of evergreens and deciduous trees sandwiched between two vivid hues of blue—the crystal clear lake and the cloudless Northern California sky—never failed to make her realize how balanced nature was. Everything had a purpose. A reason for being.

Her break had been cathartic, an ideal solution for working through her emotional upheaval. The Morrison family's lake house was an idyllic setting for soul-searching.

She positioned the chaise lounge to take advantage of the sun's angle and plopped facedown on it. Reaching behind, she undid her top and closed her eyes with her thoughts on the past few days.

Arriving on Monday afternoon in an introspective mood, her days had been spent in silent reflection that brought forth childhood memories, and in turn unlocked feelings of loneliness, of being disconnected to her surroundings. She now understood how circumstances produced them.

She'd jumped to conclusions and had assumed the worst, both ten years ago and now. That made her rather shallow and snobbish. It didn't matter that she had good reason.

She'd always been an introvert, keeping to herself or staying lost in books. Books became her friends, while her imagination eased her loneliness. She'd skipped grades, the first time going from first to third, which had been a hard social transition. It took Judith months to find a friend. The next year, when she went from third to fifth, she pretty much closed herself off socially. By then, all the girls in the class were in cliques and had been friends for several years. None seemed inclined to include

Judith in their group and she didn't know how to break into their circles. So she began the habit of being by herself, which lasted throughout high school. Maybe her parents could have intervened to help her adjust, but since Judith never complained, they were oblivious to her plight.

She'd met Kate in college when she was older, more mature, and determined to make friends. Judith kept her age a secret for two full years, not willing to risk rejection from someone who'd become so important to her.

All Judith wanted back then was to fit in and be part of a group.

After days of deep thinking, she realized how very sensitive she was to anything that made her feel different. Her virginity definitely fit that criteria. She reasoned most people had first loves during their late teens, when the emotional upheaval of romance was tossed in with everything else that adolescents face. Somehow the timing made it less traumatic. She never had that because she kept her emotions inside.

Her feelings for Dev were all too new, especially after their glorious night of lovemaking. She should've been able to deal with them at twenty-eight. Instead, she'd botched everything.

Amazing how she could now see things so well from a backward perspective.

When she'd learned about Dev's building, she'd jumped to conclusions based on emotion, had assumed the worst, and shoved reality aside to become that hurt child again, never giving him a chance to explain. The truth was, she no longer was that girl and hadn't been for many, many years.

She reassessed her life and decided what she wanted from it. Of course she wanted Dev, but she'd needed to make sure she'd be going to him without chains of the past weighing her down.

Her thoughts switched to Dev and his many livid phone messages. She loved him and knew she had to make things right between them. She sighed.

She'd been ready to leave on Wednesday, yet avoidance had kept her here. Delaying any longer would only make things worse, so she would drive home in the morning. If she didn't, he'd eventually figure out where she was and come looking for her. She could only imagine what he'd say, and she had no idea of how she'd handle him. All she knew was that it would be better if she headed him off at the pass.

Without warning, as if her thoughts had conjured him up, a voice shattered the stillness of the afternoon.

"Hello, Judith."

Stunned speechless, she put up a hand to shield her eyes from the sunlight and saw Dev, handsome as ever, wearing a polo shirt and shorts with loafers and no socks. Her focus traveled to his face, carved with an expression hard as granite. She couldn't see his eyes because he wore sunglasses, but she sensed they hid the same hard expression.

"Hello, Dev! I see you found me." Lame thing to say, but shock had stolen her capacity to think.

He shed his sunglasses and sighed, shaking his head.

She swallowed hard as his gaze slowly slid up and down her body. Warmth rushed to her cheeks at how vulnerable she was, wearing basically nothing. His glance eventually landed on her face and heated blue eyes seized hers, holding them captive. Her mind went blank and she couldn't breathe or move. She could only stare at him for endless moments.

The spell was broken when he bent to set his sunglasses on the table. Making quick use of the diversion, she stood, holding her bikini top in place, and leaned over to snatch up her cover-up.

Dev, with surprising agility, grabbed her from behind and nuzzled her neck. His cool lips sent shivers everywhere. Her heart skipped beats when his fingers skimmed over her body. Then he turned her around. Her forgotten top slid to the ground as she locked her fingers behind his neck and tugged as instinct took over. She melted into his lips, kissed him, put everything she had into her mouth and tongue, and let the kiss speak of what was in her heart. Eventually he pulled his lips from hers. A surge of disappointment flared until he dropped to the chaise lounge, taking her with him. She landed in the middle of his lap, felt his erection and stilled, embarrassed, yet utterly excited. Judith watched in dazed silence as he reached into his pocket, pulled out a ring, and slipped it on her finger.

The enormity of his actions hit her. Too shocked to think of what to say, she gawked at her hand.

Dev gave her a gentle tug while he bent and brushed his lips across hers. After he positioned her underneath him, his mouth and hands seemed to be everywhere. All coherent thought fled when his mouth became more urgent. Heat flooded from her center, moving throughout her body like lava flowing toward the sea, hot, fluid warmth, extending all the way to her fingers and toes.

She couldn't hold on to the slow moan slipping out.

How did he do that so effortlessly and so quickly? The thought dissipated into pleasure as his lips and tongue increased their tempo. She couldn't not respond, had to return his kiss in order to drive him as wild as he was driving her.

His mouth broke free, moved across her face to her ear and his tongue circled the outside, before he whispered, *"Hello, Dev! You found me?* I can't believe you put me through five days of pure hell and that's all you have to say?" He increased the pressure of his tongue on her ear. When he nipped her lobe once more, she almost came apart at the intense spurt of pleasure. Then he stopped, waited till her moans died, before whispering, "It took me a while but, yes, I finally found you."

Without giving her a chance to let the building heat coursing through her subside, his mouth captured hers again. She couldn't catch her breath. He moved too fast, wouldn't allow the excitement she felt to slow so she could grasp on to control. She melted into his warmth until he broke the kiss and his intent blue gaze snared hers.

"And now that I have, you'll never get away again. You're mine, Judith. You belong to me and I belong to you. Do you hear me?"

Judith moaned and closed her eyes. She could barely nod, since he obviously required a response. Her sentiments exactly. He belonged to her, and she planned on having him. She reached for his neck and brought him closer. Once their lips connected, she kissed him with her whole heart, no longer fearful or embarrassed, letting all the love she felt come out in the kiss.

In seconds, Dev's mouth and tongue were everywhere as were his cool hands. He knew exactly where to touch…exactly where to kiss…exactly how to prolong her pleasure.

Elation surged through her when she felt him taking off her

bikini bottoms, felt his hands move lower. His fingers were magical…his strokes heavenly. At the same time, he kissed his way to her breasts, where swirls of ecstasy his tongue and mouth elicited had more heat swamping her core.

A kaleidoscope of bliss burst forth as well as her uncontrolled moan. Prisms of vibrant color washed over her in wave after wave of pleasure.

Without breaking his kiss, Dev rose above her and managed to pull his shorts and underwear down, kicking them free. The next moment, he filled her. Her first orgasm hadn't receded. Each stroke sent her higher.

Her second orgasm hit and a scream of pleasure pierced the air. She was too overcome with the moment to realize the sound came from her own lips. A few more thrusts and Dev climaxed so powerfully his body jerked. He threw out a forceful groan before he collapsed on top of her. She was completely sated and unable to move, her legs and arms useless.

~

The passion of the joining left Dev breathless. He wondered if it would always be like this with her. She touched something deep inside of him and it brought out every tender, protective, loving, hungry, predatory instinct he had.

He rose up on his elbows and peered down at her closed eyes. "Judith, look at me," he said in a low voice. When she opened her eyes, adoration shone from them, and he sucked in a quick breath. "I love you. Please, don't ever put me through something like that again, because I don't think I'll be able to survive it."

His mouth captured hers for a soul-searing, gentle kiss. It amazed him how quickly she aroused him. Would he never get enough of her?

Finally, Judith broke the kiss. She placed her hands on the sides of his face and captured his gaze. He could see she was about to say something important. He waited.

"I love you too, Dev."

The warmth of the sentiment flowed over him. He'd never tire of hearing it. She loved him.

"But," she said. He groaned. Of course she had a but. He grinned into her shoulder when he heard what her but was. "We need to talk. You're not the only participant in this. You can't just waltz in, give me a ring, and then expect to pull me along while you bulldoze the world the way you want it. If you do, I'll drag my feet until you slow enough so I can walk or run beside you of my own free will. You got that, Devon McAllister?"

"Yeah," he said, still grinning. "Come on. We still have a few things to work out. I don't want sunburned cheeks, so let's go inside where we can be more comfortable." He kissed the top of her head and boosted himself off her, tugging her up as he went. His gaze raked over her naked form, stopping at her flushed face. "We can talk later. I'm more interested in taking up where we left off. We have all night and I'm just getting started."

He discarded his shirt and let it drop to the deck. When she reached for her cover-up, he chuckled.

At her raised eyebrow, he said, "Like that's going to help you now? Leave it. I like you naked." When her blush darkened, his grin inched wider. "There's no need to be embarrassed. I told you last time, you're going to have to get used to us both being naked and me looking at you while you're naked." He turned and taking her hand, led her through the open patio door and into the house. "Which room are you using?"

"The smaller master bedroom and bath."

He reached the bedroom with her in tow, then aimed for the bed. He kicked off his shoes before he sat down, taking her with him.

"Now, where were we? Oh yeah, I remember," he murmured, and slowly bent, brushing his lips over hers.

Dev spent leisurely moments touching her, discovering her with his mouth and tongue and fingers, in no hurry. Without understanding why, he needed to make her fully comprehend how it was between them. They belonged to each other. For all time.

As his hands approached the curls at the top of her legs, he spread her legs apart and caressed her gently. She moaned. Her hips came off the bed in response. Her hands found his head, clutching and yanking.

But Dev pushed her back down and said in a tender voice, "Stay still, I want to taste you."

He then proceeded to caress her with his tongue. She tugged

his hair harder, her moans sounding louder. When Judith bucked, screamed her release, he didn't let up. Not until her movements subsided. Dev stretched above her, but didn't enter her. Instead, he found her mouth and teased it with slow, erotic kisses. He fought her sensual moans, moving his hand to her breast, leisurely circling in unison with his mouth.

"No," he whispered fervently, when she twisted her hips into position to take him. "Not yet."

"Please! I want you inside me! Now!"

He ignored her pleas until she reached down and stroked him. When her tentative fingers captured his fullness, desire so fierce streaked through him, shattering the miniscule bit of control he had left. In a deft move, he sank inside her warmth.

Judith wrapped her arms and legs around him. He tried to keep it slow, still wanting to draw out her pleasure, but Judith's frantic movements wouldn't let him. He was lost. Where he tried to brand her with his body, she branded him with hers. The woman who met him head to head in their sensual battle had marked him for life. He knew in that moment as a flash of clarity struck. He belonged to her, heart and soul. No other would do for him. All he could do was follow her into a mind-altering release.

His heart eventually slowed its rapid beating and he could think again. Dev rolled onto his back and tucked his outside arm behind his head. He gently tugged Judith closer so she was now lying almost on top of him, with her head on his chest.

He lay there caressing her, simply enjoying the feel of having her next to him. Finally, he said, "I'm sorry I hurt you, Judith. I'm not sorry I bought the building because it brought you to me. I did intend to have my revenge. You should be happy to know my carefully made plans unraveled the first time we had dinner together. I never stood a chance after that night."

"I've already figured that out on my own," Judith said. "What I don't understand is why you needed revenge? What did I do to deserve it?"

Dev sighed. "That's complicated."

She leaned away, eyeing him intently. "Like you said, we have all night, and I'm all ears."

"Okay." He hesitated. "I don't like admitting I was wrong,

but I was. I made an error in judgment." He kissed the top of her head. "The night we met at that party changed me forever. From the moment I spotted you across the room, you held me spellbound. After spending hours talking with you, the feelings intensified. You seemed so different from all those other women I knew at school, game-playing, manipulative, vain creatures whose only goal in life was to catch a good husband. Something happened in those few hours. I fell in love. From then on, no one else would do."

He glanced at Judith, who smiled, and he couldn't resist dropping another quick kiss on her forehead before continuing. "When you ran, I couldn't understand why you hadn't been as affected as I had been, and could run out on me so easily. I was too caught up to think logically. After spending months, making several attempts to contact you and getting nowhere, I came to the only conclusion that made sense. I thought you were playing games, especially when I heard you were dating Paul. I felt foolish."

"Oh, Dev! That wasn't it at all. You frightened me. My feelings frightened me."

"I know that now. My pride was hurt, but most of all my feelings got bruised. I made an assumption based on prejudice. I was mad at myself for letting you slip past my guard. I had to have my revenge. Nothing less would do."

"But for ten years? A decade's a long time to carry a grudge over one night," she stated incredulously.

"What can I say?" A flush of embarrassment warmed his face. "My mother says I'm tenacious, and this only confirms it. Plus, I never got you out of my mind. My need to even the score only worsened over time."

"Humph, I have a hard time believing anything I could do would instill such emotion."

"Yeah? Well, let me tell you, the spark that ignites whenever we get together is unusual, at least from my experience. We share something unique and it started that night. I was determined to finish it and walk away from you as easily as you walked away from me." Then, looking down at her, a slow self-deprecating smile crept up. "Of course, I got caught in my own trap."

Smiling, she said in a teasing voice, "Well, now I feel better. I imagine that doesn't happen very often. But still, ten years?"

"It took me a while to get organized, and by then you and Paul were a couple. If it had been anyone else you were involved with, I'd have interfered, but Paul is family. If you had married him, I would have let it go."

Suddenly, Judith's bitter laughter burst forth.

"What's so funny?"

"Nothing. It's sad, actually. I used Paul and he didn't deserve it. By using his friendship as a buffer all those years to protect my heart, it kept me from you and hurt both of you. It was immature and cruel. So much wasted time." Sorrow moved over her expression. "How stupid I was to let it continue for so long. Oh, Dev, I never meant to hurt you. I got into a situation I couldn't handle and instead of trying to explain, I ran, and have been ever since."

"Hush," he said, placing a fingertip to her lips. "It's in the past, and you're caught now." He slid a hand up her arm and dropped a kiss on her shoulder. "You know, if you'd stayed back then, we'd be married and have a couple of kids by now?"

"You seem very sure of yourself. How can you be so certain?"

Bending over, he used a soft kiss until she responded to make his point, then pulled away and put on a smug smile. "That's how," he whispered, grazing her lips again and taking a nip. "That's the only thing I am certain of. You and I are well matched, Judith." At her questioning look, his smile broadened. "I keep underestimating you, but never again. You challenge me. I recognized it that night on the dance floor when you so haughtily put me in my place." He chuckled. "And no one has ever gotten the drop on me before. To be certain it doesn't happen again, I'll have to be more careful around you when you're angry."

She blushed. "Sorry, but I couldn't let you touch me. Just be glad I held back."

"Thank God! Otherwise our ability to have children may have been greatly diminished," he joked. His smile died. "Okay, I've bared my soul about my motives, what about yours? Why wouldn't you see me back then? And why did you run this time?"

Sheepishly, she looked up at him. "I had misconceptions of

my own."

"Misconceptions?"

"Don't laugh, but I thought all you wanted was sex. I was just a conquest to you."

He caught her gaze and waited. When she didn't say more, he urged, "Go on."

"If I went out with you again, I knew it would only be a matter of time before you got what you wanted."

"But why not tell me? Give me a chance?"

"Oh, Dev, look what happened after just one dance and a couple of hours of conversation. I didn't even know what was happening until it was almost too late."

"Just my luck, you'd figure it out then and not later."

"You're not helping matters," she said, laughing and slapping at his shoulder. "Let me finish." She took a deep breath and continued. "I wasn't quite ready for what you obviously were. I was afraid—of my feelings—of being hurt. I'd never had more than three dates in my entire life before we met and they were with total jerks who only wanted one thing. There you were, sweeping me off my feet, literally. Everything happened too fast. I didn't know how to slow things. Remember, I was only a seventeen-year-old virgin at the time. That alone should be enough of an excuse."

"Okay. Makes sense. We were both young and stupid, but what about six days ago? How could you not know how I felt? Did you honestly think that was only sex? Or revenge? Judith, when we made love my heart was in your hands, how could you not sense it? After what we shared, how could you run again and not give me a chance to explain?"

She cast her gaze down. He remained focused on her until she made eye contact again. He glimpsed anguish in those bright green eyes.

"I'm so sorry," she said softly. "I never meant to hurt you. I was trying to find answers to my own questions."

"I could have helped, if only you'd have let me."

"You couldn't do it for me, I had to find them on my own. I knew you wouldn't be able to back off."

He winced at her words, realizing she had a valid point.

"Dev, you overwhelm me and take my breath away. You

would have pushed away my fears and insecurities as foolish, sweeping me along with you as you've always done since that first night. I knew I overreacted after we made love and I had to deal with the reasons why because I didn't want my past to haunt my future with you. And here I am."

"Yeah, here you are—right where you're staying," he teased. Then he grew more serious. He lifted her left hand. "So, what do you think about my ring? Do you like it? Oh hell, that's not what I meant to say." He sat up and knelt on the bed before her. Taking her face in his hands, he looked into her eyes. "What I mean is…Judith, will you marry me? I promise you will never regret it, and I will always love you."

"Oh, Dev. Promises, promises!" Judith laughed. "I love the ring, and I love you."

About The Author

Sandy Loyd was born and raised in Salt Lake City, Utah. Wanderlust hit early on and she has lived a varied life since then. She joined the Army to see the world and to get an education. Living and training in four states and Germany during the three-year stint provided a cultural education. She graduated from Arizona State University with a BS in Marketing and landed a job in San Francisco that involved extensive travel throughout the United States. She's always considered San Francisco a US treasure that few other cities worldwide can compare. She's since married and moved on from her single days, but she still misses the city's diversity and beauty.

She now lives in Kentucky and 'retired' from sales after twenty years to become a stay at home mom when her son kept asking why she had to be gone all the time. She filled her days with volunteering, ending up as a PTA President in her son's elementary school. When her son moved on to Middle School, boredom set in. She wanted to be around when he came home from school, so she began to write to fill in the time. And she's been writing ever since.

Promises, Promises and the other stories in the California series are set in the Bay Area and are composites of Sandy's single life. They're fun stories of crazy friends who, like single people everywhere, are seeking that someone special to share their lives with among thousands of eligible candidates.

Here is a glimpse of the third story in the series:

JAMES

Chapter 1

"Get a good look, buddy!" Samantha Collins wanted to shout when she caught the guy's interested gaze taking a trip to the front of her blouse. And here she thought he was being polite, opening the door for her.

She made eye contact. He had the grace to flush and murmured a quick apology before his eyes darted straight ahead and his feet followed. He obviously didn't find her boring, she thought, glancing down at the blouse she'd unbuttoned in an act of defiance just minutes before entering the noisy, trendy hangout. Shaking her head in disgust and working to clear the haze of pain from her brain, she muttered, "What is it with guys? We all have to be half-undressed, otherwise they'll think we're uninteresting?"

She charged in the direction of the bar and perched on a stool with one goal. She needed a drink.

"What'll it be, sweet thing?" The bartender halted in front of her and wiped the bar in swift, easy movements.

She eyed the lanky, attractive man. Would he have called her *sweet thing* if her blouse had been fastened at its usual top button? *Probably not.*

"A shot of tequila," she said, going for something with a kick. She normally drank wine, but this abnormal situation definitely warranted Mexican courage. Her special dinner had ended in a disaster. She'd expected a proposal from the man of her dreams, not a verbal attack concerning her personality quirks.

A shot glass filled with clear liquid appeared in front of her as Charles' concerns replayed in her mind. How could he think their relationship was predictable and unexciting?

He thought she was boring? Sam slumped forward. Maybe

she was.

He hadn't actually said boring, she reminded herself. *He might as well have,* she argued back. "Sedate" and "settled" amounted to pretty much the same thing. The way he'd spoken the two words, like she was suffering from a contagious disease, really stung.

Of course she was sedate and settled. She was also precise and determined. Knew exactly what she wanted. Had her life outlined better than any AAA road map. Her trip to success began at the age of sixteen, and since then she'd spent a lot of time and effort to become someone. Someone worthy of marrying a successful man like Charles Winthrope III. Marriage to a man like him meant everything to her and, in three years' time, she'd hoped to be the mother of Charles Winthrope IV. She and Charles loved each other, for heaven's sake. Yet, he found their relationship lacking. He found *her* lacking.

Where had she gone wrong?

She downed the tequila in one swallow and blinked back tears, as more of their earlier conversation filtered through her consciousness. He'd called their relationship "tedious."

Tedious!

How could he think that? She wasn't tedious. She was an architect. A talented businesswoman. She could understand him saying they needed to spend more time together, but he'd asked for a break to think about his future. What about *her* future?

Just then the bartender stood in front of her.

"I was expecting to celebrate my engagement tonight," she offered, when his eyebrows lifted.

She cast her eyes down and stared at her empty shot glass, remembering Charles' serious expression as he'd delivered his news. At that moment, she'd kissed the thought of finding a diamond ring in her tiramisu good-bye. She might never get a ring from him.

Sam glanced up and noted a touch of sympathy in the bartender's eyes. "Do I look rigid?"

"No way." He filled a glass of beer from the tap.

Yeah, she thought, now becoming angry. How dare *he* call her *rigid*? Not a man whose bedtime routine included flossing between each tooth twice, and he counted for twenty seconds while brushing each part of his mouth to make sure he followed his dentist's advice. That was pretty damned rigid, if you asked her.

His every minute was scheduled. Just like hers. They understood each other completely. How could he now view their stable relationship as tedious? She'd even given him an opportunity to back down by reminding him of their shared values.

And his reply? She shook her head. He'd like more spontaneity. Apparently, Lucinda Thomas was spontaneous.

"I think he's got the hots for his new co-worker," she whispered. The spots of color that had hit Charles' cheeks confirmed her assumption when she'd asked him outright about the perky woman who'd never hidden her interest in Charles.

Yet, Sam had always thought he was immune to such temptation because they were so well matched. That thought set her back a bit. Maybe they were tedious together.

She nodded toward the empty shot glass. "I need another."

In moments, a second shot appeared.

So Mary Ann was right. Hadn't she warned about complacency in relationships? According to her best friend, men were vulnerable to feminine tactics, especially right before they actually committed to one specific woman. Sam hated to admit that she might have been a little too confident, a little too accepting, in just assuming everything would work out. After all, he was her perfect match, the stable dream man she'd always yearned for. They were perfect for each other. Unfortunately, an impulsive, bubbly loan officer could mar that perfection.

She wouldn't let that happen. Maybe Charles had a valid point. If their relationship needed a little spontaneity, she could do spontaneous. How hard could it be?

"Hey, Collins."

She groaned, rolling her eyes skyward. "Please, Lord, don't let it be Morrison," she said under her breath. She knew without glancing up, prayer did no good. No one called her Collins but him. She turned toward the voice and sighed.

Just what she needed to make her night a total bust—James Morrison, one of her partners in the architectural firm of Morrison, Morgan, Stone and Collins—and the last person she wanted to witness her attempt at drowning her relationship sorrows in tequila. He was the one with the relationship problems, not her.

Why oh why had she claimed, and quite smugly she might add, that she was practically engaged? The memory of her boastful conversation with James flashed through her mind as he walked up to her.

She shrugged, then swallowed the second shot. *Who cares? He'll have to get used to the new Samantha Collins along with Charles.*

She pasted her best fake smile on her face and nodded to the guy who grabbed the stool next to her as if he owned the place. Of course, the move was so like him. The man had a smooth confidence. Had a way with the ladies, too. She was immune to his early Robert Redford appeal, the same look immortalized in *Butch Cassidy and the Sundance Kid.* Those baby blues and streaked blond hair did nothing for her. She was into Charles' classic, dark looks, and he was too much of a gentleman to have a reputation. She snorted. *Until now!*

"I'd ask what you were doing here without Winthrope, but I can see for myself."

"Oh? What would that be?" She captured the bartender's notice and held up her empty glass.

"Getting drunk."

He chuckled. Ignoring the fuming glare she sent him, he took the glass out of her hand and sniffed. "What are you drinking? Looks like tequila. I never took you for a tequila kind of gal, Collins."

"Yeah? And what kind of gal do you see when you look at me?" They had a great working relationship, but he probably thought she was boring too. She definitely didn't fit the mold of women he usually dated, which was fine by her.

His hands went up in mock surrender. "That's a loaded question, and one I can't answer without matching you drink for drink."

Her aggravation vanished as an uncontrollable giggle burst free. James might be a guy who'd dated enough women since she'd met him to fill a small city's phone book, but despite her embarrassment of the situation, he did make a darned good friend. "There's the bartender. I'm sure he'll fix you right up."

"I'll pass. I still have to drive." He aimed his narrowed gaze on her. "What about you? You're not driving, are you?"

Sam shook her head. "Don't have my car. I can grab a taxi. I left Charles at Angelo's," she said, indicating a fancy restaurant a block away. "I needed air, so I walked."

"Lover's quarrel?"

She shrugged. "Something like that."

His attention moved to a spot beyond her shoulder. She watched as his eyebrows shot up and a smile covered the bottom half of his face. He nodded in the direction his eyes were focused. "Don't look now, but Charles is at seven o'clock, stalking this way. He doesn't look too happy."

Her smile faded. She straightened and swiveled around, grabbing on to the bar to steady herself. "I'm not the one who wanted a break."

"Ouch. Sounds serious."

"Nothing I can't handle."

Charles slowed to a stop in front of her. Even in the darkened bar, his face appeared flushed. "Samantha. I don't understand your behavior."

"What didn't you understand?" She tried hard not to slur her speech. "I thought I was quite clear. I read your remarks like the morning paper. You find me boring and want to break up."

"No." He blurted out. "I'm sorry I made a mess of things. My goal was to improve our relationship, not end it. I just wanted a little time to think."

Sam blew her bangs in exasperation, not really caring that her control had slipped and she was now arguing with Charles in front of Morrison. Besides, why bother hiding the truth? Their relationship did need improving. One lunch, and she'd be telling James everything anyway, only this time she'd be asking for his advice, not the other way around.

"How much time?" She met Charles' gaze and watched him fidget under her narrow-eyed scrutiny. *Let him squirm.* No way, she would make this easy on him. She noticed the hint of pink snaking up his face and smiled. "This isn't middle school, Charles. You should be mature enough to know your mind after three years and not act like an eighth grader."

He cleared his throat and looked at James.

"Don't look at Morrison. He's never progressed past high

school so he can't help you." She ignored James' disgruntled, "Hey, careful with the verbal jabs," and added, "You started this. How much time do you need? A month? Two months? A year?"

"A week or so," Charles squeaked out. "I realize now it was a stupid idea."

"No. Don't back down now." She kept her unwavering gaze on him. Eventually he glanced at the bar and studied her empty shot glass for too many seconds. She sighed. "If you need time to be sure of me, then take it. I certainly don't want you rushing into something." Oh no, she wouldn't push him, but she wouldn't let this go without giving it her best shot, either. A few weeks ought to do it. She was good at reinventing herself. If Charles wanted spontaneity, then she'd become as free spirited as a leaf blowing in the wind. "Now go away."

"Go away?" he sputtered. "I can't leave you in a bar. Come on. I'll take you home."

The bartender placed her third shot in front of her. She was starting to see double, but she had her pride. Sam wasn't going anywhere with Charles tonight. She'd walk first. She picked up her drink. "I'm not ready to leave yet and I'm still too angry with you to let you stay, so go away."

"Now who's acting like an eighth grader?"

She shrugged and downed the contents, then slammed the glass on the bar. "Answer me this. Is an eighth grader sedate and settled?"

"What?" He pushed his glasses to the bridge of his nose. The lenses magnified his soulful brown eyes, exaggerating his stunned expression.

Unwilling to let that gaze affect her, she said, "Just answer the damn question."

He cleared his throat. "I would think not."

"Then it's an improvement, isn't it?" Oh yeah. This was just the beginning. He asked for it. He'd never know what hit him, once she was done with him after three weeks.

"I'll make sure she gets home, Winthrope," James said, interrupting her gleeful thoughts.

Sam smiled at him and giggled. "You will?"

He nodded.

She patted Charles' cheek. "See? No need to worry. I'm

perfectly safe. My friend, and colleague, is taking me home."

Charles looked as if he were going to argue. Then, he sighed. "Fine. I wish I hadn't said anything. I'll call you tomorrow."

"Don't bother." She leaned back and almost lost her balance. She grabbed the bar just in time. "I don't expect to hear from you for at least three weeks."

His back went ramrod. His entire body tensed. Even his smile was stiff, but he didn't make a scene. Good old Charles, she thought, watching him. She wondered briefly if he could handle what she had in store when he got exactly what he'd asked for in the short term. Maybe this was for the better. After all, marriage did need spicing up now and then. She'd have to put that into her plans for their second anniversary.

"You're right about our relationship suffering from tedium. A break can only help us, but I guess we can talk on the phone," she said, taking pity on him.

She held out her cheek, careful not to lean too far, and he bent to kiss her.

He glanced at James. "I appreciate your seeing her home." Then, muttering something about women, he pivoted and walked out of the bar, holding his head high without looking back.

"That was interesting." James turned to her. "So, I take it you're not planning your wedding?"

A frown replaced her smile. Her mood went south in a hurry. "Silly me. I thought for sure Charles was going to propose tonight. Instead, he called me rigid. Said our relationship is tedious and I'm too predictable."

"You can be a bit predictable." When she stiffened and opened her mouth to disagree, he amended, "Except where your work is concerned."

Sam shut her mouth and stared at him in silence for a long moment, noting only sincerity in his eyes. James cared about her and he would never lord it over her about this, not like she'd secretly done with him and his relationship problems. Maybe she'd been a tad judgmental.

"It's more than that," she finally said, losing the rest of her bravado. "I told you Charles has been acting funny for weeks, just assumed his behavior was related to nerves over asking me to marry him, but I left out the part about his new loan officer.

Mary Ann says the timing's not a coincidence. Now that he asked for a break, I see her point. He says he likes her spontaneity. What if he likes more about her? She's gorgeous. What am I going to do?"

She'd never given her nondescript looks much thought. Primping was beneath Sam. So was makeup. Besides, what could Sam do to improve upon brown hair and brown eyes, other than become someone she wasn't? No, she wasn't a beauty by anyone's standards, but she had good bone structure, as her grandmother had always said. Since college, airheads with nothing but looks going for them certainly hadn't threatened her—until now.

"She's everything I'm not. What if I can't compete?" This was like high school all over again.

"Where's the Collins I know and love? What've you done with her?" James teased and pretended to search around her. "You're a creative artist and you're the woman Charles loves."

"He shouldn't have concerns. Not after three years. I've always thought we were in sync with each other. Obviously, he thinks differently."

"Maybe you match him too perfectly. He's a man. We men are simple creatures who only want to be needed. Of course, if you throw in a woman who's exciting in the bedroom, you'll have a slave for life."

"Leave it to you to make this about sex."

"I'll let you in on a little secret, Collins. Sex pretty much works on most guys."

"All I want is reliability in a mate, someone I can count on, who's stable enough to offer security." Her expression turned wistful. "It's all I've ever wanted." The memory of her bleak childhood flashed through her mind. She'd never had stability. She'd never had anyone to count on. She'd never known her dad, and her mom would never make Mother of the Year. Sam had decided early on to live her life differently and recoup everything her childhood lacked. From the first moment they started dating, she'd always been able to count on Charles. Until now.

"Well, cheer up, I'm here to help."

"You're joking, right?"

"Never been more serious in my life. Have you eaten?"

Sam ignored his question about eating, as her lips curled in disbelief. "How can a person who changes partners as often as you change your sheets help me fix my problems with Charles?"

"Ouch. You know you're exaggerating. What's more, you shouldn't offend me. I just might tell Brad and Russell we made a mistake and revoke your partnership."

She snorted. "Yeah, right." She'd made full partner only months earlier. Since her talent added a perfect mix to the firm, his threat held no more weight than a feather. Plus, their relationship had started out from the very beginning as friends, despite his penchant to go through women. In the four years she'd worked for the firm, he'd never been anything but a friend and an excellent mentor. James had also introduced her to Charles. "The only way you can help is to let me get drunk in peace."

"And that answers my question about eating." When she glared at him, willing him to leave, he only grinned. "I've never seen this side of you. Are you always this prickly when someone riles you?"

"Just being honest. I've been with Charles for three years. Your longest relationship in that time was—what? Four months?"

"Yep. Definitely hungry when you start insulting one of your peers without provocation. You shouldn't drink on an empty stomach." He stood, threw thirty dollars on the bar, and grabbed her hand to pull her off her perch. "Come on. I'll buy you dinner."

"Wait. I'm not ready to leave yet." Dizziness assaulted her as she reached for her purse and almost toppled.

"Yes, you are."

"No, I'm not." Thank God he held her hand firmly, making it easier to maintain her dignity.

"My image needs a major overhaul. I'm throwing out the old Sam and becoming more spontaneous. I plan to start by drinking a lot more tonight."

"Then we'll buy a bottle of tequila and go to my place, so you can finish. That way I can join you."

"It's Friday night. I'm sure you have better things to do than babysit me."

"Not a thing," James said, leading her to the door.

Her wobbly legs were slow to follow her brain's signals. Simply placing one foot in front of the other required intense concentration. "What happened to Veronica?"

"Same old, same old."

"Too bad. She seemed nice."

He shrugged, still tugging her along.

Unsteady, she barely kept up, thankful he still had a strong grasp on her hand, otherwise she might have embarrassed herself. She'd die before she'd let him know it. She'd also die before she'd let him know how much Charles' honesty hurt, or how that little voice in the back of her brain piped up again after a ten-year hiatus to tell her she didn't measure up. With all her success, the voice should be silenced for good. Since her pain hadn't abated, she wasn't near drunk enough. The thought of continuing at his house sounded much more appealing than going home to an empty apartment too sober, so she was glad his plans with Veronica had changed. She lived within walking distance, in the same San Mateo, California, neighborhood. Neither would have to drive.

~

James and Sam walked in silence through the parking lot to his Toyota Sequoia. He helped her inside the SUV.

"This really isn't a chick magnet. Someone like you should drive a sportier, sleeker car," she said, slurring her words, once he climbed in beside her and started the engine. "Why don't you?"

He bit the inside of his cheek to keep from laughing. "You know, Collins, I'll admit I have commitment issues, but I'm not that shallow."

"Sorry." Sam giggled. "Must be tough to go through so many women and not find one keeper in there somewhere."

James gave up the struggle to hold on to his laugh. "You're being a pain, you know? So I've had a problem finding the one? Is that a crime?" Usually, she was more understanding and less outspoken. But not tonight. The tequila had totally obliterated her normal restraint. He decided he liked her this way. He'd always liked her and felt comfortable around her. Never felt attracted to her, though. Which was a good thing because, as she'd often pointed out, his track record with women was shitty.

Beyond shitty. He made a much better friend than long-term partner. Besides, she was too set in her ways—too serious, too single-minded for his taste. He liked his women softer, especially for a lover. She was a terrific friend, even when she was being too honest. "If you continue to insult me, I'm not going to help you."

"Fine." Another giggle escaped. "I still say you should drive a sportier car."

"Why? I like this car."

"Really?"

"Yeah. It's big enough with plenty of horsepower."

"Ah! The truth finally comes out."

"What truth?" He ignored the surge of irritation her comment brought forth, put the car in gear, and backed out of the space. "I like having ample power to use the four-wheel drive for going skiing in Tahoe, and being able to haul four adults and luggage is an added bonus." He spared her a glance after turning onto the main road. "Enough about cars. Let's talk about you and Charles."

"Spoilsport."

"We're not here to poke fun at my mode of transportation," he said, braking for a red light. When the car came to a stop, he gave her his full attention. "Do you want my help or not?"

"Sure. My problem is simple." She made a face. "I'm too rigid. I doubt talking will do much."

"Talking always helps put things in perspective."

"I already have perspective. Charles is concerned about our relationship. He called it tedious…said he wants more spontaneity…that I'm too predictable."

When he didn't respond, her chin shot up and she glared at him. Her entire body straightened into one tight board. "I am not predictable."

"Of course not." He shook his head, stifling a grin at her outraged denial. In his opinion, Samantha Collins was someone he could set a clock to, she was so regimented. "Let's see. Monday you wear brown, Tuesday navy. Wednesday and Thursday you mix it up a bit with either brown, navy, or gray, but Fridays are always black."

"So, what are you? The clothes police? I happen to like those colors."

Of course she did. He rolled his eyes. "You know you could vary your pattern, go a little crazy and wear black on Monday."

"I'm organized." She broke off, considering his assessment. "And I'm a professional. I have to act the part."

"And you do—too much."

"What do you mean?" Some of the stiffness left her spine.

"I mean it wouldn't hurt to throw a little femininity into the mix. Those business suits you always wear make a guy wonder if there's really a female underneath."

"Just because I poked fun at your car doesn't mean you have to retaliate."

"I thought we were being honest. Don't think I've ever seen you in anything that shows off your feminine side. Red would look great on you." The look she sent him was priceless. "Trust me. I haven't lost any marbles. While you're at it, you should learn to relax. Enjoy life. You take everyday shit much too seriously."

When she stiffened up once more, he added quickly, not giving her a chance to interject, "When's the last time you left work early to do something frivolous?" The light turned green and he resumed driving. A half a block later, he added, "And your routine never varies. Every morning you come into the office at exactly seven forty-five with your usual cup of black Starbucks coffee and an apple. God forbid, you should ever eat an orange or drink a Coke."

"I guess I have become a little rigid in my quest for success." She leaned back into her seat and sighed. "Thank God I have three weeks to change and be more flexible." She remained silent until he turned into the Burger King parking lot. "Why are we stopping here? I thought we were going to dinner."

"It won't kill you to eat fast food."

"Yes, it will."

"Live a little. Think of this as your first exercise in flexibility."

"Studies have shown—"

"Quit reading the studies," he said. "Besides, you're in no condition to wait hours for a restaurant table, which is what it would take this time of night on a Friday." When she opened her mouth to complain, he put his finger over her lips. "Ah, ah, ah. You're being rigid. Three weeks isn't a lot of time." He grinned at her fuming glare—a glare so hot, he was sure he saw steam rising from the top of her brown hair that was tightly pulled back and held in place with its usual clip.

"I don't get what all those women see in you. You're obnoxious and pushy."

"It's my temperamental side, the artist in me. Can I help it if women love it?" He broke off and nodded toward the menu at the side of the car, ignoring her snort of disagreement. "Pick out something. FYI, I see a few nutritious items listed up there."

She told him and he ordered when the box outside his window squawked.

"See? Now was that so difficult?" he asked twenty minutes later, watching her wolf down the burger and fries like she was inhaling air, as they sat picnic style on a blanket in the living room of his San Mateo home. One thing about Collins, he thought, his gaze fixed on her as he polished off his margarita. He was always comfortable in her company. He could relax—be himself. He may give her a hard time about her inflexibility, but she was okay. Mainly because he could be an inflexible bastard at times, so they shared something in common.

"If I didn't know better, I'd say you like fast food more than you let on." He shook the frozen contents in the blender pitcher before topping off her drink, and then adding to his own.

"I guess I was hungry. I love BK Whoppers."

"Then why avoid them?" Her answer was a lift of her shoulders, which didn't satisfy his curiosity. "You don't have a weight problem, so what's wrong with enjoying a burger every now and then?"

"I'm not worried about gaining weight. I promised myself a long time ago I wouldn't do stupid things that weren't beneficial to living the best life I can. Since fast food's unhealthy, I don't eat it."

He considered her response while taking a sip of his margarita, wondering why she had this need to control her environment. Except in her designs. She gave her creativity full rein when she worked, never ceasing to amaze him with her fantastic ideas. Those two facets of her personality intrigued him.

If he was going to help her with Winthrope, he needed to get her to push past that control, get her to lighten up.

He grinned. He'd bet a month's pay Collins was even controlled while making love. He mentally rolled his eyes. Not his problem. Like he had room to make judgments. He knew he was going through some kind of weird cycle right now, especially since he'd called it off with Veronica. He sighed. He didn't want to think of that either. He shoved his errant thoughts aside and teased, "I only know of one other woman who can eat like that and never gain an ounce."

"I've seen the women you date. Most look like they've never eaten a full meal in their life, much less enjoyed it."

"You know, you just might hurt my feelings."

When she snorted and said, "Fat chance," he chuckled. Sam always gave him a hard time about his choices in women. Which was why he'd been ultra-picky with Veronica and so sure a relationship with her would be different. Yet, somehow she'd bitten the dust, just as too many others had before her, and right now he was tired of the whole dating game.

"I was talking about Kate," he said, mentioning his sister-in-law.

"How're she and the baby?" Sam grinned, paying no attention to his affronted tone. "It's been a while since I last saw her."

"Both are doing great. My godchild is six months old tomorrow."

"Spoken like a true uncle."

"Kids are fun." All teasing left his demeanor. He shook his drink and studied the contents, working to understand his unsettled mood. Was he a selfish, self-absorbed bastard who couldn't commit, as Kate had accused right before they'd broken up? She hadn't pulled any verbal punches back then, had even claimed everything in his life had come too easy, especially women.

Of course, he'd denied it. Hell, he wasn't selfish. Nor was everything handed to him. True, women did seem to find him appealing, but so what? He always put his friendships first and he gave regularly to charity. Both time and money. He just wasn't good in the relationship department. He had to admit, commitment scared him. What if he made a mistake? At times, like right now, Kate's remarks echoed in his mind and he wondered if they didn't hold too much truth. He certainly didn't want to be that type of person. He took a sip. "I can see the allure of fatherhood. Paul took to it like he was born for the role."

"Do I denote a hint of dissatisfaction?"

He shrugged, and said honestly, "Maybe."

She didn't say anything for the longest time. He was beginning to think she'd dropped the subject until she asked softly, "Do you ever wish it had been different?" When his eyebrows rose in question, she added, "That it had been you instead of Paul?"

"Sometimes I wish I had what they have." His gaze moved to the picture window, overlooking the San Francisco Bay. A blanket of fog rolled in, slowly covering the bay like a carpet. He stared through holes left in the white, billowy patches, as if what he saw held the answers to love and happiness. He just didn't think he had it in him to commit to a woman.

"I loved her but I was never in love with her," he said, of his one and only long-term relationship. He'd dated Kate for so long without committing, their prior relationship had become a running joke among his family with Paul as the main instigator. Now his brother was happily married to her.

A sigh escaped.

Yeah. He'd love to experience with someone what they had found. After seeing Paul and Kate together, he realized the emotion he'd felt for Kate had been hollow compared to what his brother felt. He was well into his thirties and had dated a broad range of women without succumbing to anything close to what he assumed love entailed. He'd tried, especially in the last three years. He simply reached a certain level in his relationships and lost interest without understanding why, yet fully understanding the consequences. Love, marriage, and fatherhood simply weren't in his future. Maybe Kate's observations weren't so far off the mark after all.

"She was easy and there. And like the bastard I am, I took advantage of it." He broke off and grunted. "Nice try, but it won't work. We're supposed to be figuring out a way to help you with Winthrope, not dissecting my failures."

"Do we have to? Thinking about him and what he said just depresses me. Mostly because he's right." Sam swirled her frozen drink, put the glass to her lips, and downed the contents in one long gulp. "You know, when you promised me tequila, margaritas weren't exactly what I had in mind."

"I happen to like my margaritas. Besides, you got your tequila."

"Yeah, but the ice and lime juice dilute it too much. Earlier, I was drinking shots and the tipsiness has worn off. Discussing failures requires more liquid courage. Unfortunately, after one of these, I'm still too sober." She held up her glass. "This is for lightweights."

"Lightweights, huh?" When she nodded, he grinned. "Can't have that." He got up and headed toward his kitchen.

"So, what're we going to do?" she asked, following. "Drink it straight out of the bottle?"

"Never let it be said that James Morrison is a lightweight. My ego won't allow it."

She leaned against the doorjamb while he picked up the knife lying on the black granite countertop and rinsed it off. He reached for a lime.

"Real limes? How impressive."

"Yeah? Stick with me, kiddo, and I'll impress the hell out of you."

"You already do."

He began cutting the lime and ignored the way her approval slid over his back, much like a warm blanket. He also tried to ignore the way her blouse stretched, outlining a pair of well-proportioned breasts as she propped her back against the doorjamb with her hands behind her.

Quit looking at her. He concentrated on cutting, but his gaze wouldn't cooperate with his brain's signal and kept moving in the direction of the open *V* of her shirt.

Funny how he'd never noticed before. He did now. Samantha Collins had a damned fine body.

Get your mind out of the gutter, Morrison. She's off-limits. Not only is she a colleague, she's a friend who's practically engaged to a nice guy—a man you know socially. Just because he's being an idiot, doesn't mean you should be a bigger idiot and take advantage.

He sighed and went back to cutting, forcing his head down so his eyes stayed focused on the limes. When done, he handed her the salt and two shot glasses. Then he grabbed the plate of limes and bottle of tequila. "Come on. We have some serious drinking to do."

~

"Okay." Sam trailed after him, as he strode from the kitchen in the direction of the sofa. He set the limes and bottle on the coffee table and relieved her of the salt and glasses.

She watched him line up the ingredients in single file in front of him and pour tequila into the glasses, before both got comfortable sitting Indian style next to each other in the space between the sofa and coffee table.

"So, what do I do first?" Excitement filled her. "Limes, salt, and tequila. I had friends who used to do this in college."

"You've never done shots of tequila before tonight?" When she shook her head, he grinned. "You really need to let loose more."

"Isn't that what I'm doing?"

"I give you an *A* for effort. Here's to fun." He held up the shot glass.

She copied his movements…licking the salt, downing the shot, and sucking on the lime.

"Whew. That's powerful."

"I aim to satisfy. You got a double shot. Can't have you calling me a lightweight."

She giggled. "I wasn't referring to you when I made the comment."

"Oh?" His eyebrows shot up; he clearly expecting her to continue.

"Yeah. I was talking about myself. I just want to make sure I do it right because I've never been drunk before."

"So, how is it you're twenty-nine and still a virgin?"

He grinned when she shot him a surprised, "What?"

"You've never had a hangover, right?" His startling blue eyes danced, drawing a desire to join him in the steps. She couldn't take her gaze off his amused smile as she tilted her head to the side. He really was charm personified.

"See! A mere virgin if you've never experienced a hangover. It's a rite of passage. So, answer my question."

"What question?" She picked up the bottle, ignoring a sudden urge to grin, and poured the next round.

He chuckled. "For a virgin, you're a natural. I'm not dropping the subject. How did you survive college without at least one hangover?"

"I couldn't risk drinking then." Her thoughts drifted to her college days—a lifetime ago. Back then, she'd had too much riding on her scholarship to ever let loose and have a good time like all her friends, who thought of college as one big party. Doing well in college was a stepping-stone to a better life and she couldn't risk screwing it up with something as stupid as drinking. Times had certainly changed since then, she realized, after her best-laid plans had veered so far off course. In fact, she'd use tonight as a catalyst to a new, spontaneous Sam. "But I'm all for it now."

"I should warn you. The side effects can be brutal."

"Oh? I think I'll survive."

"Yeah, you will, but you're going to hate me in the morning for luring you into temptation."

"You have it backward. I led you. You'll probably hate me."

"I doubt it." He tossed out another chuckle then picked up his shot glass.

"I know why I want to get drunk. I'm just not sure why you do."

"I need a reason?" He saluted her with his glass, saying, "Cheers," and followed the ritual.

"It's so unlike you." She grinned. "Come to think of it, I've never seen you drink more than two glasses of wine. So…why are you letting me lure you into temptation on a Friday when you could be with Veronica instead of me? What happened with her?"

"Does it matter?"

Her grin stretched. "Call me curious."

He shrugged. "Beats the hell out of me." Then, after a long pause, he sighed. "I felt like I was going through the motions with her, and I wasn't in the mood to do it tonight. I'm glad I found you. This is a lot more fun. The headache will be worth it."

The smile he sent made her think he really meant the sentiment, and she felt the same way. She was having the time of her life. A headache would be a small inconvenience in exchange.

Sam wasn't sure how many shots she drank; she only knew she was feeling no pain. They never did get around to talking about Charles and her inflexibility, which was fine by her.

She didn't think she could laugh any harder when James relayed the story of how his brother and sister-in-law, who were sworn enemies at the time, got together after a snowstorm stranded them for several days in Lake Tahoe.

"I want you to know, I made sure Paul suffered for stealing my girl."

"Was she?" His eyebrows rose, and she answered his implied question honestly. "Seems to me, if she'd been yours, he wouldn't have stood a chance." She needed to take her own advice. If Charles was truly hers, his loan officer didn't stand a chance either.

"Maybe. If I had thought of her as mine, I wouldn't have let him steal her. That's probably the same reason why I never seriously pursued the only other woman I've ever been totally attracted to. After getting to know her, I'd lost my chance. By the time I realized her allure, she belonged to someone else."

"No?" His comments about someone he'd never mentioned before brought her out of her thoughts and, giggling, she slapped his knee. "You mean someone actually stole your heart? Who was she?" Oh yeah. She was definitely feeling no pain when she could make such personal jokes about his love life. That he was responding in kind meant he was just as far-gone.

"No one. Just a fond memory of what might have been..." He sighed, staring wistfully at the full shot of tequila he held. "Oh, the things we do for friends," he said softly, before he finally downed the liquid and placed the glass on the table.

~

James touched her head as Sam reached across the table. She straightened abruptly, glancing at him with a question in her eyes.

"You know, if you let your hair down once in a while, it'd help." His words slurred a bit, which meant he was far too wasted, but by that point he didn't care. "Make you appear softer."

He released the clip from its usual tight grip, creating a startling effect. He couldn't take his gaze off her. He stilled the urge to run his hands through the thick, lush halo of silky softness that surrounded her face. Those lovely tresses highlighted expressive brown eyes, giving her an almost innocent appearance. She was quite pretty when she wasn't being so serious.

"I don't want to be softer. I'm fine the way I am." With an unsteady movement, she yanked her clip out of his hand, and bent to pull her long hair together.

"Charles might like you softer."

"Really?" Sam dropped her hands and drew her eyebrows together while her hair fell around her face again.

"All men do," he said, nodding. "Men want women to be women." He smiled. She looked so hopeful...so adorable...so irresistible...and, God help him, so kissable.

"Why are you looking at me like that?" Her voice came out in breathy wisps of air.

"I must be drunk." He shook his head to clear it. "All of a sudden I had an urge to kiss you."

She giggled. In seconds, her giggle erupted into uncontrollable laughter.

Though he knew she was as wasted as he, irritation swept over him as he stiffened. "You find the thought of kissing me funny?" He moved in closer. For some reason, he couldn't ignore her reaction.

"No." Her laughter died as quickly as it sprang to life. Her expression turned solemn.

Sam leaned against the sofa and ran her tongue nervously along her mouth before she bit her bottom lip, while studying him with huge, beautiful doe eyes. Her actions did nothing to ease his desire to smother her with kisses, in fact drew his attention to those pouty lips. Why had he never noticed before how perfect they were for kissing?

Whoa, back up, Morrison. This is Collins you're lusting after.

Despite the fact that her inclined position gave him an unobstructed view of a rounded, ample breast, he forced all sexual thoughts out of his brain. Yet, when she cleared her throat, sat up straight, and said too convincingly, "I'm immune to you, is all," they snuck back in and wouldn't budge. Especially after she added, "I'm not a gullible female who'll fall for a pretty face."

Her statement rankled, and his mind wouldn't let go of her implied challenge.

James had drunk too much tequila, and he knew damned well he should let her comments pass. He should stay on his course of helping her with Winthrope...he should remember they were friends. Hell, he should definitely ignore the heat now pooling in his groin at what a tempting sight she made, sprawled out next to him half exposed, with those generous, full lips begging to be kissed. Too late, he realized his biggest mistake. He should never have gotten drunk with her. Not tonight.

"So, you're immune to me?" He leaned in closer and smiled smugly at the doubt now shrouding her overconfident expression. "That's bullshit," he whispered as his mouth hovered over hers. Giving into impulse after pushing all sanity aside, he lowered his head and captured those lips. Once he leapt into craziness, Sam surprised the hell out of him. She wrapped her arms around him, pulled him closer, and inhaled his tongue in a wholly unpredictable way, sucking him in further. Nothing of her actions reminded him of his straight-laced friend, but he was too caught up in his own unexpected reaction to care.

He deepened the kiss. Savored what she offered with her tongue and mouth.

Of their own volition, his hands found her breasts. He took in the citrus scent of the limes mixed with the perfume she always wore. He'd never thought about it before, but her smell was intoxicatingly sexy, just like the feel of her. Eventually, he traced her bottom lip with his tongue. Tasted salt. Her loud moan floated somewhere above him, inciting a hunger he'd never experienced before this moment.

Stop, his mind screamed. *Before your need for her veers completely out of control and you ruin a friendship. Even you aren't that much of a selfish bastard.* Somehow, James found the strength to pull away, but he teetered on the edge of absolute insanity.

With his head mere inches above hers, he studied her expression. Her eyes were closed and a serene smile rested on her lips. How could such an unremarkable face elicit more desire, which still strummed at a fevered pace through his veins? Every cell in his body vibrated with yearning. He shouldn't want her, but he did.

Sam chose that moment to open her eyes, and the warmth spilling from them did nothing to ease his fight to stay motionless and not succumb to the lust pumping in his bloodstream.

"That was nice."

Nice...nice? "That's all you have to say? It was nice?" He'd never been so insulted. She'd given him one of the hottest kisses he'd ever had, and the only descriptive term she could use was nice?

"Okay, so you know how to kiss." She slurred the words. "I never doubted that." Her voice trailed off and her head slumped back. It took him a moment to realize she'd passed out.

James can be purchased by going to the website below.
https://www.createspace.com/3959015

Made in United States
North Haven, CT
02 March 2023

33405853R00125